A Quiet Neighborhood

George MacDonald

EDITED BY DAN HAMILTON

A Quiet Neighborhood
The Seaboard Parish
The Vicar's Daughter

VICTOR

BOOKS a division of SP Publications, Inc.
WHEATON. ILLINOIS 60187

Offices also in
Whitby, Ontario, Canada
Amersham-on-the-Hill, Bucks, England

Annals of a Quiet Neighborhood was first published in 1866 as a magazine serial in England.

Library of Congress Catalog Card Number: 84-52364
ISBN: 0-89693-328-8

VICTOR BOOKS
A division of SP Publications, Inc.
Wheaton, Illinois 60187

CONTENTS

INTRODUCTION

George MacDonald (1824-1905), a Scottish preacher, poet, novelist, fantasist, expositor, and public figure, is most well known today for his children's books—*At the Back of the North Wind*, *The Princess and the Goblin*, *The Princess and Curdie*, and his fantasies *Lilith* and *Phantastes*.

But his fame is based on far more than his fantasies. His lifetime output of more than fifty books placed him in the same literary realm as Charles Dickens, Wilkie Collins, William Thackeray, and Thomas Carlyle. He numbered among his friends and acquaintances Lewis Carroll, Mark Twain, Lady Byron, and John Ruskin.

Among his later admirers were G.K. Chesterton, W.H. Auden, and C.S. Lewis. MacDonald's fantasy *Phantastes* was a turning point in Lewis' conversion; Lewis acknowledged MacDonald as his spiritual master, and declared that he had never written a book without quoting from MacDonald.

ONE

DESPONDENCY AND CONSOLATION

I was thirty when I was made a vicar—an age at which a man might be expected to begin to grow wise—but even then I had much to learn. For then I only felt that a man had to take up his cross, whereas now I know that a man has to follow Him, and that makes an unspeakable difference.

I remember the first evening—a Saturday—in my new vicarage. I had never been there before. The weather was depressing, and grave doubts as to my place in the Church kept rising and floating about like the rain clouds. Not that I doubted the Church—I only doubted myself. Were my motives pure? What were my motives? I did not know, and therefore could not answer for their purity. Had I any right to be in the Church—to be eating her bread and drinking her wine—without knowing whether I was fit to do her work? What good might I look for as the result of my labor? How could I hope to help men live with the sense of the kingdom of heaven about them, and the expectation of something glorious at hand just outside that invisible door between the worlds? I desired to do some work worth calling work, and I did not see how to begin.

The only answer I could find was that the Church is part of God's world. He made men to work, and work of some sort must be done by every honest man. Somehow I had found myself working in the Church. I did not know that I was more fit for any other work. There was work here which I could do. With God's help, I would try to do it well.

This resolution brought me some relief, but I was still depressed. I was not married then, and firmly believed I never should be married—not from any ambition of self-denial, nor from any notion that God takes pleasure in being a hard master. But there was a lady . . . I had been refused a few months before, which I think was the best thing ever to happen to me, except one.

And so I was still depressed. For is it not depressing when the rain is falling and the steam is rising? When the river is crawling along muddily, and the horses stand stock-still with their spines in a straight line from their ears to their lowered tails?

Even so, I took my umbrella and went out, for I wanted to do my work well. I would go and fall in love, if I could, with the country round about. In my first step beyond my own gate, I was up to my ankles in mud.

I had not gone far before the rain ceased, though it was still gloomy. The road soon took a sharp turn to pass along an old stone bridge that spanned the water with a single fine arch. Through the arch I could see the swollen river stretching through the meadows, its banks bordered with pollards—poplars whose lower branches havae been trimmed away, leaving only a curious crown of leaves at the very top of the tree. Now pollards always made me miserable. In the first place, they look ill-used. In the next place, they look tame. In the third place, they look ugly. I had not then learned to honor them on the ground that they do not yield to the adversity of their circumstances. If they must be pollards, they still will be trees, and what they may not do with grace, they will yet do with bounty. Their life bursts forth, despite all that is done to repress and destroy their individuality. When you have once learned to honor anything, love is not very far off. But as I had not yet learned to honor pollards, they made me more miserable than I already was.

I stood on the bridge and, looking up and down the river through the misty air, saw two long rows of these pollards diminishing till they vanished in both directions. The sight of them took from me all power of enjoying the water beneath me, the green fields around me, or even the beauty of the the little bridge, although all sorts of bridges have been a delight to me. For I am one of those who never get rid of their infantile predilections, and to have once enjoyed making a mud bridge is to enjoy all bridges forever.

I saw a man coming along the road beyond, but I turned my back to the road, leaned my arms on the parapet of the bridge, and stood gazing where I saw no visions—namely, at those very pollards. I heard the man's footsteps coming up the crown of the arch, but I would not turn to greet him. I was in a selfish humor—surely, if ever one man ought to greet another, it was on such a comfortless afternoon. The footsteps stopped behind me, and I heard a voice, "I beg yer pardon, Sir, but be you the new vicar?"

I turned instantly and answered, "I am. Do you want me?"

Before me stood a tall old man with his hat in his hand. He smoothed his short gray hair over his forehead as he stood. His face was hued red-brown from much exposure to the weather. There was a certain look of roughness (without hardness) in it, which spoke of endurance rather than resistance, although he could evidently set his face as a flint. His features were large and a little coarse, but the smile that parted his lips when he spoke shone in his gray eyes as well, and lighted up a countenance in which a man might trust. "I wanted to see yer face, Sir, if you'll not take it amiss."

"Certainly not," I answered, pleased with the man's address, as he stood square before me, looking as modest as he was fearless. "The sight of a man's face is what everybody has a right to—but, for all that, I should like to know why you want to see my face."

"Why, Sir, you be the new vicar. You kindly told me so when I axed you."

"Well, then, you'll see my face on Sunday in church—that is, if you happen to be there."

"Yes, Sir. But you see, Sir, on the bridge here, the parson is the parson like, and I'm Old Rogers. And I looks in his face, and he looks in mine, and I says to myself, 'This is my parson.' But o' Sundays he's nobody's parson. He's got his work to do, and it mun be done, and there's an end on't."

That there was a real idea in the old man's mind was considerably clearer than his logic.

"Did you know parson that's gone, Sir? He wur a good parson. Many's the time he come and sit at my son's bedside—him that's dead and gone—for a long hour, on a Saturday night too. And then, when I see him up in the desk the next mornin', I'd say to myself, 'Old Rogers, that's the same man as sat by your son's bedside last night. Think o' that, Old Rogers!' But he didn't seem to have the same cut, somehow, and he didn't talk a bit the same. And when he spoke to me after sermon, in the churchyard, I was always of a mind to go into the church again and look up to the pulpit to see if he wur really out ov it, for this warn't the same man, you see. I always likes parsons better out o' the pulpit, and that's how I come to want to make you look at me, Sir, instead o' the water down there, afore I see you in the church tomorrow mornin'."

The old man laughed a kindly laugh, but he had set me thinking, and I did not know what to say. So, after a short pause, he resumed, "You'll be thinking me a queer kind of a man, Sir, to speak to my betters before my betters speaks to me. But mayhap you don't know what a parson is to us poor folk that has ne'er a friend more larned than theirselves but the parson. And, besides, Sir, I'm an old salt—an old man-o'-war's man—and I've been all round the world, and I ha' been in all sorts o' company, pirates and all, and I ain't a bit frightened of a parson. No—I love a parson, Sir. He's got a good telescope, and he gits to the mast-head, and he looks out. And he sings out, 'Land ahead!' or 'Breakers ahead!' and gives directions accordin'. Only I can't always make out what he says. But when he shuts up his spyglass, and comes down to the riggin', and talks to us like one man to another, then I don't know what I should do without the parson. Good evenin' to you, Sir, and welcome to Marshmallows."

The pollards did not look half so dreary. The river began to glimmer a little, and the old bridge became an interesting old bridge. I had found a friend already, that is, a man to whom I might possibly be of some use. I had learned something from him too, and I resolved to try all I could to be the same man out of the pulpit that I was in it—seeing and feeling the realities of the unseen. And in the pulpit I would be the same as I was out of it— taking facts as they are, and dealing with things as they show themselves in the world.

Before I left the bridge, the sun burst his cloudy bands and blazed out as if he had just risen from the dead, instead of being just about to sink into the grave. The whole sweep of the gloomy river answered him in gladness, and the wet leaves of the pollards quivered and glanced. The meadows offered up their perfect green, fresh and clear out of the trouble of the rain; and away in the distance, upon a rising ground covered with trees, glittered a weathercock. And when the sun had gone below the horizon, and the fields and the river were dusky once more, there the weathercock glittered still over the darkening earth, a symbol of that faith which is "the evidence of things not seen."

I stood up and wandered off the bridge and along the road. I had not gone far before I passed a house, out of which came a young woman leading a little boy. They came after me, the boy gazing at the red and gold and green of the sunset sky. As they passed me, the child said, "Auntie, I think I should like to be a painter."

"Why?" returned his companion.

"Because then," answered the child, "I could help God paint the sky."

What his aunt replied I do not know, but I went on answering him myself all the way home. Did God care to paint the sky of an evening, that a few of His children might see it? And should I think my day's labor lost if it wrought no visible salvation in the earth?

But was the child's aspiration in vain? Could I tell him God did not want his help to paint the sky? True, he could mount no scaffold against the glowing west. But might he not, with his little palette and brush, make his brothers and sisters see what he had seen? Might he not help God to paint this glory of vapor and light inside the minds of His children? Ah! If any man's work is not *with* God, its results shall be burned, ruthlessly burned, because it is poor and bad.

"So, for my part," I said to myself, "if I can put one touch of a rosy sunset into the life of any man or woman of my parish, I shall feel that I have worked with God. He is in no haste, and if I do what I may in earnest, I need not mourn if I work no great work in the earth. Let God make His sunsets—I will mottle my little fading cloud. Such be my ambition! So shall I scale the rocks in front, not leave my name carved upon those behind me."

I could not fail to see God's providence in this, that on my first attempt to find where I stood, and while I was discouraged, I should fall in with these two—an old man whom I could help and a child who could help me—the one opening an outlet for my labor and my love, and the other reminding me of the highest source of the most humbling comfort—that in all my work I might be a fellow worker with God.

TWO

MY FIRST SUNDAY
AT MARSHMALLOWS

The next morning I read prayers and preached. Never before had I enjoyed so much the petitions of the Church, which Richard Hooker calls "the sending of angels upward," or the reading of the lessons, which he calls "the receiving of angels descended from above." And whether from the newness of the parson, or the love of the service, certainly a congregation more intent or more responsive a clergyman will hardly find. But it was different in the afternoon. The people had dined, and the usual somnolence followed, nor could I find it in my heart to blame men and women who worked hard all the week for being drowsy on the day of rest. So I curtailed my sermon as much as I could, omitting page after page of my manuscript. When I came to a close, I was rewarded by agreeable surprise upon the faces round me. I resolved that in the afternoons, at least, my sermons should be as short as heart could wish.

But that afternoon there was one man of the congregation who was neither drowsy nor inattentive. I glanced toward him repeatedly and not once did I find his eyes turned away from me.

There was a small loft in the west end of the church in which stood a little organ whose voice, weakened by years of praising and possibly of neglect, had yet among a good many tones that were rough, wooden, and reedy, a few remaining mellow notes. Now this little loft was something larger than was just necessary for the organ and its ministrants, and a few of the parishioners chose to sit there. On this occasion there was but one man there.

The space below this gallery was not included in the part of the church used for the service. It was claimed by the gardener of the place—the sexton—to hold his gardening tools. There were a few ancient wood carvings lying in it, very brown in the dusky light. There were also some broken old headstones, and the kindly spade and pickaxe.

Rising against a screen which separated this mouldy portion of the church from the rest was an old monument of carved wood, once brilliantly painted, but now all bare and worn. Its gablet was on a level with the rail of the organ loft, and over it appeared the face of the man. It was a very remarkable countenance—pale and very thin, without any hair except for thick gray eyebrows that far overhung keen, questioning eyes. Short bushy hair, gray, not white, covered a well-formed head, with a high, narrow forehead. As I have said, those keen eyes looked at me all through the sermon, though I did not meet their owner until later.

My vestry door opened upon a little group of graves—poor graves without headstone or slab. Good men must have preceded me here, else the poor would not have lain so near the chancel and the vestry door. All about and beyond were stones, with here and there a monument. Mine was a large parish, and there were old and rich families in it, more of which buried their dead here than assembled their living. But close by the vestry door there was this little billowy lake of grass, and at the end of the narrow path leading from the door was the churchyard wall. But I would not creep out the back way from my people. That way might do very well to come in by; but to go out, I would use the door of the people. So I went along the church, and out by the door in the north side into the middle of the churchyard.

It lay in bright sunshine. All the rain and gloom were gone. "If one could only bring this glory of sun and grass into one's hopes for the future!" I thought, and looking down, I saw the little boy who aspired to paint the sky looking up in my face with mingled confidence and awe.

"Do you trust me, my little man?" thought I. "You shall trust me, then. But I won't be a priest to you. I'll be a big brother."

So I stooped and lifted the child and held him in my arms. And the little fellow looked at me one moment longer, and then put his arms gently round my neck. And so we were friends. I set him down, for I shuddered at the idea of the people thinking that I was showing off the clergyman. I looked at the boy. He did not say a word, but walked away to join his aunt, who was waiting for him at the gate of the churchyard. He kept his head turned toward me, and so stumbled over the grave of a child. As he fell in the hollow on the other side, I ran to pick him up. His aunt reached him at the same moment.

"O thank you, Sir!" she said, with an earnestness which seemed to me disproportionate to the deed, and carried him away with a deep blush over all her countenance.

The old man-of-war's man was waiting at the churchyard gate. His hat was in his hand, and he gave a pull to the short hair over his forehead, as if he would gladly take that off too, to show his respect for the new parson. I held out my hand gratefully, but could not close it around the hard unyielding mass of fingers. He did not know how to shake hands and left it all to me, but pleasure sparkled in his eyes.

"My old woman would like to shake hands with you, Sir," he said.

Beside him stood his old woman in a portentous bonnet. Beneath the gay yellow ribbons appeared a dusky old wrinkled face with a pair of keen black eyes, where the best beauty—that of loving-kindness—triumphed.

"I shall be in to see you soon," I said, as I shook hands with her. "I shall find out where you live."

"Down by the mill," she said, "close by it, Sir. There's one bed in our garden that always thrives, in the hottest summer, by the plash from the mill."

"Ask for Old Rogers, Sir," said the man. "Everybody knows Old Rogers. But if Your Reverence minds what my wife says, you won't go wrong. When you find the river, it takes you to the mill, and when you find the mill, you find the wheel. And when you find the wheel, you haven't far to look for the cottage, Sir. It's a poor place, but you'll be welcome."

THREE

MY FIRST MONDAY
AT MARSHMALLOWS

The next day I expected visitors from among my rich. It is fortunate that English society regards the parson as a gentleman, else he would have little chance of being useful to the upper classes. But I wanted to get a good start and see some of my poor before my rich came to see me. So, after breakfast on that lovely Monday in the beginning of autumn, I walked out to the village. I strove to dismiss from my mind every feeling of doing duty, of performing my part, and all that. I had a horror of becoming a moral policeman as much as of "doing church." I would simply enjoy the privilege of ministering. But, as no servant has a right to force his service, so I would be the neighbor only until such time as the opportunity of being the servant should show itself.

The village was as irregular as a village should be, partly consisting of those white houses with black intersecting parallelograms which still abound in some regions of our island. Just in the center, however, clustered about a house of red brick, rose a group of buildings which seemed part of some old and larger town. But round any one of three visible directions were stacks of wheat and a farmyard, while in another direction the houses went straggling away into a wood that looked very like the beginning of a forest.

From the street, the poplar-bordered stream was here and there just visible. I did not like to have it between me and my village. I could not help preferring that homely relation in which the houses are built up like swallow's nests onto the very walls of the cathedrals themselves, to the arrangement here where the river flowed between the church and the people.

15

A little way beyond the far end of the village appeared an iron gate of considerable size, dividing a lofty stone wall. Upon the top of one of the stone pillars supporting the gate stood a creature of stone, terrible enough for antediluvian heraldry.

As I passed along the street, my eye was caught by the window of a little shop, in which were arranged strings of beads and elephants of gingerbread. It was a window much broader than it was high, divided into lozenge-shaped panes. I thought to make a visit by going in and buying something. But I hesitated, because I could not think of anything I was in want of—at least that I was likely to encounter here. To be sure, I wanted a copy of Bengel's *Gnomon*, but I was not likely to find that. I wanted the fourth plate in the third volume of Law's *Bohme*, but that was not likely either. I did not care for gingerbread, and I had no little girl to take home beads to.

But why should I not go in but with a likely errand? For this reason: there are dissenters everywhere, and I could not tell but I might be going into the shop of a dissenter. Now, though nothing would have pleased me better than that all the dissenters should return to their old home in the Church, I could not endure the suspicion of canvassing or using any personal influence. Whether they returned or not—and I did not expect many would—I hoped still to stand toward every one of them as the parson of the parish, that each one might feel certain that I was ready to serve him or her at any hour. In the meantime, I could not help hesitating.

Then the door opened and out came the little boy whom I had already seen twice, and who was therefore one of my oldest friends in the place. He came across the road to see me, took me by the hand, and said, "Come and see Mother."

"Is this your mother's shop?"

"Yes."

I said no more, but accompanied him.

The place was half a shop and half a kitchen. A yard or so of counter stretched inward from the door, just as a hint to those who might be intrusively inclined. Beyond this, by the chimney corner, sat the mother, who rose as we entered. She was one of the most remarkable women I had ever seen. Her face was absolutely white except her lips and a spot upon each cheek, which glowed with a deep carmine. You would have said she had been painting, and painting very inartistically, so little was the red shaded into the surrounding white. Now this was certainly not beautiful, but when

16

I got used to her complexion, I saw that the form of her features was quite beautiful. She might indeed have been lovely but for a certain hardness which showed through the beauty. Her teeth were firmly closed and, taken with the look of the eyes and forehead, hers seemed the expression of a constant and bitter self-command. There were marks of ill health upon her as well. Her large dark eyes were burning as if the lamp of life had broken and the oil was blazing. But her manner was perfectly, almost dreadfully, quiet. Her voice was soft, low, book-proper, and chiefly expressive of indifference. She spoke without looking me in the face, but did not seem either shy or ashamed. Her figure was remarkably graceful, though too worn to be beautiful. Here was a strange parishioner for me—in a country shop too.!

The little fellow shrunk away through a half-open door that revealed a stair behind.

"What can I do for you, Sir?" said the mother. She stood on the other side of the little counter, prepared to open box or drawer at command.

"To tell the truth, I hardly know," I said. "I am the new vicar—but I do not think that I should have come in to see you just today, if it had not been that your little boy there asked me to come in and see his mother."

"He is too ready to make advances to strangers, Sir."

"Oh, but I am not a stranger to him. I have met him twice before. He is a little darling. I assure you he has quite gained my heart."

No reply for a moment. Then just, "Indeed!" and nothing more. A tobacco jar on a shelf rescued me from the most pressing portion of the perplexity—namely, what to say next.

"Will you give me a quarter of a pound of tobacco?" I said.

The woman turned, took down the jar, weighed out the quantity, wrapped it, and took the money, all without one other word than "Thank you, Sir," which was all I could return, with the same addition of "Good morning."

I walked away with my parcel in my pocket. The little boy did not show himself again, although I had hoped to find him outside.

I set out for the mill, which I had already learned was on the village side of the river. Coming to a lane leading down to the river, I followed it and then walked up a path outside the row of pollards, through a lovely meadow where brown and white cows were eating the thick deep grass. Beyond the meadow, a wood on

17

rising ground paralleled the river. The river flowed slowly on my right. Still swollen, it was of a clear brown, in which you could see the browner trout darting with such a slippery gliding that the motion seemed the result of will, without any such intermediate and complicated arrangement as brain and nerves and muscles. The water beetles went spinning about and one dragonfly made a mist about him with his long wings. The sun hung in the sky over all, pouring down life, shining on the roots of the willows, lighting up the black head of the water rat, glorifying the green lake of the grass, and giving to the whokle an ultterance of love and hope and joy which was, to him who could read it, a more certain and full revelation of God than any display of power in thunder, avalanche, or stormy sea.

I soon came within sound of the mill. Presently, crossing the stream that flowed back to the river after having done its work on the corn, I came in front of the building and looked over the half-door into the mill. The floor was clean and dusty. A few full sacks, tied at the mouth, stood about—they always look to me as if Joseph's silver cup were just inside. In the corner the flour was trickling down out of two wooden spouts into a wooden receptacle below. The whole place was full of its own faint but pleasant odor. No man was visible. The spouts went on pouring the slow torrent of flour as if everything could go on of itself with perfect propriety. I could not even see how a man could get at the stones that I heard grinding away above, except he went up the rope that hung from the ceiling. So I walked round the corner of the place and found myself in the company of the waterwheel, mossy and green with ancient waterdrops, furred and overgrown and lumpy. It was going round—slowly, indeed, and with the gravity of age, but doing its work—and casting its loose drops in a gentle rain upon a little plot of Master Rogers' garden, which was therefore full of moisture-loving flowers.

Beside the flowerbeds stood a dusty young man, talking to a young woman with a rosy face and clear honest eyes. The moment they saw me they parted. The young man came across the stream at a step, and the young woman went up toward the cottage.

"That must be Old Rogers' cottage" I said to the miller.

"Yes, Sir," he answered, looking a little sheepish.

"Was that his daughter—that nice-looking young woman you were talking to?"

"Yes, Sir, it was." And he stole a shy, pleased look at me out of the corners of his eyes.

"It's a good thing," I said, "to have an honest, experienced old mill like yours, that can manage to go on of itself for a little while now and then."

This gave a great help to his budding confidence. He laughed. "Well, Sir, it's not very often it's left to itself. Jane isn't at her father's above once or twice a week, at most."

"She doesn't live with them, then?"

"No, Sir. You see they're both hearty, and they ain't over well-to-do, and Jane lives up at the Hall, Sir. She's upper housemaid and waits on one of the young ladies. Old Rogers has seen a great deal of the world, Sir."

"So I imagine. I am just going to see him. Good morning."

I jumped across the stream and went up a little gravel walk to the cottage door. It was a sweet place to live in, with honeysuckle growing over the house, and the soft sounds of the mill wheel ever in its little porch and about its windows.

The door was open, and Dame Rogers came from within to meet me. She welcomed me, and led the way into her little kitchen. As I entered, Jane went out at the back door. But it was only to call her father, who presently came in.

"I'm glad to see ye, Sir. This pleasure comes of having no work today. After harvest there come slack times for the likes of me. People don't care about a bag of old bones when they can get hold of young men. Well, well, never mind, old woman. The Lord'll take us through somehow. When the wind blows, the ship goes; when the wind drops, the ship stops; but the sea is His all the same, for He made it; and the wind is His all the same too."

He spoke in the most matter-of-fact tone, unaware of anything poetic in what he said. To him it was just common sense.

"I am sorry you are out of work," I said. "But my garden is sadly out of order, and I must have something done to it. You don't dislike gardening, do you?"

"Well, I bean't a right good hand at garden work," answered the old man, with some embarrassment.

There was more in this than met the ear, but what I could not conjecture. I would press the point a little. So I took him at his own word.

"I won't ask you to do any of the more ornamental part," I said, "only plain digging and hoeing."

"I would rather be excused, Sir."

"I am afraid I made you think—"

"I thought nothing, Sir. I thank you kindly, Sir."

"I assure you I want the work done, and I must employ someone else if you don't undertake it."

"Well, Sir, my back's bad now—no, Sir, I won't tell a story about it. I would just rather not, Sir."

"Now," his wife broke in, "now, Old Rogers, why won't 'ee tell the parson the truth, like a man, downright? If ye won't I'll do it for 'ee. The fact is, Sir," she went on, turning to me, "the fact is, that the old parson's man for that kind o' work was Simmons, t'other end of the village. And my man is so afeard o' hurtin' e'er another, that he'll turn the bread away from his own mouth and let it fall in the dirt."

"Now, now, old 'oman, don't 'ee belie me. I'm not so bad as that. You see, Sir, I never was good at knowin' right from wrong like. I never was good, that is, at tellin' exactly what I ought to do. So, when anything comes up, I just says to myself, 'Now, Old Rogers, what do you think the Lord would best like you to do?' And as soon as I ax myself that, I know directly what I've got to do, and then my old woman can't turn me no more than a bull. But, you see, I daren't, Sir, once I axed myself that."

"Stick to that, Rogers," I said.

"Besides, Sir," he went on, "Simmons wants it more than I do. He's got a sick wife, and my old woman, thank God, is hale and hearty. And there is another thing besides, he might take it hard of you, Sir, and think it was turning away an old servant like. And then, he wouldn't be ready to hear what you had to tell him, and might, mayhap, lose a deal o' comfort. And that I would take worst of all, Sir."

"Well, well, Rogers, Simmons shall have the job."

"Thank ye, Sir," said the old man.

I rose to go. As I reached the door, I remembered the tobacco in my pocket. I had not bought it for myself. I never could smoke.

"You smoke, don't you, Rogers?" I said.

"Well, Sir, I can't deny it. It's not much I spend on baccay, anyhow, is it, Dame?"

"No, that it bean't," answered his wife.

"You see, Sir," he went on, "sailors learns many ways they might be better without. I used to take my pan o' grog with the rest of them, but I gave that up, 'cause as how I don't want it now."

" 'Cause as how," interrupted his wife, "you spend the money on tea for me instead. You wicked old man to tell stories."

"Well, I takes my share of the tea, old woman, and I'm sure it's a deal better for me. But, to tell the truth, Sir, I was a little troubled in my mind about the baccay, not knowing whether I ought to have it or not. For you see, the parson that's gone didn't more than half like it. Not as he said anything, for I was an old man. But I did hear him give a thunderin' broadside to a young chap i' the village he come upon with a pipe in his mouth. So I was in two minds whether I ought to go on with my pipe or not."

"And how did you settle the question, Rogers?"

"Why, I followed my own old chart, Sir."

"Quite right. One mustn't mind too much what other people think."

"That's not exactly what I mean, Sir. I mean that I said to myself, 'Now, Old Rogers, what do you think the Lord would say about this here baccay business?' "

"And what did you think He would say?"

"Why, Sir, I thought He would say, 'Old Rogers, have yer baccay—only mind ye don't grumble when you 'ain't got none.' "

Something in this touched me more than I can express. No doubt it was the simple reality of the relation in which the old man stood to his Father in heaven that made me feel as if the tears would come. "And this is the man," I said to myself, "whom I thought to teach! Well, the wisest learn most, and I may be useful to him after all."

As I said nothing, the old man resumed, "For you see, Sir, it is not always a body feels he has a right to spend his ha'pence on baccay, and sometimes, too, he 'ain't got none to spend."

"In the meantime," I said, "here is some that I bought for you as I came along. I hope you find it good. I am no judge."

The old sailor's eyes glistened with gratitude. "Well, who'd ha' thought it? You didn't think I was beggin' for it, Sir, surely?"

"You see I had it for you in my pocket."

"Well, that is good o' you, Sir."

"Why, Rogers, that'll last you a month!" exclaimed his wife.

"Six weeks at least, Wife," he answered. "And ye don't smoke yourself, and yet ye bring baccay to me!"

I went away resolved that Old Rogers should have no chance of "grumbling" for want of tobacco, if I could help it.

FOUR

THE COFFIN

As I went through the village, I explored a narrow lane striking off to the left. It led up to one side of the large house of which I have already spoken. As I came near, I smelt a delightful smell—that of fresh deals under the hands of the carpenter. If I were idling, that scent would draw me across many fields. I heard the sound of a saw, so I drew near, feeling as if the Lord might be working there at one of His own benches. And when I reached the door, there was my palefaced hearer of Sunday afternoon sawing a board for a coffin lid. As my shadow fell across and darkened his work, he lifted his head and saw me.

He stood upright from his labor and touched his old hat with a proud (rather than courteous) gesture. And I could not believe that he was glad to see me, although he laid down his saw and advanced to the door. It was the gentleman in him, not the man, that sought to make me welcome, hardly caring whether I saw through the ceremony or not. True, there was a smile on his lips, but the smile of a man who cherishes a secret grudge. So the smile seemed tightened, and stopped just when it was about to become hearty and begin to shine.

"I am glad I have happened to come upon you by accident," I said.

He smiled as if he did not quite believe in the accident, and considered it a part of the play between us that I should pretend it. I hastened to add, "I was wandering about the place, making some acquaintance with it, when I came upon you quite unexpectedly. I saw you in church on Sunday afternoon."

"I know you saw me, Sir," he answered, with a motion as if to return to his work, "but to tell the truth, I don't go to church very often."

I did not quite know whether to take this as proceeding from an honest fear of being misunderstood, or from a sense of being in general superior to all that sort of thing. But it would be of no good to pursue the inquiry directly. I looked, therefore, for something to say. "Your work is not always pleasant," I said, looking at the unfinished coffin.

"Well, there are unpleasant things in all trades," he answered, with an increase of bitterness in his smile.

"I didn't mean," I said, "that the work was unpleasant, only sad. It must always be painful to make a coffin."

"A joiner gets used to it, Sir, as you do to the funeral service. But, for my part, I don't see why it should be considered so unhappy for a man to be buried. This isn't such a good job, after all, this world, Sir, you must allow."

"Neither is that coffin," said I, by a sudden inspiration.

The man seemed taken aback. He looked at the coffin and then looked at me. "Well, Sir," he said, after a short pause which no doubt seemed long, "I don't see anything amiss with the coffin. I don't say it'll last till doomsday, as the gravedigger said to Hamlet; but you see, Sir, it's not finished yet."

"Thank you," I said. "That's just what I meant. You thought I was hasty in my judgment of your coffin, whereas I only said of it knowingly what you said of the world thoughtlessly. How do you know that the world is finished any more than your coffin? And how dare you say that it is a bad job?"

The same respectfully scornful smile passed over his face, as to say, "Ah! it's your trade to talk that way, so I must not be too hard on you."

"At any rate, Sir," he said, "whoever made it has taken long enough about it, a person would think, to finish anything he ever meant to finish."

"One day is with the Lord as a thousand years, and a thousand years as one day," I said.

"That's supposing," he answered, "that the Lord did make the world. For my part, I am half of a mind that the Lord didn't make it at all."

"I am very glad to hear you say so," I answered.

Hereupon I found that we had changed places a little. He

23

looked up at me, and the smile of superiority was no longer there. I was in danger of being misunderstood, however, so I proceeded at once. "Of course, it seems to me better that you should not believe God had done a thing, than that you should believe He had not done it well."

"Ah, I see, Sir. Then you will allow there is some room for doubting whether He made the world at all?"

"Yes, for I do not think an honest man, as you seem to me to be, would be able to doubt without any room whatever. That would be only for a fool. But it is just possible, as we are not perfectly good ourselves. You'll allow that, won't you?"

"That I will, Sir. God knows."

"Well, I say, as we're not quite good ourselves, it's just possible that things may be too good for us to do them the justice of believing in them."

"But there are things, you must allow, so plainly wrong!"

"So much so, both in the world and in myself, that it would be to me torturing despair to believe that God did not make the world, for then, how would it ever be put right? Therefore I prefer the theory that He has not done making it yet."

"But mightn't God have managed it without so many slips in the making? I should think myself a bad workman if I worked after that fashion."

"I do not believe there are any slips. You know you are making a coffin, but are you sure you know what God is making of the world?"

"That I can't tell, of course, nor anybody else."

"Then you can't say that what looks like a slip is really a slip, either in the design or in the workmanship. You do not know what end He has in view, and you may find someday that those slips were just the straight road to that very end."

It is a principle of mine never to push anything over the edge. When I am successful in any argument, my one dread is of humiliating my opponent. When a man reasons for victory and not for the truth in the other soul, he is sure of just one ally—the devil. The defeat of the intellect is not the object in fighting with the sword of the Spirit, but rather the acceptance of the heart. Therefore, I drew back. "May I ask for whom you are making that coffin?"

"For a sister of my own, Sir."

"I'm sorry to hear that."

"There's no occasion. I can't say I'm sorry, though she was one of the best women I ever knew."

"Why are you not sorry, then? Life's a good thing in the main, you will allow."

"Yes, when it's endurable at all. But to have a brute of a husband coming home at any hour, drunk on the money she had earned by hard work, was enough to take more of the shine out of things than churchgoing on Sundays could put in again. I'm as glad as her husband that she's out of his way at last."

"How do you know he's glad of it?"

"He's been drunk every night since she died."

"Then he's the worse for losing her?"

"He may well be. Crying like a hypocrite too over his own work!"

"A fool he must be—a hypocrite, perhaps not. A hypocrite is a terrible name to give. Perhaps her death will do him good."

"He doesn't deserve to be done any good to. I would have made this coffin for him with a world of pleasure."

"I never found that I deserved anything, not even a coffin. The only claim that I could ever lay to anything was that I was very much in want of it."

The old smile returned, as if to say, "That's your little game in the church." But I resolved to try nothing more with him at present. "This has been a fine old room once," I said, looking round the workshop.

"You can see it wasn't a workshop always, Sir. Many a grand dinner party has sat down in this room when it was in its glory. The owners little thought it would come to this—a coffin on the spot where the grand dinner was laid for them and their guests! But there is another thing about it that is odder still: my son is the last male—"

Here he stopped suddenly and his face grew very red. As suddenly he resumed, "I'm not a gentleman, Sir, but I will tell the truth. My son's not the last male descendant."

Here followed another pause. While I looked at him, I was reminded of someone else I knew, though I could not in the least determine who that might be.

"It's very foolish of me to talk so to a stranger," he resumed.

"It is very kind and friendly of you," I said. "And you yourself belong to the old family that once lived in this old house?"

"It would be no boast to tell the truth, Sir, even if it were a credit to me, which it is not. That family has been nothing but a curse to ours."

I noted that he spoke of that family as different from his, and yet implied that he belonged to it. The explanation would come in time. But the man was again silent, planing away at the lid of his sister's coffin.

"I am sure there must be many a story to tell about this old place, if only there were someone to tell them," I said at last, looking round the room once more. "I think I see the remains of paintings on the ceiling."

"You are sharp-eyed, Sir. My father says they were plain enough in his young days."

"Is your father alive, then?"

"That he is, Sir—past ninety and hearty too—though he seldom goes out of doors now. Will you go upstairs and see him? He has plenty of stories to tell about the old place, before it began to fall to pieces, like."

"I won't go today," I said, partly to secure an excuse for calling again soon. "I expect visitors myself, and it is time I were at home. Good morning."

"Good morning, Sir."

I was certain of understanding this man when I had learned something of his history. A man may be on the way to the truth just in virtue of his doubting. Lord Bacon says, "So it is in contemplation: if a man will begin with certainties, he shall end in doubts; but if he will be content to begin with doubts, he shall end in certainties." This man's doubt was evidently real, and that was much in his favor. And I could see that he was a thinking man— just one of the sort I thought I should get on with in time. At all events, here was another strange parishioner. And who could it be that he was like?

FIVE

VISITORS FROM THE HALL

When I came near my own gate, I found a carriage standing there, and a footman ringing the bell. It was an old-fashioned carriage, with two white horses who were yet whiter by age than by nature. They looked as if no coachman could get more than three miles an hour out of them, they were so fat and knuckle-kneed. I reached the door just as my housekeeper was pronouncing me absent. There were two ladies in the carriage, one old and one young.

"Ah! Here is Mr. Walton," said the old lady, in a serene voice with a clear hardness in its tone. I held out my hand to aid her descent. She had pulled off her glove to get a card out of her card case, and so put the tips of two old fingers, worn very smooth as if polished with feeling what things were like, upon the palm of my hand. I then offered my hand to her companion, a girl about fourteen, who jumped down beside her with a smile. As I followed them into the house, I took their card from the housekeeper's hand and read *Mrs. Oldcastle* and *Miss Gladwyn*.

When they were seated in the drawing room, I said to the lady, "I remember seeing you in church on Sunday morning. It is very kind of you to call so soon."

"You will always see me in church," she returned, with a stiff bow, and an expansion of deadness on her face, which I interpreted as an assertion of dignity.

"Except when you have a headache, Grannie," said Miss Gladwyn, with an arch look first at her grandmother and then at me. "Grannie has bad headaches sometimes."

27

The deadness melted a little from Mrs. Oldcastle's face as she turned with a half smile to her grandchild and said, "Yes, Pet. But you know that cannot be an interesting fact to Mr. Walton."

"I beg your pardon, Mrs. Oldcastle," I said. "A clergyman ought to know the troubles of his flock, and sympathy is one of the first demands he ought to be able to meet. I know what a headache is."

The former expression, or rather nonexpression, returned, this time unaccompanied by a bow. "I trust, Mr. Walton, that I am above any morbid necessity for sympathy. But, as you say, among the poor of your flock, it is very desirable that a clergyman should be able to sympathize."

"It's quite true what Grannie says, Mr. Walton, though you mightn't think it. When she has a headache, she shuts herself up in her own room, and doesn't even let me come near her—nobody but Sarah—and how she can prefer her to me, I'm sure I don't know." And here the girl pretended to pout, but with a sparkle in her bright gray eyes.

"The subject is not interesting to me, Pet. Pray, Mr. Walton, is it a point of conscience with you to wear the surplice when you preach?"

"Not in the least," I answered. "I think I like it rather better on the whole. But that's not why I wear it."

"Never mind Grannie, Mr. Walton. I think the surplice is lovely. I'm sure it's much like the way we shall be dressed in heaven, though I don't think I shall ever get there, if I must read the good books Grannie reads."

"I don't know that it is necessary to read any good books but *the* Good Book," I said.

"There, Grannie!" exclaimed Miss Gladwyn, triumphantly. "I'm so glad I've got Mr. Walton on my side!"

"Mr. Walton is not so old as I am, My Dear, and has much to learn yet."

I could not help feeling a little annoyed (which was very foolish, I know), and said to myself, "If it's to make me like you, I had rather not learn anymore!" but I said nothing aloud.

"Have you a headache today, Grannie?"

"No, Pet. Be quiet. I wish to ask Mr. Walton why he wears the surplice"

"Simply," I replied, "because I was told the people had been accustomed to it under my predecessor."

"But that can be no good reason for doing what is not right—that people have been accustomed to it."

"But I don't allow that it's not right. I think it is a matter of no consequence whatever. If I find that the people don't like it, I will give it up with pleasure."

"You ought to have principles of your own, Mr. Walton."

"I hope I have! And one of them is not to make mountains of molehills, for a molehill is not a mountain. A man ought to have too much to do in obeying his conscience and keeping his soul's garments clean, to mind whether he wears black or white when telling his flock that God loves them, and that they will never be happy till they believe it."

"They may believe that too soon."

"I don't think anyone can believe the truth too soon."

A pause followed, during which it became evident to me that Miss Gladwyn saw fun in the whole affair and was enjoying it thoroughly. Mrs. Oldcastle's face, on the contrary, was illegible. She resumed in a measured, still voice which she meant to be meek, I dare say, but which was really authoritative, "I am sorry, Mr. Walton, that your principles are so loose and unsettled. You will see my honesty in saying so when you find that objecting to the surplice, as I do on Protestant grounds, I yet warn you against making any change because you may discover that your parishioners are against it. You have no idea, Mr. Walton, what inroads Radicalism, as they call it, has been making in this neighborhood. It is quite dreadful. Everybody, down to the poorest, claiming a right to think for himself and set his betters right! There's one worse than any of the rest—but he's no better than an atheist—a carpenter of the name of Weir, always talking to his neighbors against the proprietors and the magistrates, and the clergy too, Mr. Walton, and the game laws, and what not. And if you once show them that you are afraid of them by going a step out of your way for their opinion about anything, there will be no end to it. The beginning of strife is like the letting out of water, as you know. *I* came to hear of it through my daughter's maid, a decent girl of the name of Rogers, and born of decent parents, but unfortunately attached to the son of one of your churchwardens, who has put him into that mill on the river."

"Who put him in the mill?"

"His own father, to whom it belongs."

"Well, it seems to me a very good match for her."

"Yes, indeed, and for him too. But his foolish father thinks the match below him, as if there was any difference between the positions of people in that rank of life! Everyone seems striving to tread on the heels of everyone else, instead of being content with the station to which God has called them. I am content with mine. I had nothing to do with putting myself there. Why should they not be content with theirs? They need to be taught Christian humility and respect for their superiors. That's the virtue most wanted at present. The poor have to look up to the rich—"

"That's right, Grannie! And the rich have to look down on the poor."

"No, my dear, I did not say that. The rich have to be kind to the poor."

"But, Grannie, why did you marry Mr. Oldcastle? Uncle Stoddart says you refused ever so many offers when you were a girl."

"Uncle Stoddart has no business to be talking about such things to a chit like you," returned the grandmother, smiling, however, at the charge which so far certainly contained no reproach.

"And Grandpa was the ugliest and the richest of them all, wasn't he, Grannie? And Colonel Markham the handsomest and the poorest?"

A flush of anger crimsoned the old lady's pale face. It looked dead no longer. "Hold your tongue," she said. "You are rude."

And Miss Gladwyn did hold her tongue but nothing else, for she was laughing all over.

The relation between these two was evidently a very odd one. It was clear that Miss Gladwyn was a spoiled child, though I could not help thinking her very nicely spoiled, as far as I saw. The old lady persisted in regarding her as a cub, although her claws had grown quite long enough to be dangerous. Certainly, if things went on thus, it was pretty clear which of them would soon have the upper hand, for Grannie was vulnerable and Pet was not.

But her granddaughter's tiger-cat play drove the old lady nearer to me. She rose and held out her hand, saying with some kindness, "Take my advice, my dear Mr. Walton, and don't make too much of your poor or they'll soon be too much for you to manage. Come, Pet, it's time to go home to lunch. And for the surplice, take your own way and wear it. I shan't say anything more about it."

"I will do what I can see to be right in the matter," I answered as gently as I could, for I did not want to quarrel with her, although I thought her both presumptuous and rude.

"I'm on your side, Mr. Walton," said the girl, with a sweet comical smile, as she squeezed my hand once more.

I led them to the carriage, and it was with a feeling of relief I saw it drive off.

The old lady certainly was not pleasant. She had a white smooth face over which the skin was drawn tight, gray hair, and rather lurid hazel eyes. I felt a repugnance toward her that was hardly to be accounted for by her arrogance to me, or by her superciliousness to the poor, although either would have accounted for much of it. I confess that I have not yet learned to bear presumption and rudeness with all the patience and forgiveness with which I ought by this time to be able to meet them. And as to the poor, I am afraid I was always in some danger of being a partisan of theirs against the rich, and that a clergyman ought never to be. Indeed, the poor rich have more need of the care of the clergyman than the others, seeing that the rich shall scarcely enter into the kingdom of heaven, and the poor have all the advantage over them in that respect.

"Still," I said to myself, "there must be some good in the woman—she can not be altogether so hard as she looks, else how should that child dare to take the liberties of a kitten with her? She doesn't look to me like one to make game of! However, I shall know a little more about her when I return her call, and I will do my best to keep on good terms with her."

I took down a volume of Plato to comfort me, and sat down in an easy chair beside the open window of my study. I began to feel as if a man might be happy, even if a lady had refused him. And there I sat, gazing out on the happy world, when a gentle wind came in as if to bid me welcome. I thought of the wind that blows where it wills, and I thanked God for the Life whose story and words are in that best of books, the Bible.

I prayed that He would make me able to speak good common heavenly sense to my people, and forgive me for feeling so cross and proud toward the unhappy old lady—for I was sure she was not happy—and make me into a rock which swallowed up the waves of wrong in its great caverns and never threw them back to swell the commotion of the angry sea whence they came. Ah! To annihilate wrong in this way—to say, "It shall not be wrong against me, so utterly do I forgive it!" Perhaps, however, the forgiveness of the great wrongs is not so true as it seems. For do we not think it is a fine thing to forgive such wrongs, and so do it rather for our own sakes than for the sake of the wrongdoer? It is dreadful not to be good, and to have bad ways inside one.

Such thoughts passed through my mind. And once more the great light went on with regard to my office, namely, that just because I was parson to the parish I must not be *the person* to myself. Therefore I prayed God to keep me from feeling stung and proud, however anyone might behave to me, for all my value lay in being a sacrifice to Him and the people.

So, when Mrs. Pearson knocked at the door, and told me that a lady and gentleman had called, I shut my book which I had just opened, and kept down as well as I could the rising grumble of the inhospitable Englishman who is apt to be forgetful to entertain strangers, at least in the parlor of his heart. And I cannot count it perfect hospitality to be friendly and plentiful toward those whom I have invited to my house, while I am cold and forbidding to those who have not that claim on my attention.

I went and received Mr. and Miss Boulderstone, who left me a little fatigued but in no way sore or grumbling. They only sent me back with additional zest to my Plato, of which I enjoyed a hearty page or two before anyone else arrived. The only other visitors I had that day were Dr. Duncan, a retired navy surgeon who practiced in the neighborhood, and Mr. Brownrigg, the church-warden.

Except Mrs. and Miss Boulderstone, I had not yet seen any common people. They were all decidedly uncommon and, as regards most of them, I could not think I should have any difficulty in preaching to them. There was some good in preaching to a man like Weir or Old Rogers, but whether there was any good in preaching to a woman like Mrs. Oldcastle I did not know.

The evening I thought I might give to my books, and thus end my first Monday in my parish, but as I said, Mr. Brownrigg, called and stayed a whole weary hour talking about matters quite uninteresting—such as the impeccable lineage of the pigs he nurtured. Really he was not an interesting man: short, broad, stout, red-faced, with an immense amount of mental inertia discharging itself in constant lingual activity about little nothings. Indeed, when there was no new nothing to be had, the old nothing would do over again to make fresh fuss about. But if I attempted to convey a thought into his mind which involved his moving round half a degree from where he stood, and looking at the matter from a new point, I found him utterly, totally impenetrable.

I could not help observing that his cheeks rose from the collar of his green coat, his neck being invisible. The conformation was just what he himself delighted to contemplate in his pigs, to which his resemblance was greatly increased by unwearied endeavors to keep himself close shaved. I could not help feeling anxious about his son and Jane Rogers. He gave a quantity of gossip about various people, evidently anxious that I should regard them as he regarded them; but in all he said concerning them, I could scarcely detect one point of significance as to character or history. I was very glad indeed when the waddling of hands—for handshaking—was over, and he was safely out of the gate. He had kept me standing on the steps for a full five minutes, and I did not feel safe from him till I was once more in my study with the door shut.

In the days following I found my poor who I thought must be somewhere, seeing the Lord had said we should have them with us always. There was a workhouse in the village, but there were not a great many in it. The poor who belonged to the place were kindly enough handled and were not too severely compelled to go into the house, though I believe in this house they would have been more comfortable than they were in their own houses.

Then I began to think it better to return Mrs. Oldcastle's visit, though I felt greatly disinclined to encounter that tight-skinned nose again, and that mouth whose smile had no light in it, except when it responded to some nonsense of her granddaughter's.

SIX

OLDCASTLE HALL

About noon on a lovely autumn day I set out for Oldcastle Hall. I walked over the old gothic bridge with a heart strong enough to meet Mrs. Oldcastle without flinching. I might have to quarrel with her—I could not tell; she certainly was neither safe nor wholesome. But this I was sure of, that I would not quarrel with her without being quite certain that I ought. I wish it were never one's duty to quarrel with anybody, I do so hate it. But not to do it sometimes is to smile in the devil's face, and that no one ought to do.

The woods on the other side of the river from my house, toward which I was now walking, were somber and rich like a life that has laid up treasure in heaven. I came nearer and nearer to them through the village, and approached the great iron gate with the antediluvian monsters on the top of its stone pillars. And awful monsters they were—are still! But they let me through very quietly, notwithstanding their evil looks: I thought they were saying to each other across the top of the gate, "Never mind—he'll catch it soon enough."

I wandered up the long winding road through the woods flanking the meadow. These woods smelt so sweet—their dead and dying leaves departing in sweet odors—that they quite made up for the absence of the flowers. And the wind—no, there was no wind, there was only a memory of wind that woke now and then in the bosom of the wood—shook down a few leaves, like the thoughts that flutter away in sighs, and then was still again. Up the slope of the hillside, the trees rose like one great rainbow-

34

billow of foliage—bright yellow, rusty red, fading bright green, and all shades of brown and purple. Multitudes of leaves lay on the sides of the path, so many that I returned to my old childish amusement of walking in them without lifting my feet, driving whole armies of them rustling before me.

At length the road brought me up to the house. It did not look such a large house as I have since found it to be, and it certainly was not an interesting house from the outside, though its surroundings of green grass and trees were beautiful. Indeed, the house itself tried hard to look ugly, failing only because the kind foiling of its efforts by the virginia creepers and ivy. But there was one charming group of old chimneys belonging to some portion behind, which indicated a very different, a very much older face upon the house, a face that had passed away to give place to this.

Once inside, I found there were more remains of the olden time than I had expected. I was led up one of those grand, square oak staircases which look like a portion of the house to be dwelt in, and not like a ladder for getting from one part to another. On the top was a fine expanse of landing, from which I was led toward the back of the house by a narrow passage, and shown into a small, dark, oak drawing room with a deep stone-mullioned window. Here I found Mrs. Oldcastle reading one of the cheap and gaudy religious books of the day. She rose and received me, and having motioned me to a seat, began to talk about the parish. I perceived at once from her tone that she recognized no other bond of connection between us but the parish.

"I hear you have been most kind in visiting the poor, Mr. Walton. You must take care that they don't take advantage of your kindness, though. I assure you, you will find some of them very grasping indeed. And you need not expect that they will give you the least credit for good intentions."

"I have seen nothing yet to make me uneasy on that score. But certainly my testimony is of no weight yet."

"Mine is. I have proved them. The poor of this neighborhood are very deficient in gratitude."

"Yes, Grannie—"

I started, but when I looked round in the direction whence the voice came, the words that followed were all rippled with sweet amusement. "Yes, Grannie, you are right. You remember how Dame Hope wouldn't take the money offered her, and dropped such a disdainful courtesy. It was so greedy of her, wasn't it?"

35

"I am sorry to hear of any disdainful reception of kindness," I said.

"Yes, and she had the coolness, within a fortnight, to send up to me and ask if I would be kind enough to lend her half a crown for a few weeks."

"And then it was your turn, Grannie! You sent her five shillings, didn't you? Oh, no, I am wrong. That was the other woman."

"Indeed, I did not send her anything but a rebuke. I told her that it would be a very wrong thing in me to contribute to the support of such an evil spirit of unthankfulness as she indulged in. When she came to see her conduct in its true light, and confessed that she had behaved very abominably, I would see what I could do for her."

"And meantime she was served out, wasn't she? With her sick boy at home, and nothing to give him?" said Miss Gladwyn.

"She made her own bed and had to lie on it."

"Don't you think a little kindness might have had more effect in bringing her to see that she was wrong?"

"Grannie doesn't believe in kindness except to me—dear old Grannie! She spoils me. I'm sure I shall be ungrateful some day, and then she'll begin to read me long lectures and prick me with all manner of headless pins. But I won't stand it, I can tell you, Grannie! I'm too much spoiled for that."

Mrs. Oldcastle was silent, why I could not tell, except it was that she knew she had no chance of quieting the girl in any other way.

(Later, I inquired of the Dame Hope and found that there had been a great misunderstanding, as I had suspected. She was really in no want at the time, and did not feel that it would be quite honorable to take money which she did not need. She had refused it, not without feeling that it was more pleasant to refuse than to accept from such a giver. Some stray sparkle of that feeling, discovered by the keen eye of Miss Gladwyn, may have given that appearance of disdain to her courtesy. When, however, her boy in service was brought home ill, she had sent to ask for what she now required on the very ground that it had been offered to her before. The misunderstanding had arisen from the total incapacity of Mrs. Oldcastle to enter sympathetically into the feelings of one as superior to herself in character as she was inferior in worldly condition.)

36

I wished to change the subject. "This is a beautiful old house," I said. "There must be strange places about it."

Mrs. Oldcastle had not time to reply, or at least did not reply, before Miss Gladwyn said, "O Mr. Walton, have you looked out the window yet? You don't know what a lovely place this is, if you haven't." She emerged from a recess in the room, a kind of dark alcove. I followed her to the window. "There!" she said, holding back one of the dingy heavy curtains with her small childish hand.

And there indeed I saw an astonishment. I had approached the house by a gentle slope, which certainly was long and winding, but had occasioned no feeling in my mind that I had reached any considerable height. And I had come up that one beautiful staircase, no more, and yet now when I looked from this window I found myself on the edge of a precipice. Below the house on this side lay a great wooded hollow. The sides were all rocky and steep, with here and there slopes of green grass. And down in the bottom, in the center of the hollow, lay a pool of water. I knew it only by its slaty shimmer through the fading green of the treetops between me and it.

"There!" again exclaimed Miss Gladwyn, "isn't that beautiful? But you haven't seen the most beautiful thing yet. Grannie, where's—ah! There she is! There's Auntie! Don't you see her down there, by the side of the pond? That pond is a hundred feet deep. If Auntie were to fall in, she would be drowned before you could jump down to get her out. Can you swim?"

Before I had time to answer, she was off again. "Don't you see Auntie down there?"

"No, I don't see her. I have been trying very hard, but I can't."

"Well, I dare say you can't. Nobody, I think, has eyes but myself. Do you see a big stone by the edge of the pond, with another stone on the top of it, like a big potato with a little one grown out of it?"

"No."

"Well, Auntie is under the trees across from that stone. Do you see her yet?"

"No."

"Then you must come down with me, and I will introduce you to her. She's much the prettiest thing here, much prettier than Grannie."

Here she looked over her shoulder at Grannie who, instead of being angry, only said, without even looking up from the book, "You are a saucy child."

Miss Gladwyn laughed merrily. "Come along," she said, and seizing me by the hand, led me out of the room, down a back staircase, across a piece of grass, and then down a stair in the face of the rock toward the pond below. The stair went in zigzags and, although rough and dangerous, was protected by an iron balustrade.

"Isn't your grandmamma afraid to let you run up and down here, Miss Gladwyn?" I said.

"Me?" she exclaimed, apparently in the utmost surprise. "That would be fun! For, you know, if she tried to hinder me—but she knows it's no use. I taught her that long ago, ten years at least. I ran away and they thought I had drowned myself in the pond. And I saw them all the time, poking with a long stick in the pond which, if I had been drowned there, never could have brought me up, for it is a hundred feet deep, I am sure. I hurt my sides trying to keep from screaming with laughter! I heard one say to the other, 'We must wait till she swells and floats!' "

"Dear me, what a peculiar child!" I thought. And yet somehow, whatever she said, even when she was most rude to her grandmother, she was never offensive. No one could have helped feeling all the time that she was a little lady. I thought I would venture a question with her. I stood at a turn of the zigzag, and looked down into the hollow, still a good way below us, where I could now distinguish the form, on the opposite side of the pond, of a woman seated at the foot of a tree and stooping forward over a book.

"May I ask you a question, Miss Gladwyn?"

"Yes, twenty if you like, but I won't answer one of them till you give up calling me Miss Gladwyn. We can't be friends, you know, so long as you do that."

"What am I to call you, then? I never heard you called by any other name than Pet, and that would hardly do, would it?"

"Oh, just fancy if you called me Pet before Grannie! That's Grannie's name for me, and nobody dares to use it but Grannie, not even Auntie. Between me and you, Auntie is afraid of Grannie. I can't think why. I never was afraid of anybody except, yes, a little afraid of Old Sarah. She used to be my nurse, you know, and Grandmamma and everybody are afraid of her, and that's just why I never do one thing *she* wants me to do. It would never do to be afraid of her, you know. There's Auntie, you see, down there just where I told you before."

"Oh, yes, I see her now. What does your aunt call you, then?"

"Why, what you must call me— my own name, of course."

"What is that?"

"Judy" She said it in a tone which seemed to indicate surprise that I should not know her name—perhaps read it of her face—as one ought to know a flower's name by looking at it. But she added instantly, glancing up in my face most comically, "I wish yours was Punch."

"Why, Judy?"

"It would be such fun, you know."

"Well, it would be odd, I must confess. What is your Auntie's name?"

"Oh, such a funny name—much funnier than Judy—Ethelwyn. It sounds as if it ought to mean something, doesn't it?"

"Yes. It is an Anglo-Saxon word, without doubt."

"What does it mean?"

"I'm not sure. I will try to find out when I go home, if you would like to know."

"Yes, that I should. I should like to know everything about Auntie. Ethelwyn. Isn't it pretty?"

"So pretty that I should like to know something more about Aunt Ethelwyn. What is her other name?"

"Why, Ethelwyn Oldcastle, to be sure. What else could it be?"

"Why, for anything I knew, Judy, it might have been Gladwyn. She might have been your father's sister."

"Might she? I never thought of that. Oh, I suppose that is because I never think about my father. And now I do think of it, I wonder why nobody ever mentions him to me, or my mother either. But I often think Auntie must be thinking about my mother. Something in her eyes, when they are sadder than usual, seems to remind me of my mother."

"You remember your mother, then?"

"No, I don't think I ever saw her. But I've answered plenty of questions, haven't I? I assure you, if you want to get me on to the catechism, I don't know a word of it. Come along."

I laughed.

"What?" she said, pulling me by the hand, "you a clergyman, and laugh at the catechism! I didn't know that."

"I'm not laughing at the catechism, Judy. I'm only laughing at the idea of putting catechism questions to you."

"You know I didn't mean it," she said, with some indignation.

"I know now," I answered. "But you haven't let me put the only question I wanted to put."

"What is it?"

"How old are you?"

"Twelve. Come along." And away we went down the rest of the stairs. When we reached the bottom, a winding path led us through the trees to the side of the pond, and along to the other side. And the thought struck me, why was it that I have never seen this aunt with the lovely name at church? Was she going to be another strange parishioner? There she sat, intent on her book. As we drew near she looked up and rose, but did not come forward.

"Aunt Wynnie, here's Mr. Walton," said Judy.

I lifted my hat and held out my hand. Before our hands met, however, a tremendous splash reached my ears from the pond. I started round. Judy had vanished. I had my coat half off, and was rushing to the pool, when Miss Oldcastle stopped me, her face unmoved except by a smile, saying, "It's only one of that frolicsome child's tricks, Mr. Walton. It is well for you that I was here, though. Nothing would have delighted her more than to have you in the water too."

"But," I said, "where is she?"

"There," returned Miss Oldcastle, pointing to the pool, in the middle of which arose a heaving and bubbling, and presently the laughing face of Judy.

"Why don't you help me out, Mr. Walton? You said you could swim."

"No, I did not," I answered. "You talked so fast, you did not give me time to say so."

"It's very cold," she returned.

"Come out, Judy dear," said her aunt. "Run home, and change your clothes. There's a dear."

Judy swam to the opposite side, scrambled out, and was off like a spaniel through the trees and up the stairs, dripping and raining as she went.

"You must be very much astonished at the little creature, Mr. Walton. There never was a child so spoiled, and never a child on whom it took less effect. I suppose such things do happen sometimes. She really is a good girl though Mamma, who has done all the spoiling, will not allow me to say she is good."

Here followed a pause for, Judy disposed of, what should I say next? And the moment her mind turned from Judy, I saw a certain stillness—not a cloud, but the shadow of a cloud—come over Miss Oldcastle's face, as if she too found herself uncomfortable, and did not know what to say next. I tried to get a glance at the book in her hand, for I should know something about her at once if I could only see what she was reading. She never came to church, and I wanted to arrive at some notion of the source of her spiritual life, for that she had such, a single glance at her face was enough to convince me. This made me even more anxious to see the book. But I could only discover that it was an old book in very shabby binding, not in the least like the books that young ladies generally have in their hands.

The two young ladies were not alike. Judy was rosy, gray-eyed, auburn-haired, sweet-mouthed. She had confidence in her chin, assertion in her nose, defiance in her eyebrows, and honesty and friendliness over all her face. No one, evidently, could have a warmer friend, and to an enemy she would be dangerous no longer than a fit of passion might last. There was nothing acrid in her and the reason, I presume, was that she had never yet hurt her conscience. (That is a very different thing from saying she had never done wrong.) She was not tall, even for her age, and just a little too plump for the immediate suggestion of grace. She would have been graceful except that impulse was always predominant, giving a certain jerkiness, like the hopping of a bird, instead of the gliding of one motion into another, such as you might see in the same bird on the wing.

There is one of the ladies. But the other—how shall I attempt to describe her?

The first thing I felt was that she was a lady-woman, and to feel that is almost to fall in love at first sight. She was graceful, rather slender, rather tall, and quite blue-eyed. But it was not upon that occasion that I found out the color of her eyes. I was so taken with her whole that I knew nothing about her parts. Yet she was blue-eyed, indicating northern extraction some centuries back perhaps. That blue was the blue of the sea that had sunk through the eyes of some sea-rover's wife and settled in those eyes of her child to be born when the voyage was over. It had been dyed so deep that it had never been worn from the souls of the race since. Her features were regular, delicate, and brave. After the grace, the dignity was the next thing I came to discover. And the only thing I did not like, I discovered last. For when the shine of the courtesy with which she received me had faded away, a certain look of negative haughtiness, of withdrawal (if not of repulsion) took its place. It was a look of consciousness of her own high breeding, a pride—not of life but of circumstance of life—which disappointed me in the midst of so much that was very lovely. Her voice was sweet, and her speech slow without drawling, and I could have fancied a tinge of sadness in it.

"This is a most romantic spot, Miss Oldcastle," I said, "and as surprising as it is romantic. I could hardly believe my eyes when I looked out of the window and saw it."

"Your surprise was the more natural in that the place itself is not natural. It *looks* pretty, but it does not have a very poetic origin. It is nothing but the quarry out of which the house was built."

"It seems to me a much more poetic origin than any convulsion of nature. From that buried mass of rock has arisen this living house, with its histories of ages and generations, and—"

Here I saw her face grow almost pallid, but her large blue eyes were still fixed on mine.

"And it seems to me," I went on, "that such a chasm is therefore more poetic. Human will, human thought, human hands in human labor and effort, have all been employed to build this house, making beautiful not only the house but also the place whence it came. It stands on the edge of its own origin, generation to generation in the same place."

Her face had grown still paler, and her lips moved as if she would speak, but no sound came from them.

"I am afraid you feel ill, Miss Oldcastle."

"Not at all," she answered, quickly. She drew herself up a little haughtily, so I drew back to the subject of our conversation.

"But I can hardly think," I said, "that all this mass of stone could be required to build the house, large as it is. A house is not solid, you know."

"No," she answered. "The original building was more of a castle, with walls and battlements. I can show you the old foundations, and the picture too, of what the place used to be. We are not what we were then. Many cottages have been built out of this old quarry, though not a stone has been taken from it for fifty years. Let me show you one thing, Mr. Walton, and then I must leave you."

"Do not let me detain you. I will go at once," I said, "though, if you would allow me, I should be more at ease if I might see you safe at the top of the stair first."

She smiled. "I am not ill, but I have duties to attend to. Let me show you this, and then you shall go back with me." She led the way to the edge of the pond and looked into it. I followed and gazed down into its depths till my sight was lost in them. I could see no bottom to the rocky shaft.

"There is a strong spring down there," she said. "Is it not a dreadful place? Such a depth!"

"Yes," I answered, "but it has not the horror of dirty water. It is clear as crystal. How does the surplus escape?"

"On the opposite side of the hill you came up, there is a well with a strong stream from it into the river."

"I almost wonder at your choosing such a place to read."

"Judy has taken all that away. Nothing in nature is strange to Judy! Look down into the water on this side. Do you see anything there against the wall of the pond?"

"I see a kind of arch or opening in the side," I answered.

"Do you also see a little barred window there, in the face of the rock, through the trees? It is the window of a little room in the rock, from which a stair leads through the rock to a sloping passage. That is the end of it you see under the water."

"Provided, no doubt," I said, "in case of siege, to procure water."

"Most likely, but not, therefore, confined to that purpose. There are more dreadful stories than I can bear to think of—"here she paused abruptly, and began anew,—"as if that house had brought death and doom out of the earth with it. There was an old burial ground here before the Hall was built."

"Have you ever been down the stair you speak of?" I asked.

"Only part of the way," she answered. "But Judy knows every step of it. If it were not that the door at the top is locked, she would have dived through that archway now, and been in her own room in half the time. The child does not know what fear means."

We moved away from the pond, toward the side of the quarry and up the open-air staircase. Miss Oldcastle accompanied me to the room where I had left her mother, and took her leave with merely a bow of farewell. I saw the old lady glance sharply from her to me, as if she were jealous of what we might have been talking about.

"Grannie, are you afraid Mr. Walton has been saying pretty

things to Aunt Wynnie? I assure you he is not of that sort. But he would have jumped into the pond after me and got his death of cold if Auntie would have let him. It *was* cold. I think I see you dripping now, Mr. Walton." There she was in her dark corner, coiled up on a couch and laughing heartily, but all as if she had done nothing extraordinary. And by her own notions and practices, what she had done was not in the least extraordinary.

Disinclined to stay any longer, I shook hands with the grandmother (with a certain invincible sense of slime) and with the grandchild (with a feeling of mischievous health, as if the girl might soon corrupt the clergyman into a partnership in pranks as well as in friendship). She followed me out of the room and danced before me down the oak staircase, clearing the portion from the first landing at a bound, turning and waiting for me. I came very deliberately, feeling the unsure contact of sole and wax. As soon as I reached her, she said in a half whisper, reaching up toward me on tiptoe, "Isn't she a beauty?"

"Who, your grandmamma?" I returned.

She gave me a little push, her face glowing with fun. But I did not expect she would take her revenge as she did. "Yes, of course," she answered, quite gravely. "Isn't she a beauty?" Then she burst into loud laughter, opened the hall door for me, and let me go without another word.

I went home very quietly, stepping with curious care over the yellow and brown leaves that lay in the middle of the road.

SEVEN

THE BISHOP'S BASIN

I have never sat down with my parishioners without finding that they actually possess a history, the most marvelous and important fact to a human being. And I have come to the conclusion, not that this was an extraordinary parish of characters, but that every parish must be extraordinary from the same cause.

The people among whom I had been today belonged in a romantic story. The Hall would hardly come into my ideas of a country parish at all. All that had happened since I looked out of the window in the old house might have been but a dream. That wooded dell was much too large for a quarry. And that madcap girl who flung herself into the pond! And was that a real book that the lady with the sea-blue eyes was reading? A commonplace book would not have been her companion at the bottom of a quarry. And that terrible pool and subterranean passage—what had their story to do with this broad daylight and dying autumn leaves? No doubt there had been such places and no doubt there were such places somewhere yet—this was one of them. But, somehow or other, it would not fit well.

I took the impression off by going to see Weir, the carpenter's old father. I found the carpenter busy as usual, working now at a window sash. "Just like life," I thought. "The other day he was closing in the outer darkness, and now he is letting in the light."

"It's a long time since you was here last, Sir," he said, but without a smile.

"Well," I answered, "I wanted to know something about all my people before I paid a second visit to any of them."

45

"All right, Sir. Don't suppose I meant to complain. Only to let you know you was welcome, Sir."

"To tell the truth, for I don't like pretenses, my visit today was more to your father. I ought to have called upon him before, only I was afraid of seeming to intrude upon you, seeing we don't exactly think the same way about some things."

A smile lighted up his face, and his answer fixed his smile in my memory. "You made me think, Sir, that perhaps, after all, we were much of the same way of thinking, only perhaps you was a long way ahead of me."

Now our opinions could hardly do more than come within sight of each other. But what he meant was right enough—the man had regard for the downright, honest way of things, and I hoped that I too had such a regard, and that the road lay open for further and more real communion between us in time to come.

"My father will be delighted to see you, I know, Sir. He can't get so far as the church on Sundays, but you'll find him much more to your mind than me. He's been putting ever so many questions to me about the new parson. I've never told him that I'd been to church since you came—I suppose from a bit of pride, because I had so long refused to go—but I don't doubt some of the neighbors have told him, for he never speaks about it now. I know he's been looking out for you, and I fancy he's begun to wonder that the parson was going to see everybody but him. It will pleasure him, Sir, for he don't see a great many to talk to."

Weir led the way through the shop and up a back stair into a large room over the workshop. There were bits of old carving about the whitewashed walls of the room. At one end stood a bed with chintz curtains and a warm-looking counterpane of rich but faded embroidery. There was a bit of carpet by the bedside, and another bit in front of the fire, and there the old man sat in a high-backed chair. He managed to rise, though bent nearly double, and tottered a few steps to meet me. He held out a thin, shaking hand and welcomed me with an air of kindly breeding rare in his station in society.

"I'm blithe to see ye, Sir," said he. "Sit ye down, Sir." He pointed to his own easy chair.

"No, Mr. Weir," I said, "The Bible tells us to rise up before the aged, not to turn them out of their seats."

"It would do me good to see you sitting in my cheer, Sir. The pains that my son Tom there takes to keep it up as the old man

46

may want it! It's a good thing I bred him to the joiner's trade, Sir. Sit ye down, Sir. The cheer'll hold ye, though I warrant it won't last that long after I be gone home. Sit ye down, Sir."

Thus entreated, I hesitated no longer, but took the old man's seat. His son brought another chair for him, and he sat down opposite the fire and close to me. Thomas went back to his work, leaving us alone.

"Ye've had some speech wi' my son Tom," said the old man, the moment he was gone, leaning a little toward me. "It's main kind o' you, Sir, to take up kindly wi' poor folks like us."

"You don't say it's kind of a person to do what he likes best," I answered. "Besides, it's my duty to know all my people."

"Oh, yes, Sir, I know that. But there's a thousand ways ov doing the same thing. I ha' seen folks, parsons and other, 'at made a great show ov bein' friendly to the poor, ye know, Sir, and all the time you could see, or tell without seein', that they didn't much regard them in their hearts, but it was a sort of accomplishment for them to be able to talk to the poor after their own fashion. But the minute an ould man sees you, Sir, he believes that you mean it, Sir, whatever it is, for an ould man somehow comes to know things like a child. They call it a second childhood, don't they, Sir? And there are some things worth growin' a child again to get hould of again."

"I only hope what you say may be true—about me, I mean."

"Take my word for it, Sir. You have no idea how that boy of mine, Tom there, did hate all the clergy till you come. Not that he's any way favorable to them yet, only he'll say nothin' again' you, Sir. He's got an unfortunate gift o' seein' all the faults first— and when a man is that way given, the faults always hides the other side, so that there's nothing but faults to be seen."

"But I find Thomas quite open to reason."

"That's because you understand him, Sir, and know how to give him his head. He tould me of the talk you had with him. You don't bait him, you don't say, 'You must come along wi' me,' but you turn and goes along wi' him. He's not a bad fellow at all, is Tom, but he will have the reason for everythink. Now I never did want the reason for everythink. I was content to be tould a many things. But Tom, you see, he was born with a sore bit in him somewheres, I don't rightly know wheres—and I don't think he rightly knows himself."

"You might give him time, for he doesn't feel at home yet. And how can he, when he doesn't know his own father?"

"I don't rightly understand you," said the old man, looking bewildered and curious.

"Till a man knows that he is one of God's family, living in God's house, with God upstairs as it were, while he works or plays below stairs, he can't feel comfortable. For a man could not be made that should stand alone like some of the beasts. A man must feel a head over him, because he's not enough to satisfy himself, you know. Thomas just wants to feel that there is a loving Father over him, who is doing things well and right."

"Ah, Sir, I fancied that you were just putting your finger upon the sore place in Tom's mind. There's no use in keeping family misfortunes from a friend like you, Sir. That boy has known his father all his life, but I was nearly half his age before I knew mine."

"Then your father and mother—" I said, and hesitated.

"Were never married, Sir," said the old man, promptly. "I couldn't help it. And I'm no less the child of my Father in heaven for it. If He hadn't made me, I couldn't ha' been their son, so that He had more to do wi' the makin' o' me than they had. I do love my mother, and I'm so sorry for my father that I love him too, Sir. And if I could only get my boy Tom to think as I do, I would die like a psalm tune on an organ, Sir."

"But it seems strange," I said, "that your son should think so much of what is so far gone by. Surely he would not want another father than you, now."

"There has been other things to keep his mind on the old affair. We have had the same misfortune all over again among the young people, and my boy Tom has a sore heart."

(I had already learned that the strange handsome woman in the little shop was the daughter of Thomas Weir, and that she was neither wife nor widow. It was a likeness to her little boy that had affected me so pleasantly when I first saw Thomas, his grandfather, and now the likeness to his great-grandfather made the other fact clear. But yet I was haunted with a flickering sense of a third likeness, which I could not identify.)

"Perhaps," I said, "he may find some good come out of that too. If we do evil that good may come, the good we looked for will never come thereby. But once evil is done, we may humbly look to Him who brings good out of evil, and wait. Is your granddaughter Catharine in bad health? She looks so delicate."

48

"She always had an uncommon look, but what she looks like now I don't know. I hear no complaints. But she has never crossed this door since we got her set up in that shop. She never comes near her father or her sister, though she would let them go and see her. I'm afraid Tom has been rather unmerciful with her. If ever he put a bad name upon her in her hearing, she wouldn't be likely to forget it. I don't believe they do more nor nod to one another when they meet in the village. There's some people made so hard that they never can forgive anythink."

"How did she get into the trouble? Who is the father of her child?"

"That no one knows for certain, though there be suspicions, and one of them no doubt correct. But I believe fire wouldn't drive his name out at her mouth, for I know my lass."

I asked no more questions, but after a short pause the old man went on.

"I sha'n't soon forget the night I first heard about my father and mother. That was a night! The wind was roaring like a mad beast about the house—not here, Sir, but the great house over the way."

"You don't mean Oldcastle Hall?"

" 'Deed I do, Sir," returned the old man. "This house here belonged to the same family at one time, though when I was born it was another branch of the family that lived in it, but even then it was something on to the downhill road."

"But," I said, fearing he might have turned aside from a story worth hearing, "do go on. The wind was blowing?"

"Eh, Sir, it was roaring—mad with rage. It would come down the chimley like out of a gun, and blow the smoke and a'most the fire into the middle of the housekeeper's room. I called the housekeeper Auntie, then, and didn't know a bit that she wasn't my aunt really. And she said, 'It was just such a night as this, leastways it was snow and not rain that was comin' down, as if the Almighty was a-going to spend all His winter stock at once.'

" 'What happened such a night, Auntie?' I said.

" 'Ay, my lad,' said she, 'ye may well ask. None has a better right. You happened, that's all. And you certainly wasn't wanted. It's my fault, if it be fault, that you're sitting there now, and not lying at the bottom of the Bishop's Basin.'

"I said, feeling cold and small, as if I had no right to be there, 'But who wanted to drown me?'

" 'It was, I make no doubt, though I can't prove it—it was your father.'

"I felt the skin go creepin' together on my head, and I couldn't speak.

" 'And now,' she said, 'it's time you knew all about it. Poor Miss Wallis! I'm no aunt of yours, though I love you dearly, because I loved your mother. She was a beauty, and better than she was beautiful. The only wrong thing she ever did was to trust your father. But I'll give you the story right through.

" 'Miss Wallis's mother and father died early, and she was left alone, and she came to us to be a governess. She never got on well with the children, for they were young and self-willed and rude, and would not learn to do as they were bid. She was a sweet creature, that she was, but nobody took any notice or care of her. The children were kept away with her in the old house, and my lady wasn't one to take trouble about anybody. And so, when the poor thing was taken with a dreadful cold, which was no wonder if you saw the state of the window in the room she had to sleep in, it fell to me to look after her. It would have made your heart bleed to see the poor thing flung all of a heap on her bed, blue with cold and coughing.

" 'I had to nurse her for a fortnight before she was able to do anything again, though she didn't shirk her work. It was a heart-sore to me to see the poor young thing, with her sweet eyes and pale face, talking away to those children that were more like wild-cats than human beings. She used to come see me evenings, and sit there without speaking, her thin white hands folded in her lap and her eyes fixed on the fire. I used to wonder what she could be thinking about.

" 'And then Miss Oldcastle, who had been at school, came home, and we had a great deal of company and visitors, and your mother's health began to come back.

" 'But then I had a blow, Samuel. It was a lovely spring night, just after the sun was down, and I wanted a drop of milk fresh from the cow, so I went through the kitchen garden to the shippen. But who was at the other end of the path but Miss Wallis, walking arm-in-arm with Captain Crowfoot who was just home from India. He was about three and thirty, a relation of the family, and the only son of Sir Giles Crowfoot. As sure as judgment no good could come of it, for the captain had not the best of characters, though he was a great favorite with everybody that knew nothing about him. He was a fine, manly, handsome fellow with a smile that, as people said, no woman could resist, though that same smile was the falsest of all the false things about him. All the time he was smiling, you would have thought he was looking at himself in a glass.

" 'They came close past me, and never saw me. At least, if he saw me he took no notice, for I don't suppose that the angel with the flaming sword would have put him out. I know she didn't see me, for her face was down, burning and smiling at once.

" 'And it was days before I saw her again. She came to my room, and without a moment of parley I said to her, "Oh, my dear, what was that wretch Captain Crowfoot saying to you?"

" ' "What have you to say against Captain Crowfoot?" says she, quite sharp-like and scornful.

" 'He was said to have gathered a power of money in India, and I don't think he would have been the favorite he was with my lady if he hadn't. Reports were about, too, of the way he had made the money—some said by robbing the poor heathen creatures, and some said speculating in horses and other things. And this one of his own servants told me, not thinking any harm or shame of it. The captain had quarreled with a young ensign in the regiment, and the captain first thrashed him most unmercifully, and then called him out for a duel. And the poor fellow could scarcely see out of his eyes, and certainly couldn't take anything like an aim. And he shot him dead, did Captain Crowfoot.

" 'So I poured out all I had against him in one breath. She turned awful pale, and shook from head to foot, and said, "I don't believe one word of it. But I'll ask him next time I see him." I knew he would not make any fuss that might bring it out in the air, and I hoped it might lead to a quarrel between them. And the next time I met her, she passed me with a nod just, and a blush instead of a smile. I knew that villain had gotten a hold of her. I could only cry, and that I did.

" 'The captain came and went for months, stopping a week each time, and came again in the autumn for the shooting and began to make up to Miss Oldcastle who had grown a fine young woman by that time. And Miss Wallis began to pine, and before long I was certain she was in a consumption. But she never spoke a word about herself or the captain.

" 'Then came the news that the captain and Miss Oldcastle were to be married in the spring. Miss Wallis took to her bed, and my lady wanted to send her away, but Miss Oldcastle spoke up for her, for she had ne'er a home to go to. I said I would take all the care and trouble of her, and my lady promised, and the poor thing was left alone. Not a word would she speak, even to me, though every moment I could spare I was with her. One day she threw her arms about my neck, and burst into a terrible fit of crying. I put my arms around her and lifted her up, and then I understood her plight, and I said, "I know now, my dear. I'll do all I can for you." It was well for her that she could go to her bed, and I thought she might die before there was any need for further concealment. But people in that condition seldom die, they say, till all is over—and she lived on, though getting weaker.

" 'The wedding day was fixed at the captain's next visit, and after that a circumstance came about that made me uneasy. A foreign servant had been constantly attending the captain. I never could abide the snake-look of the fellow, nor the noiseless way he went about the house. But this time the captain had a foreign servant-woman with him as well. The captain went away, and left the servant-woman behind, for the wedding was to take place in three weeks. Meantime poor Emily—Miss Wallis—grew fast worse. And now, with the wedding, I could see yet less of her than before, and when Miss Oldcastle sent the foreign servant to ask if she could sit with the poor girl, I did not know how to object, though I did not at all trust her. I longed to have the wedding over, that I might get rid of the servant, and take her place, and get everything prepared. The captain arrived, and his man with him. And twice I came upon the two servants in close conversation.

" 'Well, the wedding day came. The people went to church, and while they were there a terrible storm of wind and snow came on, such that the horses would hardly face it. The captain was going to take his bride home, but the storm got so dreadful no one could leave the house. The wind blew for all the world just as it blows this night, only it was snow in its mouth and not rain.

" 'After dinner was over and the ladies were gone to the drawing room, and the gentlemen had been sitting over their wine for some time, the butler, William Weir, came to my room looking scared. "Lawks, William!" says I, "whatever is the matter with you?"

" ' "Well," says he, "it's a strange wedding, it is! There's the ladies all alone in the drawing room, and the gentlemen callng for more wine, and cursing and swearing awful to hear. Swords'll be drawn afore long. And I don't a'most like goin' down them stairs alone in sich a night, ma'am. Would you mind coming with me?"

" ' "Dear me, William," says I, "a pretty story to tell your wife"—she was my own half-sister and younger than me—"that you wanted an old body like me to go and take care of you in your own cellar. But I'll go with you for, to tell the truth, it's a terrible night." And so down we went and brought up six bottles more of the best port. And I really didn't wonder, when I was down there and heard the dull roar of the wind against the rock below, that William didn't much like to go alone. When he went back with the wine, the captain said, "William, what kept you so long? Mr. Centlivre says that you were afraid to go down into the cellar."

" 'Before William could reply, Sir Giles said, "A man might well be afraid to go anywhere alone on a night like this." Whereupon the captain swore that he would go down the underground stair, and into every vault on the way, for the wager of a guinea. And a few minutes after, they were all at my door, demanding the key of the room at the top of the stair. I was just going up to see poor Emily, and I gave the captain the key, wishing with all my heart he might get a good fright for his pains. He took a jug with him, to bring some water from the well as proof he had been down. The rest went with him into the little cellar room, but wouldn't stop there, they said it was so cold. They all came into my room, where they talked as gentlemen wouldn't do if the wine hadn't got uppermost.

" 'It was some time before the captain returned. He looked as if he had got the fright I wished him. The candle in his lantern was out, and there was no water in the jug. "There's your guinea, Centlivre," says he, throwing it on the table. "You needn't ask me any questions, for I won't answer one of them."

" ' "Captain," says I, as they turned to leave the room, "I'll just hang up the key again."

" 'He started, and searched his pockets all over for it. "I must have dropped it," says he, "but it's of no consequence. You can send William for it in the morning. It can't be lost."

" 'All this time I couldn't get to see Emily. As often as I looked from my window, I saw her old west turret out there. Now I had told that servant that if anything happened, or she was worse, she must put the candle on the window, and I would come directly. But the blind was drawn down, so I thought all was right. And what with the storm keeping Sir Giles and more that would have gone home, there was no end of work and contrivance, for we were nothing too well provided with blankets and linen in the house. There was always more room than money in it.

" 'So it was past twelve before they had all gone to bed—the bride and the bridegroom in the crimson chamber, of course. At last I crept into Emily's room. There was no light there, and my own candle had blown out. I spoke, but no one answered. Then I heard such a shriek from the crimson chamber that it made me all creep like worms. Doors were opened, and lights came out, with everybody looking terrified. And the door of the crimson chamber opened too, and the captain bawled out to know what was the matter—though I'm certain the cry came from that room and that he knew more about it than anyone else did. I got a light and ran back, and there was Emily lying white and motionless. A baby had been born, but no baby was to be seen. Though she was still warm, your mother was quite dead.

" 'Then I saw it all. Without waiting to be afraid, I ran to the underground stairs, and found the door standing open. I had not gone down more than three turnings, when I heard a cry, and just about halfway down, there lay a bundle in a blanket. And how you ever got over the state I found you in, Samuel, I can't think. But I caught you up and ran to my room and locked the door, and did the best for you I could. The breath wasn't out of you, though it well might have been. And then I laid you before the fire, and by that time you had begun to cry a little. I wrapped you up in a blanket and made my way with you to Mrs. Wier. William opened the door to me, and saw the bundle in my arms. "Mrs. Prendergast," says he, "I didn't expect it of you."

" ' "Hold your tongue," I said. "You would never talk such nonsense if you had the grace to have any of your own." I went into the bedroom and shut the door and left him out there in his shirt. My sister and I soon got everything arranged, and before morning I had made all tidy. Your poor mother was lying as sweet a corpse as ever an angel saw, and no one could say a word against her. She was buried down there in the churchyard, close by the vestry door,' said my aunt, Sir, and all our family have been buried there since, my son Tom's wife among them, Sir."

"But what was that cry in the house?" I asked. "And what became of the servant-woman?"

"The woman was never seen again, and what that cry was my

aunt never would say. She seemed to know, although Captain and Mrs. Crowfoot denied all knowledge of it. But the lady looked dreadful, she said, and was never well again, and died at the birth of her first child. That was the present Mrs. Oldcastle's father, Sir."

"But why should the woman have left you on the stair, instead of drowning you in the well at the bottom?"

"There was some mystery about that. All my aunt would say was, 'The key was never found, Samuel. I had to get a new one made.' So I was brought up as her nephew, though people were surprised that William Weir's wife should have a child, and nobody know she was expecting.

"Well, with all the reports of the captain's money, none of it showed in this old place, which began to crumble away. If it hadn't been a well-built place to begin with, it wouldn't be standing now. It's very different now. Why, all behind was a garden with terraces and fruit trees and flowers to no end. I remember it as well as yesterday—nay, a great deal better, for I don't remember yesterday at all."

His story interested me greatly, but only tended to keep up the sense of distance between my experience at the Hall and the work I had to do among my other people.

I left the old man with thanks and walked home thinking of many things. I shut myself up in my study and tried in vain to read a sermon of Jeremy Taylor. I fell fast asleep over it, and woke refreshed.

EIGHT

WHAT I PREACHED

During the suffering and disappointment at which I have already hinted, I sought consolation from the New Testament. To my surprise, I discovered that I could not read the Epistles at all—I did not then care an atom for the theology which had interested me before. Now that I was in trouble, what to me was that philosophical theology? All reading of the Book is not reading of the Word. It was Jesus Christ, and not theology, that filled the hearts of the men who wrote those Epistles—Jesus Christ, whom I found not in the Epistles but in the Gospels. And until we understand the Gospel, the good news of Jesus Christ—until we understand Him, until we have His Spirit—all the Epistles are to us a sealed book.

The Gospels then took hold of me as never before. I found out that I had known nothing at all—that I had only a certain surface knowledge which tended to ignorance, because it fostered the delusion that I did know. Know that Man, Christ Jesus? Ah! Lord, I would go through fire and water to sit at Thy table in Thy kingdom, but dare I say now I *know* Thee?

I found, as I read, that His very presence in my thoughts smoothed the troubled waters of my spirit, so that even while the storm lasted, I was able to walk upon them to go to Him. And when those waters became clear, I most rejoiced in their clearness because they mirrored His form.

And therefore, when I was once more in a position to help my fellows, what could I want to give them but the Saviour Himself? I took the story from the beginning and told them about the Baby.

And I followed the life on, trying to show them how He felt, what His sayings meant, as far as I understood them myself. Where I could not understand them, I just told them so and said I hoped for more light by and by, because I knew that only as I did my duty would light go up in my heart. And I told them that if they would try to do their duty, they would find more understanding than from any explanation I could give them.

And so I went on from Sunday to Sunday. The number of people who slept grew fewer and fewer, until at last it was reduced to Mr. Brownrigg and an old washerwoman. She stood so much all the week that sitting down was like going to bed, and she never could do it without going to sleep. I therefore called on her every Monday morning, and had five minutes' chat with her as she stood at her washtub, thinking that if I could once get her interested, she might be able to keep awake a little while at the beginning of the sermon. I never got so far as that, however. The only fact that showed me I had made any impression upon her, beyond the pleasure she always manifested when I appeared, was that whereas all my linen had been very badly washed at first, a decided improvement took place after a while, gradually extending itself till even Mrs. Pearson was unable to find any fault with the sleepy woman's work.

For Mr. Brownrigg, I am not sure that the sense of any one sentence ever entered into his brain—I dare not say his mind or heart.

Before long I was also sure of seeing the pale face of Thomas Weir perched, like that of a man beheaded for treason, upon the gablet of the old tomb. I continued to pay him visits. The man was no more an atheist than David was when he saw the wicked spreading like a green bay tree and was troubled at the sight. He only wanted a God in whom he could trust. And if I succeeded at all in making him hope that there might be such a God, it is to me one of the most precious seals of my ministry.

It was getting very near Christmas, and there was one person whom I had never yet seen at church—Catharine Weir. I had told my housekeeper to buy whatever she could from her, instead of going to the larger shop in Marshmallows. Mrs. Pearson had grumbled a good deal, saying how could the things be so good out of a poky shop like that? But I told her I did not care if the things were not quite as good. It would be of more consequence to Catharine to have the custom, than it would be to me to have the sugar in my morning tea one or even two shades whiter.

So I had kept up a connection with her, although I saw that any attempt at conversation was so distasteful to her that it must do harm until something should have brought about a change in her feelings, though what feeling wanted changing I could not at first tell. I came to the conclusion that she had been wronged, and that this wrong, operating on a nature similar to her father's, had drawn all her mind to brood over it. The world itself would seem then to have wronged her, and to speak of religion would only rouse her scorn, and make her feel as if God Himself, if there were a God, had wronged her too. Evidently she had that peculiarity of being unable, once possessed by one set of thoughts, to get rid of them again or to see anything except in the shadow of these thoughts. I had no doubt that she was ashamed in the eyes of society, and that this prevented her from appearing where it was unnecessary, especially in church.

I could do nothing more than wait for a favorable opportunity. I could invent no way of reaching her yet, for I had found that kindness to her boy was regarded as an insult to her. I should have been greatly puzzled to account for his being such a sweet little fellow, had I not known that he was with his aunt and grandfather a great deal.

I should also say that on three occasions before Christmas I had seen Judy look grave. She was always quite well-behaved in church, though restless. But on these occasions she was not only attentive, but grave.

On the other hand, I never saw Mrs. Oldcastle change countenance or expression in church.

NINE

THE ORGANIST

I should explain that on the afternoon of my second Sunday at Marshmallows, I had been standing in the churchyard, casting a long shadow in the light of the declining sun. I was reading the inscription upon an old headstone, when I heard a door open and shut again before I could turn. I saw at once that it must have been a little door in the tower, almost concealed from where I stood by a deep buttress. I had never seen the door open, and had never inquired about it, supposing it led merely into the tower.

After a moment it opened again, and out came a man whom no one could pass without looking after him. Tall and strongly built, he had the carriage of a military man, a large face with regular features, and large clear gray eyes. His beard, which descended halfway down his breast, would have been white as snow except for a slightly yellowish tinge. His eyebrows were very dark, just touched with the frost of winter. His hair, too, as I saw when he lifted his hat, was still wonderfully dark. His clothes were all black, very neat and clean but old-fashioned, bearing signs of use and time and careful keeping. It flashed into my mind that this must be the organist who played so remarkably. I would have spoken to him, but something in the manner in which he bowed to me prevented me, and I let him go.

The sexton came out directly after, and I asked him who the gentleman was.

"That is Mr. Stoddart, Sir," he answered. "He's played our organ for the last ten years, ever since he come to live at Oldcastle Hall."

And then it dawned that I heard Judy mention her Uncle Stoddart. But how could he be her uncle? "Is he a relation of the family?" I asked.

"He's a brother-in-law, I believe, of the old lady, Sir—been in the military line in the Indies or somewhere."

Although I had intended to inquire after Mr. Stoddart when I left the vicarage to go to the Hall, and had even thought of him when sitting with Mrs. Oldcastle, I never thought of him again after going with Judy, and I left the house without having made a single inquiry after him.

And now, after all this time, I resolved to call on him the following week, and did. When I rang the doorbell at the Hall and inquired for Mr. Stoddart, the butler stared at me, and answered with some hesitation, "Mr. Stoddart never calls upon anyone, Sir."

"I am not complaining of Mr. Stoddart," I answered, wishing to put the man at his ease.

"But nobody calls upon Mr. Stoddart," he returned.

"That's very unkind of somebody, surely," I said.

"But he doesn't want anybody to call upon him, Sir."

"Ah! that's another matter. I didn't know that. However, as I have come without knowing his dislike, perhaps you will take him my card, and say that I should like to thank him in person for his exquisite voluntary on the organ last Sunday."

"I will try, Sir," he answered. "But won't you come upstairs, Sir, while I take this to Mr. Stoddart?"

"No, I thank you," I answered. "I came to call upon Mr. Stoddart only, and I will wait here in the hall."

The man withdrew, and I sat down on a bench and amused myself with looking at the portraits about me. One particularly pleased me. It was the portrait of a young woman, very lovely but with an expression both sad and scared. It was remarkably like Miss Oldcastle. (I learned afterward that it was the portrait of Mrs. Oldcastle's grandmother, that very Mrs. Crowfoot mentioned in Weir's story. It had been made about six months after her marriage, and about as many before her death.)

The butler returned with a request to follow him. He led me up the grand staircase, through a passage, up a narrow staircase, across a landing, then up a straight, steep, narrow stair. At the top I found myself in a small cylindrical lobby, papered in blocks of stone and lighted by a conical skylight. There was no door to be seen. My conductor gave a push against the wall. Certain blocks yielded, and others came forward. A door revolved on central pivots, and we were admitted to a chamber crowded with books from floor to ceiling. From the center of the ceiling radiated a number of strong beams supporting bookshelves. On each side of those I passed under, I could see the gilded backs of books standing together.

"How does Mr. Stoddart reach those books?" I asked my conductor.

"I don't exactly know, Sir," whispered the butler. "I believe, however, he does not use a ladder."

There was no one in the room, and I saw no entrance but that by which we had entered. The next moment, however, a nest of shelves revolved in front of me, and there stood Mr. Stoddart with outstretched hand.

"You have found me at last, Mr. Walton, and I am glad to see you," he said.

He led me into an inner room, much larger than the one I had passed through.

"I am glad," I replied, "that I did not know your unwillingness to be intruded upon. Had I known it, I should have been yet longer a stranger to you."

"You are no stranger to me. I have heard you read prayers, and I have heard you preach."

"And I have heard you play, so you are no stranger to me either."

"I must say about this report of my unsociable disposition that I encourage it, but I am very glad to see you, notwithstanding. I was so bored with visits after I came—visits which were to me utterly uninteresting—that I was only too glad when the unusual nature of some of my pursuits gave rise to the rumor that I was mad. The more people say I am mad, the better pleased I am, so long as they are satisfied with my own mode of shutting myself up, and do not attempt to carry out any fancies of their own in regard to my personal freedom."

Like the outer room, this one was full of books from floor to ceiling.

"What a number of books you have!" I observed.

"Not a great many," he answered. "But they are almost personal acquaintances, as I have bound a couple of hundred or so of them myself. I don't think you could tell the work from a tradesman's. I'll give you a guinea for the poor box if you pick out three of my bindings consecutively."

I accepted the challenge. I could not bind a book but I consider myself to have a keen eye for the outside finish. After looking over the backs of a great many, I took one down, examined a little further, and presented it.

"You are right. Now try again."

Again I was successful, although I doubted.

"And now for the last," he said.

Once more I was right.

"There is your guinea," said he, a little mortified.

"No," I answered, "I do not feel at liberty to take it because, to tell the truth, the last was a mere guess."

Mr. Stoddart looked relieved. "You are more honest than most of your profession," he said. "But I am far more pleased to offer you the guinea upon the smallest doubt of you having won it."

"I have no claim upon it."

"What! Couldn't you swallow a small scruple like that for the sake of the poor even? Well, I don't believe you could. Oblige me by taking this guinea for your poor. But—I am glad you weren't sure of that last book."

I took the guinea, and put it in my purse.

"But," he resumed, "you won't do, Mr. Walton. You're not fit for your profession. You won't tell a lie for God's sake. You won't dodge about a little to keep all right between Jove and his weary parishioners. You won't cheat a little for the sake of the poor! You wouldn't even bamboozle a little at a bazaar!"

"I should not like to boast of my principles," I answered. "But assuredly I would not favor a fiction to keep a world out of hell. The hell that a lie would keep any man out of is doubtless the very best place for him to go to. It is truth, yes, *The Truth* that saves the world."

"You are right, I dare say. You are more sure about it than I am, though."

"Let us agree where we can first of all, and that will make us able to disagree, where we must, without quarreling."

"Good," he said. "Would you like to see my workshop?"

"Very much indeed," I answered.

He pushed a compartment of books. It yielded, and we entered a small closet. In another moment I found myself rising, and in yet a moment we were on the floor of an upper room.

"What a nice way of getting upstairs!" I said.

"There is no other way to this room," answered Mr. Stoddart. "I built it myself and there was no room for stairs. This is my shop. Here I read anything I want to read, write anything I want to write, bind my books, invent machines, and amuse myself generally. Take a chair."

I obeyed and began to look about me. There were many books in detached bookcases, and various benches against the walls between—one a bookbinder's, another a carpenter's. A third had a turning lathe, and a fourth had an iron vice fixed on it. And there were several tables of chemical apparatus—flasks, retorts, sand baths, and such, while in a corner stood a furnace.

"What an accumulation of ways and means you have about you," I said, "and all, apparently, to different ends."

"All to the same end, if my object were understood. I have theories of education. I think a man has to educate himself into harmony. Therefore, he must open every possible window by which the influences of the All may come in upon him. I do not think any man complete without a perfect development of his mechanical faculties, for instance."

"I do not object to your theory, provided you do not put it forward as a perfect scheme of human life. If you did, I should have some questions to ask you about it, lest I should misunderstand you."

He smiled what I took for a self-satisfied smile. There was nothing offensive in it, but it left me without anything to reply to. No embarrassment followed, however, for a rustling motion in the room attracted my attention, and I saw, to my surprise and confusion, Miss Oldcastle. She was seated in a corner, reading from a quarto lying upon her knees.

"Oh! You didn't know my niece was here? I forgot her when I brought you up, else I would have introduced you."

"That is not necessary, Uncle," said Miss Oldcastle, closing her book.

I was by her instantly. She slipped the quarto from her knee and took my offered hand.

"Are you fond of old books?" I said.

"Some old books," she answered.

"May I ask what you were reading?"

"I will answer you—under protest," she said with a smile. "It is a volume of Jakob Bohme."

"I bought his works as I passed through London last, and found that one of the plates is missing from my copy."

"Which plate is it? It is not very easy, I understand, to procure a perfect copy. One of my uncle's sets has no two volumes bound alike. Each must have belonged to a different set."

"I can't tell you what the plate is. But there are only three of those very curious unfolding ones in my third volume, and there should be four."

"I should always like things to be perfect myself," she returned.

"Doubtless," I answered, and thought it better to try another direction. "How is Mrs. Oldcastle?" I asked, feeling the inner reproach of hypocrisy.

"Quite well, thank you," she answered, in a tone of indifference, which either implied that she saw through me or shared my indifference.

"And Miss Judy?" I inquired.

"A little savage, as usual."

"Not the worse for her wetting, I hope."

"Oh! Dear no. There never was health to equal that child's. It belongs to her savage nature."

"I wish some of us were more of savages, then," I returned, for I saw signs of exhaustion in her eyes which moved my sympathy.

"You don't mean me, Mr. Walton, I hope, for if you do I assure you your interest is quite thrown away. Uncle will tell you I am as strong as an elephant." But a shadow passed over her face, as though she felt she ought not to be the subject of conversation.

When I glanced away from Miss Oldcastle in slight embarrassment, I saw Judy in the room. Miss Oldcastle rose and said, "What is the matter, Judy?"

"Grannie wants you," said Judy.

As Miss Oldcastle left the room, Judy turned to me.

"How do you do, Mr. Walton?" she said.

"Quite well, thank you, Judy," I answered. "Your uncle admits you to his workshop, then?"

"Yes, indeed. He would feel rather dull, sometimes, without me. Wouldn't you, Uncle Stoddart?"

"Just as the horses in the field would feel dull without the gadfly, Judy," said Mr. Stoddart.

Judy was gone in a moment, leaving Mr. Stoddart alone with me. He had been busy at one of his benches, filing away at a piece of brass for a very curious machine. He turned and said to me, "I wonder what speech I shall make next, to drive *you* away, Mr. Walton."

"I am not so easily got rid of, Mr. Stoddart," I answered. "And as for taking offense, I don't like it, and therefore I never take it. But tell me what you are doing now."

"I have been working for some time at an attempt after perpetual motion, but, I must confess, I have not yet succeeded." He threw down his file on the bench. "But this, you will allow, would have made a very pretty machine."

"Pretty, I will allow," I answered, "as distinguished from beautiful, for I can never dissociate beauty from use."

"You say that! With all the poetic things you say in your sermons! For I am a sharp listener, and none the less such for that you do not see me. I have a loophole for seeing you. I flatter myself that I am the only person in the congregation on a level with you. I cannot contradict you, and you cannot address me."

"Do you mean, then, that whatever is poetical is useless?" I asked.

"Do you assert that whatever is useful is beautiful?" he retorted.

"Whatever subserves a noble end must in itself be beautiful."

"Then a gallows must be beautiful because it subserves the noble end of ridding the world of malefactors?" he returned promptly.

"I do not see anything noble in the end," I answered. "If the machine got rid of malefaction, it would indeed have a noble end. But if it only compels it to move on, as a constable does, from this world into another, I do not, I say, see anything so noble in that end. The gallows cannot be beautiful, for an inevitable necessity is very different from a noble end. To cure the diseased mind is the noblest of ends. To make the sinner forsake his ways, and the unrighteous man his thoughts, is the loftiest of designs. But to punish him for being wrong, however necessary it may be for others, cannot be called noble. But I ask you a question now: what is the immediate effect of anything poetic upon your mind?"

"Pleasure," he answered.

"And is pleasure good or bad?"

"Sometimes the one, sometimes the other."

"In itself?"

"I should say bad."

"I should not."

"Are you not, by your very profession, more or less an enemy of pleasure?"

"On the contrary, I believe that pleasure is good, and does good, and urges to good. Care is the evil thing."

"Strange doctrine for a clergyman."

"Now, do not misunderstand me, Mr. Stoddart. That might not hurt you, but it would distress me. Pleasure obtained by wrong is poison and horror. But it is not the pleasure that hurts; it is the wrong that is in it that hurts—the pleasure hurts only as it leads to more wrong. If you could make everybody happy, half the evil would vanish from the earth."

"Then why does not God destroy evil, at such a cheap and pleasant rate?"

"Because He wants to destroy all the evil, not the half of it, and destroy it so that it shall not grow again, which it would be sure to do very soon if it had no antidote but happiness. As soon as men got used to happiness, they would begin to sin again, and so lose it all."

But here I saw that I had lost Mr. Stoddart, so I went back to the original question.

"If I say poetic things in the pulpit, it is because true things come to me in poetic forms. Therefore, I am free to say as many poetic things as shall be of the highest use, namely to embody and reveal the true."

There was no satisfactory following out of the argument on either side. I don't like argument, and I don't care for victory. If I had my way, I would never argue, but only set forth what I believe, and so leave it to work its own way.

I thought it was time for me to take leave. But I could not bear to run away with the last word, as it were, so I said, "You put plenty of poetry yourself into that voluntary you played last Sunday. I am so much obliged to you for it!"

"Oh! that fugue. You liked it, did you?"

"More than I can tell you."

"Shall I tell you what I was thinking of while playing that fugue?"

"I should like to hear."

"I had been thinking, while you were preaching, of the many fancies men had worshiped for the truth—now following this, now following that, ever believing they were on the point of laying hold upon her, and going down to the grave as empty-handed as they came. Multitudes followed where nothing was to be seen, with arms outstretched in all directions, some clasping vacancy to their bosoms, some reaching on tiptoe over the heads of their neighbors, and some with hanging heads, and hands clasped behind their backs, retiring hopeless from the chase."

"Strange!" I said, "for I felt so full of hope while you played!"

"The multitude was full of hope, vain hope, to lay hold upon the truth. And you, being full of the main expression, and in sympathy with it, did not heed the undertones of disappointment, or the sighs of those who turned their backs on the chase. Just so it is in life."

"I am no musician," I returned, "to give you a musical counter to your picture. But I see a man tilling the ground in peace, and the form of Truth standing behind him, and folding her wings closer and closer over and around him as he works on at his day's labor."

"Very pretty," said Mr. Stoddart, and said no more.

"Suppose," I went on, "that a person knows that he has not laid hold on the truth—is that sufficient ground for his making any further assertion than that he has not found it?"

"No. But if he has tried hard and has not found anything that he can say is true, he cannot help thinking that most likely there is no such thing."

"Suppose," I said, "that nobody has found the truth. Is that sufficient ground for saying that nobody ever will find it? Or that there is no such thing as truth to be found? Are the ages so nearly done that no chance remains? Surely, if God has made us to desire the truth, He has some truth to cast into the gulf of that desire. Shall God create hunger and no food? But possibly a man may be looking the wrong way for it. You may be using the microscope when you ought to open both eyes and lift up your head. Or a man may be finding some truth which is feeding his soul when he does not think he is finding any. You know *The Faerie Queene*. Think how long the Red-cross Knight traveled with the Lady Truth without learning to believe in her, and how much longer still without ever seeing her face. For my part, may God give me strength to follow till I die. Only I will venture to say this, that it is not by any agony of the intellect that I expect to discover truth."

"But does not," he asked, gently lowering his eyes upon mine after a moment's pause, "does not your choice of a profession imply that you have, and hold, and therefore teach the truth?"

"I profess only to have caught glimpses of her white garments—those, I mean, of the abstract truth of which you speak. But I have seen that which is eternally beyond her—the ideal in the real, the living truth. Not the truth that I can *think,* but the truth that thinks itself, that thinks me, that God has thought, that God is, the truth being true to itself, and to God, and to man—Christ Jesus, my Lord, who knows and feels and does the truth. I have seen Him, and I am both content and unsatisfied, for in Him are hid all the treasures of wisdom and knowledge. Thomas a Kempis said, 'He to whom the eternal Word speaks is set free from a press of opinions.' "

I rose and held out my hand to Mr. Stoddart. He rose likewise and took it kindly, conducted me to the room below and, ringing the bell, committed me to the care of the butler.

As I approached the gate I met Jane Rogers coming back from the village. I stopped and spoke to her. Her eyes were very red.

"Nothing amiss at home, Jane?" I said.

"No, Sir, thank you," answered Jane, and burst out crying.

"What is the matter, then? Is your—"

"Nothing's the matter with nobody, Sir."

"Something is the matter with you."

"Yes, Sir. But I'm quite well."

"I don't want to pry into your affairs—but if you think I can be of any use to you, mind you come to me."

"Thank you kindly, Sir," said Jane. Dropping a courtesy, she walked on with her basket.

I went to her parents' cottage. As I came near the mill, the young miller was standing in the door with his eyes fixed on the ground, while the mill went on hopping behind him. But when he caught sight of me, he turned and went in, as if he had not seen me.

"Has he been behaving ill to Jane?" thought I.

As he evidently wished to avoid me, I passed the mill without looking in at the door, and went on to the cottage where I lifted the latch and walked in. Both the old people were there, and both looked troubled, though they welcomed me none the less kindly.

"I met Jane," I said, "and she looked unhappy, so I came on to hear what was the matter."

"You oughtn't to be troubled with our small affairs," said Mrs. Rogers.

"If the parson wants to know, why the parson must be told," said Old Rogers, smiling cheerily, as if he at least would be relieved by telling me.

"I don't want to know," I said, "if you don't want to tell me. But can I be of any use?"

"I don't think you can, Sir, leastways I'm afraid not," said the old woman.

"I am sorry to say, Sir, that Master Brownrigg and his son has come to words about our Jane, and it's not agreeable to have folks' daughter quarreled over in that way," said Old Rogers. "What'll be the upshot of it I don't know, but it looks bad now. For the father he tells the son that if ever he hears of him saying one word to our Jane, out ov the mill he goes, as sure as his name's Dick. Now it's rather a good chance, I think, to see what the young fellow's made of, Sir. So I tells Mrs. Rogers here, and so I told Jane, but neither of 'em seems to see the comfort of it somehow. But the New Testament do say a man shall leave father and mother, and cleave to his wife."

"But she ain't his wife yet," said Mrs. Rogers to her husband, whose drift was not yet evident.

"No more she can be, 'cept he leaves his father for her."

"And what'll become of them then, without the mill?"

"You and me never had no mill, yet here we be, very nearly ripe now, ain't us, Wife?"

"Medlar-like, Old Rogers, I doubt—rotten before we're ripe," replied his wife.

"Nay, nay, old 'oman. Don't 'e say so. The Lord won't let us rot before we're ripe, anyhow. That I be sure on."

"But, anyhow, it's all very well to talk. Thou knows how to talk, Rogers. But how will it be when the children comes, and no mill?"

"To grind 'em in, old 'oman?"

I was listening with real interest and much amusement, and Mrs. Rogers turned to me.

"I wish you would speak a word to Old Rogers, Sir. He never will speak as he's spoken to. He's always overmerry or overserious. He either takes me up short with a sermon, or he laughs me out of countenance."

Now I was pretty sure that Rogers' conduct was simple consistency, and that the difficulty arose from his always acting upon the plainest principles of truth and right. His wife, good woman—for the bad leaven of the Pharisees could not rise much in her some-how—was always reminding him of certain precepts of behavior to the oblivion of principles. "A bird in the hand is worth two in the bush," and "Marry in haste, repent in leisure," "When want comes in at the door, love flies out at the window," were among her favorite sayings, although not one of them was supported by her own experience. She had married in haste herself and never, I believe, had once thought of repenting of it, although she had had more than the requisite leisure for doing so. And many was the time that want had come in at her door, and the first thing it always did was to clip the wings of love and make him less flighty, and more tender and serviceable. So I could not even pretend to read her husband a lecture.

"He's a curious man, Old Rogers," I said, "but as far as I can see, he's in the right of the main. Isn't he, now?"

"Oh, yes, I dare say. I think he's always right about the rights of the thing, you know. But a body may go too far that way. It won't do to starve, Sir."

"I don't think anyone can go too far in the right way."

"That's just what I want my old 'oman to see, and I can't get it into her, Sir. If a thing's right, it's right, and if a thing's wrong, why, wrong it is. The helm must either be to starboard or port, Sir."

"But why talk of starving?" I said. "Can't Dick work? Who could think of starting that nonsense?"

"Why, my old 'oman here. She wants 'em to give it up and wait for better times. The fact is, she don't want to lose the girl."

"But she hasn't got her at home now."

"She can have her when she wants her though, leastways after a bit of warning, whereas, if she was married, and the consequences a follerin' at her heels, like a man-o'-war with her convoy, she would find she was chartered for another port, she would."

"Well, you see, Sir, Rogers' and me's not so young as we once was, and we're likely to be growing older every day. And if there's a difficulty in the way of Jane's marriage, why, I take it as a godsend."

"How would you have liked such a godsend, Mrs. Rogers, when you were going to be married to your sailor here? What would you have done?"

"Why, whatever he liked, to be sure. But then, you see, Dick's not my Rogers."

"But your daughter thinks about him the same way you did about this dear old man when he was young."

"Young people may be in the wrong. I see nothing in Dick Brownrigg."

"But young people may be right sometimes, and old people may be wrong sometimes."

"I can't be wrong about Rogers."

"No, but you may be wrong about Dick."

"Don't you trouble yourself about my old 'oman, Sir. She allus was awk'ard in stays, but she never missed them yet. When she's said her say, round she comes in the wind like a bird, Sir."

"There's a good old man to stick up for your old wife!" she said. "Still, I say they may as well wait a bit. It would be a pity to anger the old gentleman."

"What does the young man say to it?" I asked.

"Why, he says like a man he can work for her as well's the mill, and he's ready, if she is."

"I am very glad to hear such a good account of him. I shall look in and have a little chat with him. Good morning, Mrs. Rogers."

"I'll see you across the stream, Sir," said the old man, following me out of the house.

"You see, Sir," he resumed, as soon as we were outside. "I'm always afeard of taking things out of the Lord's hands. It's the right way, surely, that when a man loves a woman, and has told her so, he should act like a man, and do as is right. And isn't that the Lord's way? And can't He give them what's good for them? Mayhap they won't love each other the less in the end if Dick has a little bit of hard work. I wouldn't like to anger the old gentleman, as my wife says, but if I was Dick, I know what I would do. But don't 'e think hard of my wife, Sir, for I believe there's a bit of pride in it. She's afeard of bein' supposed to catch at Richard Brownrigg because he's above us, you know, Sir, and I can't altogether blame her, only we ain't got to do with the look o' things, but with the things themselves."

"I understand you quite, and I'm very much of your mind. You can trust me to have a little chat with him, can't you?"

"That I can, Sir."

I bade him good-day, jumped across the stream, and went into the mill, where Richard was tying the mouth of a sack as gloomily as the brothers of Joseph must have tied their sacks after his silver cup had been found.

"Why did you turn away from me as I passed half an hour ago, Richard?" I said cheerily.

"I beg your pardon, Sir. I didn't think you saw me."

"But supposing I hadn't? But I won't tease you. I know all about it. Can I do anything for you?"

"No, Sir. You can't move my father. It's no use talking to him. He never hears a word anybody says. He never hears a word you say 'o Sundays, Sir. He won't even believe the newspaper about the price of corn. It's no use talking to him, Sir."

"You wouldn't mind if I were to try?"

"No, Sir. You can't make matters worse. No more can you make them any better, Sir."

"I don't say I shall talk to him, but I may, if I find a fitting opportunity."

"He's always worse—more obstinate—that is, when he's in a good temper. So you may choose your opportunity wrong. But it's all the same. It can make no difference."

"What are you going to do, then?"

"I would let him do his worst. But Jane doesn't like to go against her mother. I'm sure I can't think how she should side with my father against both of us. He never laid her under any such obligation, I'm sure."

"There may be more ways than one of accounting for that. You must mind, however, and not be too hard on your father. You're quite right in holding fast to the girl, but mind that vexation does not make you unjust."

"I wish my mother were alive. She was the only one that ever could manage him. How she contrived to do it nobody could think—but manage him she did, somehow or other."

"I dare say he prides himself on not being moved by talk. But has he ever had a chance of knowing Jane, of seeing what kind of girl she is?"

"He's seen her over and over."

"But seeing isn't always believing."

"It certainly isn't with him."

"If he could only know her! But don't you be too hard on him. And don't do anything in a hurry. Give him a little time, you know. Mrs. Rogers won't interfere between you and Jane, I am pretty sure. But don't push matters till we see. Good-by."

"Good-by, and thank you kindly, Sir. Ain't I to see Jane in the meantime?"

"If I were you, I would make no difference. See her as often as you used, which I suppose was as often as you could. I don't think that her mother will interfere. Her father is all on your side."

I called on Mr. Brownrigg but, as his son had forewarned me, I could make nothing of him. He didn't see, when the mill was his property and Dick was his son, why he shouldn't have his way with them. His son might marry any lady in the land, and he wasn't going to throw himself away.

All my missiles of argument were lost, as it were, in a bank of mud. My experience in the attempt, however, did a little to reconcile me to his going to sleep in church, for I saw that it could make little difference whether he was asleep or awake. He, and not Mr. Stoddart in his organ sentry box, was the only person whom it was absolutely impossible to preach to. I might preach *at* him, but *to* him—no.

TEN

MY CHRISTMAS PARTY

As Christmas drew near, my heart glowed with gladness, and the question came pressingly—could I not do something to make it more truly a holiday of the Church for my parishioners? That most of them would have a little more enjoyment on it than they had all the year through, I had ground to hope. But I wanted to connect this gladness in their minds with its source, the love of God manifested in the birth of the Son of man. But I would not interfere with the Christmas Day at home. I resolved to invite my parishioners to spend Christmas Eve at the vicarage.

I therefore had a notice affixed to the church door, and resolved to send out no personal invitations, so that I might not give offense by accidental omission. The only person thrown into perplexity by this mode of proceeding was Mrs. Pearson.

"How many am I to provide for, Sir?" she asked, with an injured air.

"For as many as you ever saw in church at one time," I said. "And if there should be too much, why, so much the better. It can go to make Christmas Day the merrier at some of the poorer houses."

She looked discomposed, for she was not of an easy temper. But she never *acted* from her temper—she only *looked* or *spoke* from it. "I shall want help," she said at length.

"As much as you like, Mrs. Pearson. I can trust you entirely."

Her face brightened, and the end showed that I had not trusted her amiss.

I was a little anxious about the result of the invitation, partly because it indicated the amount of confidence my people placed in me. But, although no one said a word to me about it beforehand except Old Rogers, as soon as the hour for the party arrived, the people began to come. And the first I welcomed was Mr. Brownrigg.

I had had all the rooms on the ground floor prepared for their reception. Tables of provision were set out in every one of them. My visitors had tea or coffee and plenty of bread and butter when they arrived. The more solid supplies were reserved for the later part of the evening. I soon found myself with enough to do. But before long I had a very efficient staff—for, after having had occasion once or twice to mention something of my plans for the evening, I found my labors gradually diminish, and yet everything seemed to go right. Good Mr. Boulderstone, in one part, had cast himself into the middle of the flood of people, and stood there immovable both in face and person, turning its waters toward the barn. In the barn, Dr. Duncan was doing his best, and that was simply something first-rate, to entertain the people till all should be ready. From a kind of instinct, and almost without knowing it, these gentlemen had taken upon them to be my staff, and very grateful I was.

When I came and saw the goodly assemblage, I could not help rejoicing that my predecessor had been so fond of farming that he had rented land and built this large barn, so I might make a hall to entertain my friends. For how can a man be *the person* of a parish if he never entertains his parishioners? And really, though it was lighted only with candles round the walls, and I had not been able to do much for the decoration of the place, I thought it looked very well, and my heart was glad—just as if the Babe had been coming again to us that same night. And is He not always coming to us afresh in every childlike feeling that awakes in the hearts of His people?

It was amusing to watch Mr. Boulderstone's honest though awkward endeavors to be at ease with everyone. Dr. Duncan was just a sight worth seeing. Very tall and stately, he was talking now to this old man, now to that young woman, and every face toward which he turned glistened. There was no condescension about him. He was as polite and courteous to the one as to another, and the smile that every now and then lighted up his old face was genuine and sympathetic. No one could have known by his behavior that he was not at court.

I felt more certain than ever that a free mingling of all classes would do more than anything else toward binding us all into a wise, patriotic nation, and keep down that foolish emulation which makes one class ape another from afar. It would refine the roughness of the rude, and enable the polished to see that public matters might also be committed into the hands of the honest workman.

There was no one there to represent Oldcastle Hall. And Catharine Weir was likewise absent. But how could I have everything a success at once?

After we had spent awhile in pleasant talk, and when I thought nearly all were with us, I got up on a chair and said, "Kind friends, I am very grateful to you for honoring my invitation as you have done. Permit me to hope that this meeting will be the first of many, and that it may grow the yearly custom in this parish of gathering in love and friendship upon Christmas Eve. When God comes to man, man looks round for his neighbor. When man departed from God in the Garden of Eden, the only man in the world ceased to be the friend of the only woman in the world. Instead of seeking to bear her burden, he became her accuser to God, in whom he saw only the Judge, unable to perceive that the infinite love of the Father had come to punish him in tenderness and grace. But when God in Jesus comes to men, brothers and sisters spread forth their arms to embrace each other, and so to embrace Him. We all need to become little children like Him, to cease to be careful about many things, and trust in Him, seeking only that He should rule, and that we should be made good like Him. What else is meant by, 'Seek ye first the kingdom of God and His righteousness, and all these things shall be added unto you'? Instead of doing so, we seek the things God has promised to look after for us, and refuse to seek the thing He wants us to seek—a thing that cannot be given us except we seek it. But tonight, at least, let all unkind thoughts, all hard judgments of one another, all selfish desires after our own way, be put from us, that we may welcome the Babe into our very bosoms, so that when He comes among us He may not be troubled to find that we are quarrelsome, and selfish, and unjust."

I came down from the chair, and shook hands with Mr. Brownrigg, and there was some meaning in the grasp with which he returned mine.

First of all, we sang a hymn about the Nativity, and then I read an extract from a book of travels, describing the interior of an

Eastern cottage, probably much resembling the inn in which our Lord was born, the stable being scarcely divided from the rest of the house. I felt that to open the inner eyes even of the brain, enabling people to see in some measure the reality of the old lovely story, might help to open the yet deeper spiritual eyes which alone can see the meaning and truth dwelling in and giving shape to the outward facts. And the extract was listened to with all the attention I could wish, except, at first, from some youngsters at the farther end of the barn who became, however, perfectly still as I proceeded.

After this followed conversation, during which I talked a good deal to Jane Rogers, paying her particular attention indeed, with the hope of a chance of bringing old Mr. Brownrigg and her together in some way.

"How is your mistress, Jane?" I said.

"Quite well, Sir, thank you. I only wish she was here."

"I wish she were. But perhaps she will come next year."

"I think she will. I am almost sure she would have liked to come tonight, for I heard her say—"

"I beg your pardon, Jane, for interrupting you, but I would rather not be told anything you may have happened to overhear," I said, in a low voice.

"O sir," returned Jane, blushing a dark crimson, "it wasn't anything in particular."

"Still, if it was anything on which a wrong conjecture might be built"—I wanted to soften it to her—"it is better that one should not be told it. Thank you for your kind intention, though. And now, Jane," I said, "will you do me a favor?"

"That I will, Sir, if I can."

"Sing that Christmas carol I heard you sing last night to your mother."

"I didn't know anyone was listening, Sir."

"I know you did not. I came to the door with your father, and we stood and listened."

She looked very frightened. But I would not have asked her had I not known that she could sing like a bird. "I am afraid I shall make a fool of myself," she said.

"We should all be willing to run that risk for the sake of others," I answered.

"I will try, then, Sir."

So she sang, and her voice soon silenced the speech all round.

"You have quite a gift of song, Jane," I said.

"My father and mother can both sing."

Mr. Brownrigg was seated on the other side of me, listening with some interest. His face was ten degrees less stupid than it usually was. I fancied I saw even a glimmer of some satisfaction in it. I turned to Old Rogers.

"Sing us a song, Old Rogers," I said.

"I'm no canary at that, Sir, and, besides, my singing days be over. I advise you to ask Dr. Duncan there. He can sing."

I rose and said to the assembly, "My friends, if I did not think God was pleased to see us enjoying ourselves, I should have no heart for it myself. I am going to ask our dear friend Dr. Duncan to give us a song. If you please, Dr. Duncan."

"I am very nearly too old," said the doctor, "but I will try."

His voice was certainly a little feeble, but the song was not much the worse for it, and genuine applause followed. I turned to Miss Boulderstone, from whom I had borrowed a piano, and asked her to play a country dance for us. But first I said—not getting up on a chair this time—"Some people think it is not proper for a clergyman to dance. I mean to assert my freedom from any such law. If our Lord chose to represent, in His Parable of the Prodigal Son, the joy in heaven over a repentant sinner by the figure of 'music and dancing,' I will hearken to Him rather than to men, be they as good as they may."

For I had long thought that the way to make indifferent things bad was for good people not to do them.

And, so saying, I stepped up to Jane Rogers, and asked her to dance with me. She blushed so dreadfully that, for a moment, I was almost sorry I had asked her. But she put her hand in mine at once—and if she was a little clumsy, she yet danced very naturally—an honest girl, and friendly to me in her heart.

But to see the faces of the people! While I had been talking, Old Rogers had been drinking in every word. To him it was milk and strong meat in one. But now his face shone with a father's gratification besides. And Richard's face was glowing too. Even old Mr. Brownrigg looked with a curious interest upon us, I thought.

Meantime Dr. Duncan was dancing with one of his own patients, old Mrs. Trotter, to whose wants he ministered far more from his table than from his surgery. I have known that man, hearing of a case of want, to send the fowl he was about to dine upon, untouched, to those whose necessity was greater than his.

And Mr. Boulderstone had taken out old Mrs. Rogers, and young Mr. Brownrigg had taken Mary Weir. Thomas Weir did not dance at all, but looked on kindly.

"Why don't you dance, Old Rogers?" I said, as I placed his daughter in a seat beside him.

"Did you ever see an elephant go up the futtock shrouds?"

"No, I never did."

"I thought you must, Sir, to ask me why I don't dance. You won't take my fun ill, Sir? I'm an old man-o'-war's man, you know, Sir."

"I should have thought, Rogers, that you would have known better by this time than make such an apology to me."

"God bless you, Sir. An old man's safe with you—or a young lass either, Sir," he added, turning with a smile to his daughter.

I turned and addressed Mr. Boulderstone. "I am greatly obliged to you, Mr. Boulderstone, for the help you have given me this evening. I've seen you talking to everyone, just as if you had to entertain them all."

"Well, I thought it wasn't a time to mind one's p's and q's exactly, and it's wonderful how one gets on without them. I hate formality myself."

The dear fellow was the most formal man I had ever met.

"Why don't you dance, Mr. Brownrigg?"

"Who'd care to dance with me, Sir? I don't care to dance with an old woman, and a young woman won't care to dance with me."

"I'll find you a partner, if you will put yourself in my hands."

"I don't mind trusting myself to you, Sir."

So I led him to Jane Rogers. She stood up in respectful awe before the master of her destiny. There were signs of calcitration in the church warden when he saw where I was leading him. But when he saw the girl stand trembling before him, whether it was that he was flattered by the signs of his own power, accepting them as homage, or that his hard heart actually softened a little, I cannot tell, but after a perceptible hesitation he said, "Come along, my lass, and let's have a hop together."

She obeyed very sweetly.

"Don't be too shy," I whispered to her as she passed me.

And the church warden danced very heartily with the lady's-maid.

I then asked him to take her into the house and give her something to eat in return for her song. He yielded somewhat awkward-ly, and what passed between them I do not know. But when they returned, she seemed less frightened, and when the company was parting, I heard him take leave of her with the words, "Give us a kiss, my girl, and let bygones be bygones."

Which I heard with delight. For had I not been a peacemaker? And should I not feel blessed? But the understanding was brought about simply by making people meet—compelling them, as it were, to know something of each other.

I took care that we should have dancing in moderation. Indeed, we had only six country dances during the evening. And between the dances I read two or three of Wordsworth's ballads to them. For I thought if I could get them to like poetry and beautiful things in words, it would not only do them good, but would help them to see what is in the Bible, and therefore to love it more. For I never could believe that a man who did not find God in other places, as well as in the Bible would ever find Him there at all. And I have always thought that to find God in other books enables us to see clearly that He is more in the Bible than in any other book, or all other books put together.

After supper we had a little more singing. And, to my satisfac-tion, nothing came to my eyes or ears during the whole evening that was undignified or ill-bred. Of course, I knew that many of them must have two behaviors, and that now they were on their good behavior. But I thought the oftener such were put on their good behavior, the more it would give them the opportunity of finding out how nice it was. It might make them ashamed of the other at last.

Before we parted I gave each guest a sheet of Christmas carols, gathered from the older portions of our literature. For to my mind, most of the modern hymns are neither milk nor meat but mere wretched imitations. There were a few curious words and idioms in these, but I thought it better to leave them as they were. They might set them inquiring, and give me an opportunity of interest-ing them further, sometime or other, in the history of a word; in their ups and downs of fortune, words fare very much like human beings.

ELEVEN

MY CHRISTMAS SERMON

I never asked questions about the private affairs of any of my parishioners, except if they individually asked me for advice. Hence, I believe, they became the more willing that I should know. But I heard a good many things, notwithstanding, for I could not be constantly closing lips as I had done with Jane Rogers. Among other things, I learned that Miss Oldcastle went most Sundays to the neighboring town of Addicehead to church. Now I had often heard of the ability of the rector, and although I had never met him, I was prepared to find him a cultivated if not an original man. Yet I confess that I heard this news with a pang, which I discovered to be jealousy. It was no use asking myself why I should be jealous; there the ugly thing was. So I went and told God I was ashamed, and begged Him to deliver me from the evil, because His was the kingdom and the power and the glory. And He took my part against myself, for He waits to be gracious.

But there was one stray sheep of my flock that appeared in church for the first time on the morning of Christmas Day—Catharine Weir. She did not sit beside her father, but in the most shadowy corner of the church, yet near the organ loft. She could have seen her father if she had looked up, but she kept her eyes down the whole time, and never even lifted them to me. The spot on one cheek was much brighter than that on the other, and made her look very ill.

I took my text from the Sermon on the Mount—St. Matthew the sixth chapter, and part of verses twenty-four and twenty-five: " 'Ye cannot serve God and mammon. Therefore I say unto you,

Take no thought for your life.'

"When the Child whose birth we celebrate grew up to be a Man, He said this. Did He mean it? He meant it altogether and entirely. When people do not understand what the Lord says, instead of searching deeper for a meaning which will be evidently true and wise, they comfort themselves by thinking He could not have meant it altogether, and so leave it. Or they think that if He did mean it, He could not expect them to carry it out. Let it not be so with us this day. Let us seek to find out what our Lord means, that we may do it.

"*Mammon,* you know, means *riches.* Now, riches are meant to be the slave—not even the servant of man, and not the master. If a man serve his own servant—anyone who has no just claim to be his master—he is a slave. But here he serves his own slave.

"But how can a man *serve* riches? Why, when he says to riches, 'Ye are my god.' When he feels he cannot be happy without them. When he schemes, and dreams, and lies awake thinking about them. When he will not give to his neighbor for fear of becoming poor himself. When he wants to have more—and to know he has more—than he can need. When he honors those who have money because they have money, or when he honors in a rich man what he would not honor in a poor man. Still more when his devotion to his god makes him oppressive to those over whom his wealth gives him power, or when he becomes unjust in order to add to his stores.

"How will it be with such a man when he finds that the world has vanished, and he is alone with God? There lies the body in which he used to live. He cannot now even try to bribe God with a check. The angels will not bow down to him. And the poor souls of hades, who envied him the wealth they had lost before, rise up as one man to welcome him, rejoicing in the mischief that has befallen him, and saying, 'Art thou also become one of us?' He can no longer deceive himself in his riches. And so even in hell he is something nobler than he was on earth, for he worships his riches no longer. He cannot. He curses them.

"Terrible things to say on Christmas Day! But if Christmas Day teaches us anything, it teaches us to worship God and not mammon, to worship Spirit and not matter, to worship love and not power.

" 'Ye cannot serve God and mammon. Therefore I say unto you, Take no thought for your life.'

82

"Why are you to take no thought? Where are you now, poor man? Brooding over the frost? Will it harden the ground so that the God of the sparrows cannot find food for His sons? Where are you now, poor woman? Sleepless over the empty cupboard and tomorrow's dinner, because you have no bread? Have you forgotten the five loaves among the five thousand, and the fragments that were left? Oh ye of little faith!

"But I may be too hard upon you. I know well that our Father sees a great difference between the man who is anxious about his children's dinner (or even about his own) and the man who is only anxious to add another ten thousand pounds to his much goods laid up. But you ought to find it easy to trust in God for your daily bread.

"But how is the work of the world to be done, if we take no thought? We are nowhere told not to take thought. We *must* take thought—but what about? Why, about our work. What are we not to take thought about? Why, about life. The one is our business, the other God's. A man's business is just to do his duty. God takes upon Himself the feeding and the clothing. Will the work of the world be neglected if a man thinks of his work, his duty, God's will to be done, instead of what he is to eat and drink and how he is to be clothed?

"I *should* like to know a man who just minded his duty and troubled himself about nothing, who did his own work and did not interfere with God's. How nobly he would work—not for reward but because it was the will of God! What peace would be his! What a friend he would be! How sweet his sympathy! And his mind would be so clear he would understand everything. His eye being single, his whole body would be full of light. No fear of his ever doing a mean thing—he would die in a ditch rather. It is this fear of want that makes men do mean things. They are afraid to part with their precious lord—mammon. He gives no safety against such a fear. One of the richest men in England is haunted with the dread of the workhouse.

"But I think I hear my troubled friend who does not love money—and yet cannot trust in God out and out—I hear her say, 'I believe I could trust Him for myself, but it is the thought of my children that is too much for me.' Ah! Woman! She whom the Saviour praised so pleasedly was one who trusted Him for her daughter. 'Be it unto thee even as thou wilt.' Do you think you love your children better than He who made them? Is not your love what it is because He put it into your heart first? You did not create that love. God sent it. He loves them a thousand times better than you do—be sure of that.

"But don't we see people die of starvation sometimes? Yes. But if you did your work in God's name and left the rest to Him, that would not trouble you. You would say, 'If it be God's will that I should starve, I can starve as well as another.' And your mind would be at ease. 'Thou wilt keep him in perfect peace whose mind is stayed on Thee, because he trusteth in Thee.' Of that I am sure. It may be good for you to go hungry and barefoot, but it must be utter death to have no faith in God. We do not know why here and there a man may be left to die of hunger, but I do believe that they who wait upon the Lord shall not lack any good. What it may be good to deprive a man of till he knows and acknowledges whence it comes, it may be still better to give him when he has learned that every good and every perfect gift is from above, and cometh down from the Father of lights.

"It has been well said that no man ever sank under the burden of the day. It is when tomorrow's burden is added to the burden of today that the weight is more than a man can bear. If you find yourselves so loaded, remember: it is your own doing, not God's. He begs you to leave the future to Him, and mind the present. What more or what else could He do to take the burden off you? Money in the bank wouldn't do it. He cannot do tomorrow's business for you beforehand to save you from fear about it. What else is there but to tell you to trust in Him? Walk without fear, full of hope and courage, and strength to do His will, waiting for the endless good which He is always giving as fast as He can get us able to take it in.

"Pain and hunger are evils, but if faith in God swallows them up, do they not so turn into good? I say they do. I have never been too hungry, but I have had trouble which I would gladly have exchanged for hunger and cold and weariness. Some of you have known hunger and cold and weariness. Do you not join with me to say, 'It is well, and better than well, whatever helps us know the love of Him who is our God'?

"And this One is the Baby whose birth we celebrate this day. Was this a condition to choose—that of a baby? Did He not thus cast the whole matter at once upon the hands and heart of His Father? Sufficient unto a baby's day is the need thereof; he toils not, neither does he spin, and yet he is fed and clothed and loved and rejoiced in.

"But let us look at what will be more easily shown, how, namely, He did the will of His Father, and took no thought for the morrow after He became a man. Remember how He forsook His trade when the time came for Him to preach. Preaching was not a profession then. There were no monasteries or vicarages or stipends then. Yet witness for the Father the garment woven throughout—the ministering of women, the purse in common! Hardworking men and rich ladies were ready to help Him, and did help Him with all that He needed. Did He then never want? Yes, once at least, for a little while only.

"He was hungered in the wilderness. 'Make bread,' said Satan. 'No,' said our Lord. He could starve, but He could not eat bread that His Father did not give Him, even though He could make it Himself. He had come hither to be tried. But when the victory was secure, lo! the angels brought Him food from His Father. Which was better, to feed Himself or be fed by His Father? He sought the kingdom of God and His righteousness, and the bread was added unto Him.

"Do you feel inclined to say in your hearts, 'It was easy for Him to take no thought, for He had the matter in His own hands'? But there is nothing very noble in a man's taking no thought, except it be from faith. If there were no God to take thought for us, we should have no right to blame anyone for taking thought. You may fancy the Lord had His own power to fall back upon. But that would have been to Him the one dreadful thing—that His Father should forget Him! No power in Himself could make up for that. He feared nothing for Himself, and never once employed His divine power to save Himself from His human fate. Let God do that for Him if He saw fit. To fall back on Himself, God failing Him— that would be to declare heaven void, and the world without a God. He did not come into the world to take care of Himself.

"His need was not to be fed and clothed, but to be one with the Father, to be fed by His hand, clothed by His care. This was what the Lord wanted, and what we too often need without wanting it. He never once used His power for Himself. God would mind all that was necessary for Him, and our Lord would mind the work His Father had given Him to do. And, my friends, this is the secret of a blessed life, the one thing every man comes into this world to learn. With what authority it comes to us from the lips of Him who knew all about it, and ever did as He said!

"Now you see that He took no thought for the morrow. And in the name of the Holy Child Jesus, I call upon you, this Christmas Day, to cast care to the winds, and trust in God; to receive the message of peace and goodwill to men; to yield yourselves to the Spirit of God, that you may be taught what He wants you to know; to remember that the one gift promised without reserve to those who ask it—the one gift worth having, the gift which makes all other gifts a thousandfold in value—is the gift of the Holy Spirit, the Spirit of the Child Jesus, who will take of the things of Jesus and show them to you, make you understand them, so that you shall see them to be true, and love Him with all your heart and soul, and your neighbors as yourselves."

I had more than ordinary attention during my discourse. At one point I saw the bent head of Catharine Weir sink yet lower upon her hands. After a moment, however, she sat more erect than before, though she never lifted her eyes to meet mine. She was not present to my mind when I spoke the words that so far had moved her. Indeed, had I thought of her, I could not have spoken them.

As I came out of the church, my people crowded about me with outstretched hands and good wishes. One woman, the aged wife of a more aged laborer, called from the outskirts of the little crowd. "May the Lord come and see ye every day, Sir. And may ye never know the hunger and cold as me and Tomkins has come through."

"Amen to the first of your blessing, Mrs. Tomkins, and hearty thanks to you. But I daren't say Amen to the other part of it after what I've been preaching, you know."

"But there'll be no harm if I say it for ye, Sir?"

"No, for God will give me what is good, even if your kind heart should pray against it."

"Ah! Sir, ye don't know what it is to be hungry *and* cold."

"Neither shall you anymore, if I can help it."

"God bless ye, Sir. But we're pretty tidy just now."

When I reached my own study I sat down by a blazing fire. Let me, if I may, be ever welcomed to my room in winter by a glowing hearth, in summer by a vase of flowers. If I may not, let me then think how nice they would be and bury myself in my work.

I soon fell into a dreamy state (which a few mistake for thinking, because it is the nearest approach they ever make to it) and in this reverie I kept staring about my bookshelves. I am very fond of books. Do not mistake me. I do not mean that I love reading. I

86

hope I do. That is no fault—a virtue rather than a fault. But, as the old meaning of the word *fond* was foolish, I use that word: I am foolishly fond of the bodies of books as distinguished from their souls. I do not say that I love their bodies as divided from their souls—I should not keep a book for which I felt no respect or had no use. But I delight in seeing books about me, books even of which there seems to be no prospect that I shall have time to read a single chapter. I confess that if they are nicely bound, so as to glow and shine in a firelight, I like them ever so much the better. I suspect that by the time books (which ought to be loved for the truth that is in them) come to be loved as articles of furniture, the mind has gone through a process which the miser's mind goes through— that of passing from the respect of money because of what it can do, to the love of money because it is money. I have not yet reached the furniture stage, and I do not think I ever shall. I would rather burn them all.

The thought suddenly struck me that I had promised Judy to find out what her aunt's name meant in Anglo-Saxon. I got down my dictionary and discovered that Ethelwyn meant Home-Joy or Inheritance. A lovely meaning.

And I went off into another reverie for my half hour. Then I got up and filled my pockets with little presents for my poor people, and set out to find them in their homes. Several families had asked me to take my Christmas dinner with them but, not liking to be thus limited, I had answered each that I would not, if they would excuse me, but would look in some time or other in the course of the evening.

I was variously received, but always with kindness. Mrs. Tomkkins looked as if she had never seen so much tea together before, though there was only a couple of pounds of it. Her husband received a pair of warm trousers none the less cordially that they were not quite new, the fact being that I found I did not myself need such warm clothing this winter as I had needed last. I did not dare to offer Catharine Weir anything, but I gave her little boy a box of watercolors in remembrance of the first time I saw him, though I said nothing about that. His mother did not thank me. She told little Gerard to do so, however, and that was something. And, indeed, the boy's sweetness would have been enough for both.

When I reached Old Rogers' cottage, I found not merely Jane there with her father and mother (which was natural on Christmas

Day, with no company at the Hall) but my little Judy as well.

"Why, Judy!" I exclaimed, "you here?"

"Yes. Why not, Mr. Walton?" she returned, holding out her hand.

"I know no reason why I shouldn't see a Sandwich Islander here. Yet I might express surprise if I did find one, might I not?"

Judy pretended to pout, and muttered something about comparing her to a cannibal. But Jane took up the explanation.

"Mistress had to go off to London with her mother today, Sir, quite unexpected, on some banking business, I fancy, from what I—I beg your pardon, Sir. They're gone anyhow, whatever the reason may be, and so I came to see Father and Mother, and Miss Judy would come with me."

"She be very welcome," said Mrs. Rogers.

"How could I stay up there with Sarah? I wouldn't be left alone with her for the world. She'd have me in the Bishop's Pool before you came back, Janey dear."

"That wouldn't matter much to you, would it, Judy?" I said.

"She's a white wolf, that old Sarah, I know!" was all her answer.

"But what will the old lady say when she finds you brought the young lady here?" asked Mrs. Rogers.

"I didn't bring her, Mother. She would come."

"Had they actually to go away on the morning of Christmas Day?" I said.

"They went anyhow, whether they had to do it or not, Sir," answered Jane.

"Aunt Ethelwyn didn't want to go till tomorrow," said Judy. "She said something about coming to church this morning, but Grannie said they must go at once. It was very cross of old Grannie. Think what a Christmas Day is to me without Auntie, and with Sarah! But I don't mean to go home till it's quite dark. I mean to stop here with dear Old Rogers—that I do."

The latch was gently lifted, and in came young Brownrigg, so I thought it was time to leave my best Christmas wishes and take myself away. Old Rogers came with me to the millstream as usual.

"It 'mazes me, Sir," he said, "a gentleman o' your age and bringin'-up, to know all that you tould us this mornin'. It 'ud be no wonder, now, for a man like me, come to be the shock o' corn fully ripe—leastways yellow and white enough outside, if there bean't much more than milk inside it yet—it'ud be no mystery for a man like me, who'd been brought up hard, and tossed about well nigh all the world over—why, there's scarce a wave on the Atlantic but knows Old Rogers!

"It 'ud be a shame of a man like me not to know as you said this morning, Sir—leastways I don't mean able to say it right off as you do, Sir. But not to know it, after the Almighty had been at such pains to beat it into my hard head just to trust in Him and fear nothing and nobody—captain, bosun, devil, sunk rock, or breakers ahead, but just to mind Him and stand by the wheel, or hang on for that matter. For, you see, what does it signify whether I go to the bottom or not, so long as I didn't skulk? Or rather," and here the old man took off his hat and looked up, "so long as the Great Captain has His way, and things is done to His mind? But how ever a man like you, goin' to the college, and readin' books, and warm o' nights, and never knowin' what it was to be downright hungry, how ever you come to know all those things is just past my comprehension, except by a double portion o' the Spirit, Sir. And that's the way I account for it, Sir.

"I had to learn it all without book, as it were, though you know I had my old Bible that my mother gave me, and without that I should not have learned it at all."

"You have had more of the practice, and I more of the theory, but if we had not had both, we should neither of us have known anything about the matter. I never was content without trying at least to understand things—and if they are practical things, and you try to practice them at the same time as far as you do understand them, there is no end to the way in which the one lights up the other. I suppose that is how, without your experience, I have more to say about such things than you could expect. The only difference is that though I've got my clay and my straw together, and they stick pretty well as yet, my brick is not half so well baked as yours, old friend, and it may crumble away yet, though I hope not."

"I pray God to make both our bricks into stones of the New Jerusalem, Sir. I think I understand you quite well. To know about a thing is of no use except you do it. Besides, as I found out when I went to sea, you never can know a thing till you do it, though I thought I had a tidy fancy about some things beforehand. It's better not to be quite sure that all your seams are caulked, and so to keep a lookout on the bilge pump,—isn't it, Sir?"

During most of the conversation we were standing by the mill water which was half frozen over. The ice from both sides came toward the middle, leaving an empty space between, along which the dark water showed itself, hurrying away as if in fear of its life from the white death of the frost. The wheel stood motionless, and the drip from the mill over it in the sun had frozen the shadow into icicles, making the wheel look like its own gray skeleton. The sun was getting low, and I should want all my time to see my other friends before dinner, for I would not willingly offend Mrs. Pearson on Christmas Day by being late.

"I must go, Old Rogers," I said, "but I will leave you something to think about till we meet again. Find out why our Lord was so much displeased with the disciples, whom He knew to be ignorant men, not knowing what He meant when He warned them against the leaven of the Pharisees. I want to know what you think about it. You'll find the story told both in the sixteenth chapter of St. Matthew and the eighth of St. Mark."

"Well, Sir, I'll try, that is, if you will tell me what you think about it afterward, so as to put me right if I'm wrong."

"Of course I will, if I can find out an explanation to satisfy me. But it is not at all clear to me now. In fact, I do not see the connecting links of our Lord's logic in the rebuke He gives them."

"How am I to find out then, Sir, knowing nothing of logic at all?" said the old man, his rough worn face summered over with his childlike smile.

"There are many things which a little learning, while it cannot really hide them, may make you less ready to see all at once," I answered, shaking hands with Old Rogers, and then springing across the rock with my carpetbag in my hand.

By the time I had got through the rest of my calls, the fogs were rising from the streams and the meadows to close in upon my first Christmas Day in my own parish. How much happier I was than when I came such a few months before! The only pang I felt that day was as I passed the monsters on the gate leading to Oldcastle Hall. Should I be honored to help only the poor of the flock? Was I to do nothing for the rich, for whom it is so hard to enter into the kingdom of heaven?

To these people at the Hall I did not seem acceptable. I might in time do something with Judy, but the old lady was still so dreadfully repulsive to me that it troubled my conscience to feel how I disliked her. Mr. Stoddart seemed nothing more than a dilettante in religion as well as in the arts and sciences—music always excepted. I did not understand Miss Oldcastle yet—and she was so beautiful! I thought her more beautiful every time I saw her. But I never appeared to make the least progress toward any real acquaintance with her thoughts and feelings. I longed to do something for these rich of my flock, for it was dreadful to think of their being poor inside, if not outside.

Perhaps I ought to have been as anxious about poor Farmer Brownrigg as about the beautiful lady. But the farmer had given me good reason to hope for some progress in him, after the way he had given in about Jane Rogers. Positively I had caught his eye during the sermon that very day. And we are nowhere told to love everybody alike, only to love everyone who comes within our reach as ourselves.

I made Mrs. Pearson sit down with me to dinner, for Christmas Day was not a time to dine alone. Ever since, I have had my servants dine with me on Christmas Day.

When we had finished our dinner, and I was sitting alone drinking a cup of tea before going out again, Mrs. Pearson came in and told me that little Gerard Weir wanted to see me. The little fellow entered, looking very shy, and clinging first to the door and then to the wall.

"Come, my dear boy," I said, "and sit down by me." He came directly and stood before me.

"Please, Sir," he said, putting his hand in his pocket, "Mother gave me some goodies, and I kept them till I saw you come back, and here they are, Sir."

I said, "Thank you," and I ate them up, every one of them, that he might see me at them before he left the house. And the dear child went off radiant.

Then I went out again, and made another round of visits. Those whom I could not see that day I saw on the following days between it and the new year, and so ended my Christmas holiday with my people.

TWELVE

THE AVENUE

After Christmas I found myself in closer relationship to my parishioners. I visited, of course, at the Hall, as at the farmhouse in the
country and the cottages in the village. I did not come to like Mrs.
Oldcastle better, and there was one woman in the house whom I
disliked still more—that Sarah whom Judy had called in my hearing a white wolf. Her face was yet whiter than that of her mistress,
only it was not smooth like hers—its whiteness came apparently
from smallpox which had so thickened the skin that no blood
could shine through. I seldom saw her—only, indeed, caught a
glimpse of her now and then as I passed through the house.

Nor did I make much progress with Mr. Stoddart. He always
had something friendly to say, and some theosophical theory to
bring forward. He was a great reader of mystical books, and yet
the man's nature seemed cold. It was sunshiny, but not sunny. His
intellect was rather a lambent flame than genial warmth. He could
make things, but he could not grow anything. And when I came to
see that he had had more than anyone else to do with the education of Miss Oldcastle, I understood her a little better. For to
teach speculation instead of devotion, mysticism instead of love,
word instead of deed, is surely repressive to the nature meant for
sunbright activity. My chief perplexity continued to be how he
could play the organ as he did.

I have not much more to tell about this winter. As out of a
whole changeful season only one day will cling to the memory, so
of that winter nothing more of nature or human nature occurs to
me worth recording. I will pass on to the summer season, though

the early spring will detain me with the relation of a single incident.

I was on my way to the Hall to see Mr. Stoddart. I wanted to ask him whether something could not be done beyond his exquisite playing to rouse the sense of music in my people. Now I had, I confess, little hope of moving Mr. Stoddart in the matter; but if I should succeed, I thought it would do him good to mingle with his humble fellows in the attempt to do them a trifle of good.

It was just beginning to grow dusk. The wind was blustering in gusts among the trees. There was just one cold bar of light in the west, and the east was one gray mass, while overhead the stars were twinkling. The grass and all the ground about the trees was very wet. The time seemed more dreary somehow than the winter. Rigor was past, and tenderness had not come, for the wind was cold without being keen, and whirled about me as if it wanted me to join in its fierce play.

Suddenly I saw, in a walk that ran along the avenue, Miss Oldcastle struggling against the wind. I had supposed her with her mother in London, whither their journeys had been not infrequent since Christmas. And why should she be fighting with the wind, so far from the house, with only a shawl drawn over her head?

Passing between two great tree trunks, I was by her side in a moment. But the noise of the wind prevented her from hearing my approach, and when I uttered her name, she started violently and, turning, drew herself up very haughtily, in part to hide her tremor.

"I beg your pardon," I said. "I have startled you dreadfully."

"Not in the least," she replied, but without moving, and still with a curve in her form like the neck of a frayed horse.

"I was on my way to call on Mr. Stoddart," I said.

"You will find him at home, I believe."

"I fancied you and Mrs. Oldcastle in London."

"We returned yesterday."

Still she stood as before. I made a movement in the direction of the house. She seemed as if she would walk in the opposite direction.

"May I not walk with you to the house?"

"I am not going in just yet."

"Are you protected enough for such a night?"

"I enjoy the wind."

I bowed and walked on. What else could I do?

I cannot say that I enjoyed leaving her behind me in the gathering dark, the wind blowing her about with no more reverence than if she had been a bush of privet. Nor was it with a light heart that I bore her repulse as I slowly climbed the hill to the house.

Sarah opened the glass door, her black, glossy, restless eyes looking out of her white face from under the gray eyebrows. I knew at once by her look beyond me that she had expected to find me accompanied by her young mistress. I did not volunteer any information.

As I had feared, I found that, although Mr. Stoddart seemed to listen with some interest to what I said about the music in the church, I could not bring him to the point of making any practical suggestion, or of responding to one made by me, and I left with the conviction that he would do nothing to help me. Yet during the whole of our interview he had not opposed a single word I said. He was like clay too much softened with water to keep the form into which it has been modeled. He would take some kind of form easily, and lose it yet more easily. I did not show all my dissatisfaction, however, for that would only have estranged us. It is not required, nay, it may be wrong, to show all we feel or think. What is required of us is *not* to show what we do *not* feel or think, for that is to be false.

I left the house in a gloomy mood. I know I ought to have looked up to God and said, "These things do not reach to Thee, my Father. Thou art ever the same. I rise above my small as well as my great troubles by remembering Thy peace, and Thy unchangeable godhood to me and all Thy creatures." But I did not come to myself all at once. The thought of God had not come, though it was sure to come. I was brooding over the littleness of all I could do, and feeling that sickness which sometimes will overtake a man in the midst of the work he likes best, when the unpleasant parts of it crowd upon him and his own efforts—especially those made from the will without sustaining impulse—come back upon him with a feeling of unreality, decay, and bitterness, as if he had been unnatural and untrue, and putting himself in false relations by false efforts for good. I know this all came from selfishness—thinking about myself instead of about God and my neighbor. But so it was. And I was walking down the avenue, now very dark, with my head bent to the ground. I started at the sound of a woman's voice and, looking up, saw by the starlight the dim form of Miss Oldcastle before me.

She spoke first.

"Mr. Walton, I was very rude to you. I beg your pardon."

"Indeed, I did not think so. I only thought what a blundering, awkward fellow I was to startle you as I did. You have to forgive me."

"I fancy"—and here I know she smiled—"I fancy I have made that even, for you must confess I startled you now."

"You did, but in a very different way. I annoyed you with my rudeness. You only scattered a swarm of bats that kept flapping their skinny wings in my face."

"What do you mean? There are no bats at this time of year."

"Not outside. In 'winter and rough weather' they creep inside, you know."

"Ah! I ought to understand you. But I did not think you were ever like that. I thought you were too good."

"I wish I were. I hope to be someday. I am not yet, anyhow. And I thank you for driving the bats away."

"You make me the more ashamed of myself to think that perhaps my rudeness had a share in bringing them. Yours is, no doubt, thankless labor sometimes."

She seemed to make the last remark just to prevent the conversation from returning to her as its subject.

The wind rose again with a gush in the trees. Was it fancy? Or, as the wind moved the shrubbery, did I see a white face? And could it be the White Wolf?

I spoke aloud, "But it is cruel to keep you standing here in such a night. You must be a real lover of nature to walk in the dark wind."

"I like it. Good night."

So we parted. I gazed into the darkness after her, though she disappeared at the distance of a yard or two. I would have stood longer, had I not still suspected the proximity of Judy's Wolf, which made me turn and go home.

I met Miss Oldcastle several times before the summer, but her old manner remained, or rather had returned, for there had been nothing of it in the tone of her voice in that interview, if interview it could be called where neither could see more than the other's outline.

THIRTEEN

YOUNG WEIR

By slow degrees the summer bloomed. Green came instead of white, rainbows instead of icicles. I often wandered in the fields and woods, with a book in my hand at which I often did not look the whole day, and which yet I liked to have with me. And I seemed somehow to come back with most on those days in which I did not read. I prepared almost all my sermons that summer in the open country, but had another custom before I preached them—to spend the Saturday evening not in my study but in the church. It was always clean and ready for me after midday, so that I could be alone there as soon as I pleased.

This fine old church was not the expression of the religious feeling of my time. There was a gloom about it—a sacred gloom, I know, and I loved it—but such gloom was not in my feeling when I talked to my flock. The place soothed me, tuned me to a solemn mood of gentle gladness; but, had I been an architect, and had I had to build a church, I am certain it would have been very different from this. For I always found the open air the most genial influence upon me. Our Lord seemed so much to delight in the open air, and late in the day, as well as early in the morning, He would climb the mountain to be alone with His Father.

I therefore sought to bridge this difference, to find an easy passage between the open air and the church, so as to bring into the church the fresh air and the gladness over all. I thought my sermon over again in the afternoon sun slanting through the stained window, pacing up and down the solemn old place, hanging my thought here on a cricket, there on a corbel, and now on the gable point over which Weir's face would gaze next morning. And when the next day came, I found the forms around me so interwoven with the forms of my thought, that I felt almost like one of the old monks who had built the place.

One lovely Saturday, I had been out all morning. I had my Greek Testament with me, and I read when I sat and thought when I walked. I was planning to preach about the cloud of witnesses and explain this did not mean persons looking at our behavior—as if any addition could be made to the awfulness of the fact that the eye of God was upon us—but witnesses to the truth, people who did what God wanted them to do, come of it what might, whether a crown or a rack, scoffs or applause. When I came home I had an early dinner, and then betook myself to my Saturday resort.

All through the slowly fading afternoon, the autumn of the day when the colors are richest and the shadows long and lengthening, I paced my solemn, old-thoughted church. Sometimes I sat in the pulpit, looking on the ancient walls which had grown up under men's hands that men might be helped to pray, and I thought how many witnesses to the truth had knelt in those ancient pews. And my eye was caught by a yellow light that gilded the apex of the font cover, which had been wrought like a flame or a bursting blossom, and then by a red light all over a white marble tablet in the wall—the red of life and the cold hue of the grave. And this red light did not come from any work of man, but from the great window of the west, which little Gerard Weir wanted to help God to paint. And I lingered on till the night had come—till the church only gloomed about me and had no shine—and then I found my spirit burning up the clearer, as a lamp which has been flaming all the day with light unseen becomes a glory in the room when the sun is gone down.

At length I felt tired and would go home. Yet I lingered for a few moments in the vestry, thinking what hymns would harmonize best with the things I wanted to make my people think about. It was now quite dark out-of-doors. Suddenly I heard a moan and a sob, I listened, but heard nothing more, and concluded I had deceived myself. So I left the church by my vestry door and took my way along the path through the clustered graves.

Again I heard a sob. This time I was sure of it. And there lay something dark upon one of the grassy mounds. I approached it, but it did not move. I spoke. "Can I be of any use to you?" I said.

"No," returned an almost inaudible voice.

Though I did not know whose was the grave, I knew that no one had been buried there very lately, and if the grief were for the loss of the dead, it was more than probably aroused to fresh vigor by recent misfortune. I stopped and, taking the figure by the arm, said, "Come with me, and let us see what can be done for you."

Then I saw that it was a youth, perhaps scarcely more than a boy. And as soon as I saw that, I knew that his grief could hardly be incurable. He returned no answer, but rose at once to his feet and submitted to be led away. I took him the shortest road to my house through the shrubbery, brought him into the study, made him sit down in my easy chair and rang for lights and wine, for the dew had been falling heavily and his clothes were quite dank. But when the wine came he refused to take any.

"But you want it," I said.

"No, Sir, I don't, indeed."

"Take some for my sake, then."

"I would rather not, Sir."

"Why?"

"I promised my father a year ago, when I left for London, that I would not drink anything stronger than water. I can't break my promise now."

"That wasn't your father's grave I found you upon, was it?"

"No, Sir, it was my mother's. You know my father very well, Thomas Weir."

"Ah! He told me he had a son in London. Then what is the matter? Your father is a good friend of mine and would tell you you might trust me."

"I don't doubt it, Sir. But you won't believe me any more than my father."

The boy was of middle size but evidently not full grown. His dress was very decent. His face was pale and thin, and revealed a likeness to his father. He had blue eyes that looked full at me and, as far as I could judge, an honest and sensitive nature. I was therefore emboldened to press for his story.

"I cannot promise to believe whatever you say. But if you tell me the truth, I like you too much already to be in great danger of doubting you, for you know the truth has a force of its own."

"I thought so till tonight," he answered. "But if my father would not believe me, how can I expect you to do so, Sir?"

"Your father may have been too much troubled by your story to do it justice. It is not a bit like your father to be unfair."

"No, Sir. And so much the less chance of your believing me."

Somehow his talk prepossessed me still more in his favor, and I became more and more certain that he would yet tell me the truth. "Come, try me," I said.

"I will, Sir. But I must begin at the beginning."

"Begin where you like. I have nothing more to do tonight, and you may take what time you please. But I will ring for tea first, for I daresay you have not made any promise about that."

A faint smile flickered on his face. He was evidently beginning to feel a little more comfortable.

"When did you arrive from London?" I asked.

"About two hours ago, I suppose."

"Bring tea, Mrs. Pearson, and that cold chicken and ham, and plenty of toast. We are both hungry." Mrs. Pearson gave a questioning look at the lad and departed to do her duty.

When she returned with the tray and we were left alone, I would not let him say a word till he had made a good meal. Few troubles will destroy a growing lad's hunger; indeed, it has always been to me a marvel how the feelings and the appetite affect each other.

After the tea things had been taken away, I put the candles out, for I thought that he might find it easier to tell his story in the moonlight. So, sitting by the window, he told his tale. The moon lighted up his pale face as he told it and gave a wild expression to his eyes.

He had, he told me, filled a place in the employment of Messrs. Bates and Co., large silk mercers, linen drapers, etc., etc., in London. His work at first was to accompany one of the carts which delivered purchases, but they took him at length into the shop to wait behind the counter. This he did not like so much but, as it was considered a rise in life, he made no objection to the change.

He seemed to himself to get on pretty well. He soon learned all the marks on the goods understood by the shopmen, and within a few months believed that he was found generally useful. He had as yet no distinct department allotted to him, but was moved from place to place as business might demand.

"I confess," he said, "that I was not always satisfied with what was going on about me. I could not help doubting if everything was done on the square, as they say. But nothing came plainly my way, and so I could honestly say it did not concern me. But one day while I was showing a lady some handkerchiefs, she said she did not believe they were French cambric. Knowing little about it, I said nothing. But happening to look up, I caught sight of the shopwalker—the man who shows customers where to go for what they want and sees that they are attended to. He was a fat man, dressed in black, with a great gold chain which they say in the shop is only copper gilt. He was standing staring at me. From that day I often caught him watching me, as if I had been a customer suspected of shoplifting. I only thought he was disagreeable, and tried to forget him.

"The day before yesterday, two ladies, an old lady and a young one, came into the shop, and wanted to look at some shawls. I am sure the two were Mrs. and Miss Oldcastle of the Hall. They wanted to buy a cashmere for the young lady. I showed them some but they wanted better. I brought the best we had. They asked the price and I told them. They said they were not good enough and wanted to see some more. I told them they were the best we had. They looked at them again, said the shawls were not good enough, and left the shop without buying a thing. I proceeded to take the shawls upstairs again and, as I went, I passed the shopwalker whom I had not observed. 'You're for no good, young man!' he said, with a nasty sneer.

" 'What do you mean by that?' I asked, for his sneer made me angry.

" 'You'll know before tomorrow,' he answered, and walked away.

"That same evening, as we were shutting up shop, I was sent for to the manager's room. The moment I entered, he said, 'You won't suit us, young man, I find. You had better pack up your box tonight, and be off tomorrow. There's your quarter's salary.'

" 'What have I done?' I asked in astonishment, and yet with a vague suspicion.

" 'It's not what you've done, but what you won't do,' he answered. 'Do you think we can afford to keep you here and pay you wages to send people away from the shop without buying? If you do, you're mistaken. You may go.'

" 'But what could I do?' I said. 'I suppose that spy. . . .'

" 'Now, now, young man, none of your sauce!' said Mr. Barlow 'Honest people don't think about spies.'

" 'I thought it was for honesty you were getting rid of me,' I said.

"Mr. Barlow rose to his feet, his lips white, and pointed to the door. 'Take your money and be off. And mind you don't refer to me for a character. After such impudence I couldn't in conscience give you one.' Then, calming down a little when he saw I turned to go, 'You had better take to your hands again, for your head will never keep you. There, be off!' he said, pushing the money toward me and turning his back to me. I could not touch it.

" 'Keep the money, Mr. Barlow,' I said. 'It will make up for what you've lost by me.' And I left the room at once.

"While I was packing my box, one of my chums came in, and I told him all about it. He laughed and said, 'What a fool you are, Weir! You'll never make your daily bread. If you knew what I know, you'd have known better. Mr. Barlow was serving some ladies himself. They wanted the best Indian shawl they could get. None of those he showed them were good enough, for the ladies really didn't know one from another. They always go by the price you ask, and Mr. Barlow knew that well enough. He sent me upstairs for the shawls, and as I brought them he said, "These are the best imported, Madam." There were three ladies, and one shook her head, and another shook her head, and they all shook their heads. And then Mr. Barlow was sorry that he had said they were the best. But you won't catch him in a trap. He's too old a fox for that. He looked close down at the shawls, as if he were shortsighted, though he could see as far as any man. "I beg your pardon, ladies," said he, "you're right. I am quite wrong. What a stupid blunder to make! And yet they did deceive me. Here, Johnson, take these shawls away. I will fetch the thing you want myself, ladies." He chose out three or four shawls, of the nicest patterns, from the very same lot, marked in the very same way, folded them differently, and gave them to me to carry down. "Now, ladies, here they are!" he said. "These are quite a different thing, as you will see—and, indeed, they cost half as much again." In five minutes they bought two of them, and paid just half as much more than he asked for them the first time. That's Mr. Barlow! And that's what you should have done if you had wanted to keep your place.' But I assure you, Sir, I could not help being glad to be out of it."

"But there is nothing in all this to be miserable about," I said. "You did your duty."

"It would be all right, Sir, if Father believed me. I don't want to be idle, I'm sure."

101

"Does your father think you do?"

"I don't know what he thinks. He won't speak to me. I told my story—as much of it as he would let me, at least—but he wouldn't listen to me. He only said he knew better than that. I couldn't bear it. He always was rather hard on us. I'm sure if you hadn't been so kind to me, Sir, I don't know what I should have done by this time. I haven't another friend in the world."

"Yes you have. Your Father in heaven is your friend."

"I don't know that, Sir. I'm not good enough."

"That's quite true. But you would never have done your duty if He had not been with you. Everything good comes from the Father of lights. Everyone who walks in any light walks in His light, for there is no light—only darkness—from below. Man, apart from God, can generate no light."

"I think I understand. But I didn't feel good at all in the matter. I didn't see any other way of doing."

"So much the better. We ought never to feel good. We are but unprofitable servants at best. There is no merit in doing your duty; you would have been a poor wretched creature not to do as you did. And now, instead of making yourself miserable over the consequences of it, you ought to bear them like a man, with courage and hope, thanking God that He has made you suffer for righteousness' sake and denied you the success and the praise of cheating. I will go to your father at once and find out what he is thinking about it, for no doubt Mr. Barlow has written to him with his version of the story. Perhaps he will be more inclined to believe you when he finds that I believe you."

"Oh, thank you, Sir!" cried the lad, and jumped up from his seat to go with me.

"No," I said, "you had better stay where you are. I shall be able to speak more freely if you are not present. Here is a book to amuse yourself with. I do not think I shall be long gone."

But I was longer gone than I thought I should be.

When I reached the carpenter's house I found, to my surprise, that he was still at work. By the light of a single tallow candle beside him on the bench, he was plowing away at a groove. He looked up, but, without even greeting me, dropped his pale face again and went on with his work.

"What!" I said, cheerily. "Working so late?"

"Yes, Sir."

"It is not unusual with you, I know."

"It's all a humbug!" he said, fiercely, but coldly. He stood erect
from his work, and turned his white face full on me, though his
eyes dropped. "It's all a humbug, and I don't mean to be hum-
bugged anymore. Tell me that a God governs the world! What
have I done, to be used like this?"

I thought with myself how I could retort for his young son:
"What has he done to be used like this?" I could only stand and
wait. "It would be wrong in me to pretend ignorance," I said. "I
know all about it"

"He has been to you, has he? But you don't know all about it,
Sir. The impudence of the young rascal! Me to be treated like this!
One child a. . . ." Here came a terrible break in his speech. But he
tried again. "And the other a. . . . " Instead of finishing the sentence he drove his plow fiercely through the groove, splitting off
some inches of the wall of it at the end.

"If anyone has treated you so," I said, "it must be the devil, not
God."

"But if there were a God, He could have prevented it all."

"Mind what I said to you once before—He hasn't done yet. And
there is another enemy in His way as bad as the devil—ourselves.
When people want to walk their own way without God, God lets
them try it. And then the devil gets a hold of them. But God won't
let him keep them. As soon as they are 'wearied in the greatness of
their way,' they begin to look about for a Saviour. And then they
find God ready to pardon, ready to help, not breaking the bruised
reed but leading them to His own self manifest. God is tender—
just like the prodigal son's father—only with this difference, that
God has millions of prodigals, and never gets tired of going out to
meet them and welcome them back, every one as if he were the
only prodigal son He had ever had. There's a Father indeed! Have
you been such a father to your son?"

"The prodigal didn't come with a pack of lies. He told his father
the truth, bad as it was."

"How do you know that your son didn't tell you the truth? All
the young men that go from home don't do as the prodigal did.
Why should you not believe what he tells you?"

He handed me a letter. I took it and read:

"Sir—It has become our painful duty to inform you that your
son has this day been discharged from our employment, his conduct not being such as to justify the confidence hitherto reposed in
him. It would have been contrary to the interests of the establish-

ment to continue him longer behind the counter, although we are not prepared to urge anything against him beyond the fact that he has shown himself absolutely indifferent to the interests of his employers. We trust that the chief blame will be found to lie with certain connections of a kind easily formed in large cities, and that the loss of his situation here may be punishment sufficient, if not for justice, yet to make him consider his ways and be wise. We enclose his quarter's salary, which the young man rejected with insult, and we remain, etc., Bates and Co."

"And," I exclaimed, "this is what you found your judgment of your own son upon! You reject him unheard, and take the word of a stranger! I don't wonder you cannot believe in your Father when you behave so to your son. I don't say your conclusion is false— though I don't believe it—but I do say the grounds you go on are anything but sufficient."

"You don't mean to tell me that a man of Mr. Barlow's standing, who manages one of the largest shops in London, and whose brother is mayor of Addicehead, would slander a poor lad like that!"

"O you mammon-worshiper!" I cried. "Because a man runs one of the largest shops in London, and his brother is mayor of Addicehead, you take his testimony and refuse your son's! I did not know the boy till this evening—but I call upon you to bring back to your memory all that you have known of him from his childhood, and then ask yourself whether there is not at least as much probability of his having remained honest as of the master of a great London shop being infallible in his conclusions."

The pale face of the carpenter was red as fire, for he had been acting contrary to all his own theories of human equality, and that in a shameful manner. Still, whether convinced or not, he would not give in. He only drove away at his work, which he was utterly destroying. His mouth was closed tight, and his eyes gleamed over the ruined board with a light which seemed to have more obstinacy in it than contrition.

"Ah, Thomas!" I said, "if God had behaved to us as you have behaved to your boy-be he innocent, be he guilty—there's not a man or woman of all our lost race would have returned to Him from the time of Adam till now. I don't wonder that you find it difficult to believe in Him."

And with those words I left the shop, determined to overwhelm the unbeliever with proof, and put him to shame before his own soul whence, I thought, would come even more good to him than to his son. For there was a great deal of self-satisfaction mixed up with the man's honesty, and the sooner that had a blow the better. It was pride that lay at the root of his hardness. He visited the daughter's fault upon the son. His daughter had disgraced him— her he had never forgiven—and now his pride flung his son out after her upon the first suspicion. His imagination had filled up all the blanks in the wicked insinuations of Mr. Barlow. His pride paralyzed his love. He thought more about himself than about his children. It was a lesser matter that they should be guilty than that he, their father, should be disgraced.

Thinking over all this, and forgetting how late it was, I found myself halfway up the avenue of the Hall. I wanted to find out whether the ladies were Mrs. and Miss Oldcastle. What a point if they were! I should not then be satisfied except I could prevail on Miss Oldcastle to accompany me to Thomas Weir. So eager was I that it was not till I stood before the house that I saw clearly the impropriety of attempting anything further that night. One light only was burning, and that on the first floor.

As I turned to go down the hill again, I saw a corner of the blind drawn aside, and a face peeping out—whose, I could not tell. This was uncomfortable, for what could be taking me there at such a time? But I walked steadily away, certain I could not escape recognition, and determining to refer to this ill-considered visit when I called again.

I lingered on the bridge as I went home. Not a light was to be seen in the village except one over Catharine Weir's shop. There were not many restless souls in my parish, not so many as there ought to be. Yet gladly would I see the troubled in peace—not a moment, though, before their troubles should have brought them where the weary and heavy-laden can alone find rest to their souls.

I had little immediate comfort to give my young guest, but I had plenty of hope. I told him he must stay in the house tomorrow, for it would be better to have the reconciliation with his father over before he appeared in public.

So the next day neither Weir was at church.

As soon as the afternoon service was over, I went to the Hall and was shown into the drawing room. It looked down upon the lawn, where Mrs. Oldcastle sat reading. A little way off sat Miss Oldcastle, with a book on her knee, but her gaze fixed on the landscape before her. I caught glimpses of Judy flitting among the trees, never a moment in one place.

Fearful of having an interview with the old lady alone, which was not likely to lead to what I wanted, I stepped out on the terrace, and thence down the steps to the lawn below. The servant had just informed Mrs. Oldcastle of my visit when I came near. She drew herself up in her chair, and evidently chose to regard my approach as an intrusion.

"I did not expect a visit from you today, Mr. Walton, you will allow me to say."

"I am doing Sunday work," I answered. "Will you kindly tell me whether you were in London on Thursday last? But stay— allow me to ask Miss Oldcastle to join us."

Without waiting for an answer, I went to Miss Oldcastle and begged her to come and listen to something in which I wanted her help. She rose courteously, though without cordiality, and accompanied me to her mother who sat with perfect rigidity watching us.

"Again let me ask," I said, "if you were in London on Thursday?"

Though I addressed the old lady, the answer came from her daughter. "Yes, we were."

"Were you in Bates and Co.'s, in Dublin Street?"

But now, before Miss Oldcastle could reply, her mother interposed. "Are we charged with shoplifting, Mr. Walton? Really, one is not accustomed to such cross-questioning, except from a lawyer."

"Have patience with me for a moment," I returned. "I am not going to be mysterious for more than two or three questions. Please tell me whether you were in that shop or not."

"I believe we were," said the mother.

"Yes, certainly," said the daughter.

"Did you buy anything?"

"No. We—" Miss Oldcastle began.

"Not a word more," I exclaimed, eagerly. "Come with me at once."

"What do you mean, Mr. Walton?" said the mother, with a sort of cold indignation, while the daughter looked surprised, but said nothing.

"I beg your pardon for my impetuosity, but much is in your power at this moment. The son of one of my parishioners has come home in trouble. His father, Thomas Weir—"

"Ah!" said Mrs. Oldcastle, in a tone considerably at strife with refinement. But I took no notice.

"His father will not believe his story. The lad thinks you are the ladies whom he was serving when he got into trouble. I am so confident he tells the truth, that I want Miss Oldcastle to be so kind as to accompany me to Weir's house—"

"Really, Mr. Walton, I am astonished at your making such a request!" exclaimed Mrs. Oldcastle. "To ask Miss Oldcastle to accompany you to the dwelling of the ringleader of all the *canaille* of the neighborhood!"

"It is for the sake of justice," I interposed.

"That is no concern of ours. Let them fight it out between them. I am sure any trouble that comes of it is no more than they all deserve. A low family—men and women!"

"I assure you, I think very differently. However, neither your opinion nor mine has anything to do with the matter." Here I turned to Miss Oldcastle and went on. "It is a chance which seldom occurs in one's life, Miss Oldcastle—a chance of setting wrong right by a word. As a minister of the Gospel of truth and love, I beg you to assist me with your presence to that end."

I would have spoken more strongly, but I knew that her word given to me would be enough without her presence. At my last words, Mrs. Oldcastle rose to her feet, her face whiter than usual.

"You dare to persist! You take advantage of your profession to drag my daughter into a vile dispute between people of the lowest class—against the positive command of her only parent! Have you no respect for her position in society? For her sex? *Mister Walton,* you act in a manner unworthy of your cloth."

I had stood with as much self-possession as I could muster, and I believe I should have borne it all quietly but for that last word. If there is one epithet I hate more than another, it is that execrable word *cloth* used for the office of a clergyman.

"Madam," I said, "I owe nothing to my tailor, but I owe God my whole being, and my neighbor all I can do for him. 'He that loveth not his brother is a murderer,' or murderess, as the case may be."

At the word *murderess,* her face became livid and she turned without reply. By this time her daughter was halfway to the house. She followed her. And here was I left to go home, with the full knowledge that, partly from trying to gain too much, and partly from losing my temper, I had at best a mangled and unsatisfactory testimony to carry back to Thomas Weir.

I walked away, round the end of the house and down the avenue, and the farther I went the more mortified I grew. It was not merely the shame of losing my temper, though that was a shame—and with a woman too, merely because she used a common epithet!—but I saw that it must appear very strange to the carpenter that I had not learned anything decisive in the matter. It only amounted to this—that Mrs. and Miss Oldcastle were in the shop on the very day on which Weir was dismissed. It proved that so much of what he had told me was correct, nothing more.

In fact, I had lost all the certain good of my attempt, in part from the foolish desire to produce a conviction *of* Weir, rather than *in* Weir, which should be triumphant and melodramatic, and—must I confess it?—should punish him for not believing in his son when I did, forgetting in my selfishness that not to believe in his son was unspeakable punishment enough.

I felt humiliated, and humiliation is a very different condition of mind from humility. Humiliation no man can desire, for it is shame and torture. Humility is the true, right condition of humanity—peaceful, divine. And yet a man may gladly welcome humiliation when it comes, if he finds that it has turned him right round, with his face away from pride and toward humility. To me there came an effective dissolution of the bonds both of pride and humiliation, and I became nearly as anxious to heal Weir's wounded spirit as I was to work justice for his son.

I was still walking slowly, with burning cheek and downcast eyes, away from the great house (which seemed to be staring after me down the avenue with all its window-eyes) when suddenly my deliverance came. At a sharp turn, where the avenue changed into a winding road, Miss Oldcastle stood waiting for me, the glow of haste upon her cheek, and the firmness of resolution upon her lips.

"Mr. Walton, what do you want me to do? I would not willingly refuse, if it is, as you say, my duty to go with you."

"I cannot be positive about that," I answered. "I think I put it too strongly. But it would be a considerable advantage, I think, if you would go with me and let me ask you a few questions in the presence of Thomas Weir."

"I will go."

"A thousand thanks. But how did you manage to—" Here I stopped, not knowing how to finish the question.

"You are surprised that I came, notwithstanding Mamma's objection to my going? Do you think obedience to parents is to last forever? The honor is, of course. But I am surely old enough to be right in following my conscience at least."

"You mistake me. That is not the difficulty at all. Of course you ought to do what is right against the highest authority on earth, which I take to be the parental. What I am surprised at is your courage."

"Not because of its degree, only that it is mine!" And she sighed. She was quite right, and I did not know what to answer. "I know I am cowardly. But, if I cannot dare, I can bear. Is it not strange? With my mother looking at me, I dare not say a word, dare hardly move against her will. And it is not always a good will. I cannot honor my mother as I would. But the moment her eyes are off me I can do anything, knowing the consequences perfectly, and just as regardless of them. Once she kept me shut up in my room, and sent me only bread and water, for a whole week to the very hour. Not that I minded that much, but it will let you know a little of my position in my own home. That is why I walked away before her. I saw what was coming."

And Miss Oldcastle drew herself up with more expression of pride than I had yet seen in her, revealing to me that perhaps I had misunderstood the source of her apparent haughtiness. I could not reply for indignation. My silence must have been the cause of what she said next.

"Ah! You think I have no right to speak so about my own mother! Well! But indeed I would not have done so a month ago."

"If I am silent, Miss Oldcastle, it is that my sympathy is too strong. There are mothers and mothers, and for a mother not to be a mother is too dreadful." She made no reply. "Perhaps—and I shall feel more honest when I have said it—the only thing I feel should be altered in your conduct is that you should dare your mother. Do not think that my meaning is a vulgar one. If it were, I should at least know better than to utter it to you. What I mean is that you ought to be able to be and do the same before your mother's eyes that you are and do when she is out of sight."

"I *know* that. I know it *well*. But you do not know what a spell she casts upon me, how impossible it is to do as you say."

"Difficult, I allow. Impossible, not. You will never be free till you do."

We walked in silence for some minutes. At length she said, "My mother's self-will amounts to madness, I do believe. I have yet to learn where she would stop of herself."

"All self-will is madness," I returned. "To want one's own way, just and only because it is one's own way, is the height of madness."

"Perhaps. But when madness has to be encountered as if it were sense, it makes it no easier to know that it is madness."

"Does your uncle give you no help?"

"He is as frightened of her as I am! He dares not even go away. He did not know what he was coming to when he came to Oldcastle Hall. Dear Uncle! I owe him a great deal. But for any help of that sort, he is of no more use than a child. I believe Mamma looks upon him as half an idiot. He can do anything or everything but help one to live, to *be* anything. O me! I *am* so tired!" And the proud lady burst out crying.

By this time we were at the gate, and as soon as we had passed the guardian monstrosities, we found the open road an effectual antidote to tears. When we came within sight of the old house where Weir lived, Miss Oldcastle became again a little curious as to what I required of her.

"Trust me," I said. "There is nothing mysterious about it. Only I prefer the truth to come out fresh in the ears of the man most concerned."

"I do trust you," she answered. And we knocked at the house door.

Thomas Weir himself opened the door, with a candle in hand. He looked very much astonished to see his lady visitor. He asked us in, politely enough, and ushered us into the large room upstairs. There sat the old man, as I had first seen him, by the side of the fire. He received us with more than politeness—with courtesy— and I could not help glancing at Miss Oldcastle to see what impression this family of "low, freethinking republicans" made upon her. It was easy to discover that the impression was of favorable surprise. But I was as much surprised at her behavior as she was at theirs. Not a haughty tone was to be heard in her voice, not a haughty movement to be seen in her form. She accepted the chair offered her and sat down by the fireside, perfectly at home, only that she turned toward me, waiting for what explanation I might think proper to give.

Before I had time to speak, however, old Mr. Weir broke the silence. "I've been telling Tom, Sir, as I've told him many a time afore, as how he's a deal too hard with his children."

"Father!" interrupted Thomas angrily.

"Have patience a bit, my boy," persisted the old man, turning again toward me. "Now, Sir, he won't even hear young Tom's side of the story, and I say that boy won't tell him no lie if he's the same boy he went away."

"I tell you, Father," again began Thomas, but this time I interposed, to prevent useless talk beforehand.

"Thomas," I said, "listen to me. I have heard your son's side of the story. Because of something he said, I went to Miss Oldcastle and asked her whether she was in that shop last Thursday. That is all I have asked her, and all she has told me is that she was. I know no more than you what she is going to reply to my questions now, but I have no doubt her answers will correspond to your son's story."

I then put my questions to Miss Oldcastle, whose answers amounted to this: that they had wanted to buy a shawl; that they had seen none good enough; that they had left shop without buying anything; and that they had been waited upon by a young man who, while perfectly polite and attentive to their wants, did not seem to have the ways or manners of a London shoplad. And that was all.

"I think, Mr. Walton, if you have done with me, I ought to go home now," said Miss Oldcastle.

"Certainly," I answered. "I will take you home at once. I am greatly obliged to you for coming."

"Indeed, Sir," said the old man, rising with difficulty, "we're obliged to both you and the lady more than we can tell. To take such a deal of trouble for us! But you see, Sir, you're one of them as thinks a man's got his duty to do one way or another, whether he be clergyman or carpenter. God bless you, Miss. You're of the right sort, which you'll excuse an old man, Miss, as'll never see ye again till ye've got the wings as ye ought to have."

Miss Oldcastle smiled very sweetly and answered nothing, but shook hands with them both and bade them good-night. Weir could not speak a word—he could hardly even lift his eyes. But a red spot glowed on each of his pale cheeks, making him look very like his daughter Catharine, and I could see Miss Oldcastle wince and grow red too with the grip he gave her hand. But she smiled again none the less sweetly.

"I will see Miss Oldcastle home, and then go back to my house and bring the boy with me," I said as we left.

It was some time before either Miss Oldcastle or I spoke. The sun was setting, the sky, the earth, and the air were lovely with rosy light, and the world full of that peculiar calm which belongs to the eveing of the day of rest. Surely the world ought to wake better on the morrow.

"Not very dangerous people, those, Miss Oldcastle." I said at last.

"I thank you very much for taking me to see them," she returned, cordially.

"You won't believe all you may happen to hear against the working people now?"

"I never did."

"There are ill-conditioned, cross-grained, low-minded, selfish, unbelieving people among them. God knows it. But there are ladies and gentlemen among them too."

"That old man is a gentleman."

"He is. And the only way to teach them all to be such is to be such to them. The man who does not show himself a gentleman to the working people—why should I call them the poor? Some of them are better off than many of the rich, for they can pay their debts and do it—"

I had forgot the beginning of my sentence.

"You were saying that the man who does not show himself a gentleman to the poor—"

"Is no gentleman at all, only a gentle without the man; and if you consult my namesake, old Izaak, you will find what that is."

"I will look. I know your way now. You won't tell me anything I can find out for myself."

"Is it not the best way?"

"Yes. Because, for one thing, you find out so much more than you look for."

"Certainly that has been my own experience."

"I am very glad you asked me to go tonight."

"If people only knew their own brothers and sisters, the kingdom of heaven would not be far off."

I do not think Miss Oldcastle quite liked this, for she was silent thereafter. And we had now come close to the house.

"I wish I could help you," I said.

"In what?"

"To bear what I fear is waiting you."

"I told you I was equal to that. It is where we are unequal that we want help. You may have to help me someday—who knows?"

I left her most unwillingly on the porch, though rejoicing in my heart over her last words. (Although I do happen to know how she fared that night after I left, the painful record is not essential to my story.)

Later, when young Tom and I came to his father's house and entered the room, his grandfather rose and tottered to meet him. His father made one step toward him and then hesitated. Of all conditions of the human mind, that of being ashamed of himself must have been the strangest to Thomas Weir. His fall had been from the pinnacle of pride. I call it Thomas Weir's fall, for surely to behave in an unfatherly manner to both daughter and son—the one sinful, and therefore needing the more tenderness; the other innocent, and therefore claiming justification—and to do so from pride, and hurt pride, was fall enough. And now, if he was humbled in the one instance, there would be room to hope he might become humble in the other. But I had soon to see that for a time, his pride, driven from its entrenchment against his son, only retreated with all its forces into the other against his daughter.

Before a moment had passed, however, justice overcame so far that he held out his hand and said, "Come, Tom, let bygones be bygones."

But I stepped between. "Thomas Weir," I said, "I have too great a regard for you—and you know I dare not flatter you—to let you off this way, or rather leave you to think you have done your duty when you have not done the half of it. You have done your son a wrong, a great wrong. How can you claim to be a gentleman—I say nothing of being a Christian, for there you make no claim—if, having done a man wrong you don't beg his pardon?"

He did not move a step. But young Tom stepped hurriedly forward, and, catching his father's hand in both of his, cried out, "My father shan't beg my pardon. I beg yours, Father, for everything I ever did to displease you, but I wasn't to blame in this. I wasn't, indeed."

"Tom, I beg your pardon," said the hard man, overcome at last. "And now, Sir," he added, turning to me, "will you let bygones be bygones between my boy and me?" There was just a touch of bitterness in his tone.

"With all my heart," I replied. "But I want just a word with you in the shop before I go."

"Certainly," he answered, stiffly.

113

"Thomas, my friend," I said, when we got into the shop, laying my hand on his shoulder, "will you after this day that God has dealt hardly with you? There's a son to give thanks for on your knees! Thomas, you have a strong sense of fair play in your heart, and you give fair play neither to your own son nor yet to God Himself. You close your doors and brood over your own miseries and the wrongs people have done you—whereas, if you would but open those doors, you might come out unto the light of God's truth, and see that His heart is as clear as sunlight toward you. You won't believe this, and therefore you can't quite believe that there is a God at all. If you would but let Him teach you, you would find your perplexities melt away like the snow in the spring, till you could hardly believe you had ever felt them. No arguing will convince you of a God, but let Him once come in, and all argument will be tenfold useless to convince you that there is no God. Give God justice. Try Him as I have said. Good night."

He did not return my farewell with a single word, but the grasp of his strong rough hand was earnest and loving. I felt that it was better I could not see his face in the dark.

I went home as peaceful in my heart as the night whose curtains God had drawn about the earth.

FOURTEEN

MY PUPIL

In the middle of the following week I was returning from a visit I had made to Tomkins and his wife, when I met Dr. Duncan.

"Well, Dr. Duncan," I said, "busy as usual fighting the devil?"

"Ah! My dear Mr. Walton," returned the doctor—and a kind word from him went a long way into my heart—"I know what you mean. You fight the devil from the inside, and I fight him from the outside. My chance is a poor one."

"It would be, perhaps, if you were confined to outside remedies. But what an opportunity your profession gives you of attacking the enemy from the inside as well! And you have this advantage over us, that no man can say it belongs to your profession to say such things, and therefore disregard them."

"Ah! Mr. Walton, I have too great a respect for your profession to dare interfere with it. The doctor in *Macbeth*, you know, could

> Not minister to a mind diseased,
> Pluck from the memory a rooted sorrow,
> Raze out the written troubles of the brain,
> And with some sweet oblivious antidote
> Cleanse the stuff'd bosom of that perilous stuff
> Which weighs upon the heart.

"What a memory you have! But do you think I can do that anymore than you?"

"You know the best medicine to give, anyhow. I wish I always did. But you see we have no *theriaca* now."

115

"Well, we have. For the Lord says, 'Come unto Me and I will give you rest.'"

"There! I told you! That will meet all diseases."

"There comes to my mind a line of Chaucer. You have mentioned *theriaca* and I quoted our Lord's words. Chaucer brings the two together, for the word *triacle* is merely a corruption of *theriaca*, the unfailing cure for everything. 'Crist, which that is to every harm triacle.'"

"That is in Chaucer?"

"Yes. In the Man of Law's Tale."

"I have just come from referring to the passage I quoted from Shakespeare. And I mention that because I want to tell you what made me think of the passage: I have been to see Catharine Weir. I think she is not long for this world. She has a bad cough, and her lungs are going."

"I am not surprised. But I do wish I had got a hold of her before, that I might be of some use to her now. Is she in immediate danger?"

"No, but I have no expectation of her recovery. Very likely she will just live through the winter and die in the spring. Those patients so often go as the flowers come! All her coughing, poor woman, will not cleanse *her* stuffed bosom either. For that perilous stuff weighs on her heart as well as on her lungs."

"Ah, dear! What is it, Doctor, that weighs upon her heart? Is it shame, or what is it? She is so uncommunicative that I hardly know anything at all about her yet."

"I cannot tell. She has the faculty of silence."

"If she would talk at all, one would have a chance of knowing something of the state of her mind, and so might give her some help."

"Perhaps she will break down all at once and open her mind to you. I have not told her she is dying. I think a medical man ought at least to be quite sure before he dares to say such a thing. I have known a long life injured, to human view at least, by the medical verdict in youth of imminent death."

"Certainly one has no right to say what God is going to do with anyone till he knows it beyond a doubt. Illness has its own peculiar mission, independent of any association with coming death, and may often work better when mingled with the hope of life. But could you not suggest something, Dr. Duncan, to guide me in trying to do my duty by her?"

"I cannot. We don't know what she is thinking. How can I prescribe without some diagnosis? I do not think anything will save her life, as we say; but you have taught us to think of the life that belongs to the spirit as the life, and I do believe confession would do everything for that."

"Yes, if made to God. But I will grant that communication of one's sorrows or sins to a wise brother of mankind may help to deepen confession to the Father in heaven. But we must not hurry things. She will perhaps come to me of herself before long. But I will call and inquire after her."

We parted, and I went at once to Catharine Weir's shop. She received me much as usual, which was hardly to be called receiving at all. Her eyes were full of a stony brilliance, and the flame of the consuming fire glowed upon her cheeks more brightly than ever. Her hand trembled, but her demeanor was perfectly calm.

"I am sorry to hear you are complaining, Miss Weir," I said.

"I suppose Dr. Duncan told you so, Sir. But I am quite well. I did not send for him. He called of himself, and wanted to persuade me I was ill."

I understood that she felt injured by his interference. "You should attend to his advice, though. He is a prudent man, and not in the least given to alarming people without cause."

She returned no answer. So I tried another subject. "What a fine fellow your brother is! Has your father found another place for him yet?"

"I don't know. My father never tells me any of his doings."

"But don't you go and talk to him sometimes?"

"No. He does not care to see me."

"I am going there now. Will you come with me?"

"Thank you. I never go where I am not wanted."

"But it is not right that father and daughter should live as you do. Suppose he may not have been so kind to you as he ought, you should not cherish resentment against him for it. That only makes matters worse, you know."

"I never said that he had been unkind to me."

"And yet you let every person in the village know it."

"How?" Her eyes had no longer the stony glitter.

"You are never seen together. You scarcely speak when you meet. Neither of you crosses the other's threshold."

"It is not my fault."

"It is not all your fault, I know. But do you think you can go to

117

a heaven at last where you will be able to keep apart from each other, he in his house and you in your house, without any sign that it was through this father on earth that you were born into the world which the Father in heaven redeemed by the gift of His own Son?"

She was silent. After a pause, I went on. "I believe in my heart that you love your father. I could not believe otherwise of you. And you will never be happy till you have made it up with him. Have you done him no wrong?"

At these words her face turned white with anger—all but those spots on her cheekbones, which shone out in dreadful contrast to the deathly paleness of the rest of her face. Then the returning blood surged violently from her heart, and the red spots were lost in one crimson glow. She opened her lips to speak but, changing her mind, turned and walked haughtily out of the shop and closed the door behind her.

I waited, hoping she would recover herself and return; but, after ten minutes had passed, I thought it better to go away.

As I had told her, I was going to her father's shop. There I was received very differently. There was a certain softness in the manner of the carpenter, with the same heartiness in the shake of his hand which had accompanied my last leave-taking. I had purposely allowed ten days to elapse before I called again, to give time for the unpleasant feelings associated with my interference to vanish. And now I had something in my mind about young Tom.

'Have you got anything for your boy yet, Thomas?"

"Not yet, Sir. There's time enough. I don't want to part with him just yet. There he is, taking his turn at what's going. Tom!"

And from the farther end of the large shop, where I had not observed him, now approached young Tom, looking quite like a workman in his canvas jacket.

"Well, Tom, I am glad to find you can turn your hand to anything."

"I must be a stupid, Sir, if I couldn't handle my father's tools," returned the lad.

"I don't know that quite. My father is a lawyer, and I never could read a chapter in one of his books."

"Perhaps you never tried, Sir."

"Indeed I did, and no doubt I could have done it if I had made up my mind to it. But I never felt inclined to finish the page. And that reminds me why I called today. Thomas, I know that lad of yours is fond of reading. Can you spare him from his work for an hour or so before breakfast?"

"Tomorrow, Sir?"

" 'Tomorrow, and tomorrow, and tomorrow,' " I answered, "and there's Shakespeare for you."

"Of course, Sir, whatever you wish," said Thomas, with a perplexed look, in which pleasure seemed to long for confirmation.

"I want to give him some direction in his reading. When a man is fond of any tools, and can use them, it is worthwhile showing him how to use them better."

"Oh, thank you, Sir!" exclaimed Tom, his face beaming with delight.

"That is kind of you, Sir! Tom, you're a made man!" cried the father.

"So," I went on, "if you will let him come to me for an hour every morning, till he gets another place, say from eight to nine, I will see what I can do for him."

Tom's face was as red with delight as his sister's had been with anger. And I left the shop somewhat consoled for the pain I had given Catharine, which grieved me without making me sorry that I had occasioned it.

I had intended to try to do something from the father's side toward a reconciliation with his daughter, but I saw I had blocked up my own way. I could not bear to offer to bribe him. The first impression would be that I had a professional end to gain—that the reconciling of father and daughter was a sort of parish business of mine, and that I had smoothed the way to it by offering a gift. This was just what would irritate such a man, and I resolved to bide my time.

When Tom came, I asked him if he had read any Wordsworth. I always give people what I like myself, because that must be wherein I can best help them. I was anxious, too, to find out what he was capable of.

I therefore chose one of Wordsworth's sonnets, the one entitled, "Composed During a Storm," telling him to let me know when he considered that he had mastered the meaning of it. It was fully half an hour before Tom rose. I had not been uneasy about the experiment after ten minutes had passed, and after that time was doubled I felt certain of some measure of success. It was clear that Tom did not understand the sonnet at first, but I was delighted that he at least knew that he did not know, for that is the very next step to knowing.

"Well, Tom," I said, "have you made it out?"

"I can't say I have, Sir. I'm afraid I'm very stupid, for I've tried hard. I must just ask you to tell me what it means. But I must tell you one thing, Sir. Every time I read it over—twenty times, I dare say—I thought I was lying on my mother's grave, as I lay that terrible night. And then, at the end, there you were standing over me and saying, 'Can I do anything to help you?'"

I was struck with astonishment. For here in a wonderful manner I saw the imagination outrunning the intellect and manifesting to the heart what the brain could not yet understand. There was a hidden sympathy of the deepest kind between the life experience of the lad and the embodiment of such life experience on the part of the poet. He went on. "I am sure, Sir, I ought to have been at my prayers then, but I wasn't, so I didn't deserve you to come. But don't you think God is sometimes better to us than we deserve?"

"He is just everything to us, Tom, and we don't and can't deserve anything. Now I will try to explain the sonnet to you."

I had always had an impulse to teach, but not for the teaching's sake—for the attempt to fill skulls with knowledge had always been to me a desolate dreariness. But the moment I saw a sign of hunger, an indication of readiness to receive, I was invariably seized with a kind of passion for giving. I now proceeded to explain the sonnet as well as I could.

Tom said, "It is very strange, Sir. But, now that I have heard you say what the poem means, I feel as if I had known it all the time, though I could not say it."

Here at least was no common mind. The hour before breakfast extended into two hours after breakfast as well. Nor did this take up too much of my time, for the lad was capable of doing a great deal for himself under the sense of help at hand. His father, so far from making any objection to the arrangement, was delighted with it. Nor do I believe that the lad did less work in the shop for it—I learned he worked regularly till eight o'clock every night.

I had the lad fresh in the morning, clearheaded, with no mists from the valley of labor to cloud the heights of understanding. From the exercise to the mind it was a pleasant and relieving change to turn to bodily exertion. I am certain that he both thought and worked better, because he both thought and worked. But it would have been quite a different matter if he had come to me after the labor of the day. He would not than have been able to think nearly so well. Labor, sleep, thought, labor again, seems to me to be the right order.

Having exercised him in the analysis of literature—I mean helped him to take them to pieces that, putting them together again, he might see what kinds of things they were—I resolved to try something fresh with him.

By the end of three months, my pupil, without knowing any other Latin author, was able to read any part of the first book of the *Aeneid*—to read it tolerably in measure, and to enjoy the poetry of it—and this not without a knowledge of the declensions and conjugations. As to the syntax, I made the sentences themselves teach him that. As an end, all this was of no great value. But as a beginning it was invaluable, for it made and kept him hungry for more. In most modes of teaching, the beginnings are such that, without pressure, no boy will return to them.

Through the whole of that summer and the following winter I went on teaching Tom Weir. His father, though his own book learning was but small, had enough insight to perceive that his son was something out of the common, and that any possible advantage he might lose by remaining in Marshmallows was considerably more than balanced by the instruction from the vicar.

FIFTEEN

DR. DUNCAN'S STORY

On the second Sunday after that—which was surprising to me when I considered our last parting—Catharine Weir was again in church.

I was endeavoring to enforce the Lord's Prayer by making them think about the meaning of the words they were so familiar with. I had come to the petition, "Forgive us our debts, as we forgive our debtors," with which I naturally connected the words of our Lord that follow: "For if ye forgive men their trespasses, your Heavenly Father will also forgive you; but if ye forgive not men their trespasses, neither will your Father forgive your trespasses." I tried to show that even were it possible with God to forgive an unforgiving man, the man himself would not be able to believe that God did forgive him, and therefore he could get no comfort, or help, or joy of any kind from the forgiveness. Hatred or revenge or contempt, or anything that separates us from man, separates us from God too. To the loving soul alone does the Father reveal Himself, for love alone can understand Him. It is the peacemakers who are His children.

This I said, thinking of no one more than another of my audience. But as I closed my sermon, I could not help fancying that Mrs. Oldcastle looked at me with more than her usual fierceness. I forgot all about it, however, for I never seemed to myself to have any hold of, or relation to, that woman. When I called upon her next, after the interview last related, she behaved much as if she had forgotten all about it, which was not likely.

In the end of the week after that sermon, I was passing the Hall

122

gate on my usual Saturday walk, when Judy saw me and came out of the lodge. "Mr. Walton," she said, "how could you preach at Grannie as you did last Sunday?"

"I did not preach at anybody, Judy."

"O Mr. Walton!"

"You know I didn't, Judy. You know that if I had, I would not say I had not."

"Yes, yes, I know that perfectly," she said, seriously, "but Grannie thinks you did."

"How do you know that?"

"I can read her face—not so well as plain print, but as well as what Uncle Stoddart calls black letter, at least. I know she thought you were preaching at her, and her face said, 'I shan't forgive you, anyhow. I never forgive, and I won't for all your preaching.' That's what her face said."

"I am sure she would not say so, Judy."

"Oh, no, she would not say so. She would say, 'I always forgive, but I never forget.' That's a favorite saying of hers."

"But, Judy, don't you think it is rather hypocritical of you to say all this to me about your grandmother when she is so kind to you, and you seem such good friends with her?"

She looked up in my face with an expression of surprise.

"It is all true, Mr. Walton," she said.

"Perhaps. But you are saying it behind her back."

"I will go home and say it to her face directly." And she turned to go.

"No, no, Judy, I did not mean that," I said, taking her by the arm.

"I won't say you told me to do it. I thought there was no harm in telling you. Grannie is kind to me, and I am kind to her. But Grannie is afraid of my tongue, and I mean her to be afraid of it. It's the only way to keep her in order. Darling Aunt Wynnie! It's all she's got to defend her. If you knew how Grannie treats her sometimes, you would be cross with her yourself, Mr. Walton, for all your goodness and your white surplice."

And to my yet greater surprise, the wayward girl burst out crying and, breaking away from me, ran through the gate and out of sight among the trees, without once looking back.

I pursued my walk, my meditations somewhat discomposed. Would she go home and tell her grandmother what she had said to me? And, if she did, would it not widen the breach beyond which

Ethelwyn stood, out of the reach of my help?

I walked quickly on to leave the little world of Marshmallows behind me, and be alone with nature and my Greek Testament. Hearing the sound of horsehoofs on the road, I glanced up and saw a young man approaching upon a good seviceable hack. He turned into my road and passed me. He was pale, with a dark mustache, and large dark eyes; sat his horse well and carelessly; had fine features of the type commonly considered Grecian, but thin, and expressive chiefly of conscious weariness. He wore a white hat with crepe upon it, white gloves, and long, military boots. All this I caught as he passed me. I saw him stop at the lodge of the Hall, ring the bell, and then ride through the gate. I confess I did not quite like this, but I got over the feeling so far as to be able to turn to my Testament when I had crossed the stile.

I came home another way, after one of the most delightful days I had ever spent. Having reached the river in the course of my wandering, I came down the side of it toward Old Rogers' cottage, loitering and looking, quiet in heart and soul and mind, because I had committed my cares to Him who careth for us. I was gazing over the stump of an old pollard on which I was leaning, down on a great bed of white water lilies that lay on the broad slow river, here broader and slower than in most places. And then came a hand on my shoulder and, turning, I saw the gray head and white smock of my friend Old Rogers, and I was glad that he loved me enough not to be afraid of the parson and the gentleman.

"I've found it, Sir, I do think," he said, his brown furrowed old face shining.

"Found what, Old Rogers?" I returned.

"Why He was displeased with the disciples for not knowing what He meant about the leaven of the Pharisees. It was all dark to me for days. For it appeared to me very nat'ral that, seeing they had no bread in the locker, and hearing tell of leaven which they weren't to eat, they should think it had summat to do with their having none of any sort. But He didn't seem to think it was right of them to fall into the blunder. For why then? A man can't be always right. He may be like myself, a foremastman with no schoolin' but what the winds and the waves puts into him, and I'm thinkin' those fishermen the Lord took to so much were something o' that sort. 'How could they help it?' I said to myself, Sir. And from that I came to ask myself, 'Could they have helped it?' If they couldn't, He wouldn't have been vexed with them. And all at once, Sir, this mornin', it came to me. And when I saw you, Sir, a readin' upon the lilies, I couldn't help runnin' out to tell you. Isn't it a satisfaction, Sir, when yer dead reckonin' runs ye right in betwixt the cheeks of the harbor? I see it all now."

"Well, I want to know, Old Rogers. I'm not so old as you, and so I may live longer; and every time I read that passage, I should like to be able to say to myself, 'Old Rogers gave me this.' "

"I only hope I'm right, Sir. It was just this: their heads was full of their dinner because they didn't know where it was to come from. If their hearts had been full of the dinner He gave to the five thousand hungry men, women, and children, they wouldn't have been uncomfortable about not having a loaf. And so they wouldn't have been set upon the wrong tack when He spoke about the leaven of the Pharisees and Sadducees, and they would have known in a moment what He meant."

"You're right! You must be right, Old Rogers. It's as plain as possible!" I cried, rejoiced at the man's insight. "Thank you. I'll preach about it tomorrow. I thought I had got my sermon, but I was mistaken; you had got it."

But I was mistaken again. I had not got my sermon yet.

I walked with him to his cottage and left him, after a greeting with the "old woman." Passing then through the village, and seeing by the light of her candle Catharine Weir behind her counter, I went in. I thought Old Rogers' tobacco must be nearly gone, and I might safely buy some more. Catharine's manner was much the same as usual. But, as she was weighing my purchase, she broke out all at once, "It's no use your preaching at me, Mr. Walton. I cannot, I will not forgive. I will do anything but forgive. And it's no use."

"It is not I that say it, Catharine. It is the Lord Himself. And I was not preaching at you. I was preaching to you as much as to anyone there, and no more. Just think of what He says, not what I say."

"I can't help it. If He won't forgive me, I must go without it. I can't forgive."

I saw that good and evil were fighting in her, and felt that no words of mine could be of further avail at the moment. The words of our Lord had laid hold of her and that was enough for this time. All I could venture to say was, "I won't trouble you with talk, Catharine. Our Lord wants to talk to you. It is not for me to interfere. But please remember, if ever you think I can serve you in

125

any way, you have only to send for me."

She murmured a mechanical thanks and handed me my parcel. I paid for it, bade her good-night, and left the shop.

"O Lord," I said in my heart, as I walked away, "what a labor Thou hast with us all! Shall we ever, someday, be all and quite, good like Thee? Help me. Fill me with Thy light, that my work may all go to bring about the gladness of Thy kingdom."

And now I found that I wanted very much to see my friend Dr. Duncan. He received me with stately cordiality, and a smile that went further than all his words of greeting.

"Come, now, Mr. Walton, I am just going to sit down to my dinner, and you must join me. I think there will be enough for us both. There is, I believe, a chicken for us, and we can make up with cheese and a glass of my own father's port. He was fond of port, though I never saw him with one glass more than the registered tonnage. He always sat light on the water."

We sat down to our dinner, so simple and so well-cooked that it was just what I liked. We chattered away concerning many things, and I happened to refer to Old Rogers.

"What a fine old fellow that is!" said Dr. Duncan.

"Indeed he is," I answered. "He is great comfort and help to me. I don't think anybody but myself has an idea what there is in that old man."

"The people in the village don't quite like him though, I find. He is too ready to be down on them when he sees things going amiss. The fact is, they are afraid of him."

"Something as the Jews were afraid of John the Baptist, because he was an honest man and spoke not merely his own mind, but the mind of God in it."

"Just so. I believe you're quite right. Do you know, the other day, happening to go into Weir's shop to get him to do a job for me, I found him and Old Rogers in an argument? Keen as Weir was, and far surpassing Rogers in correctness of speech, and precision as well, the old sailor carried too heavy metal for the carpenter. It evidently annoyed Weir, but such was the good humor of Rogers, that he could not, for very shame, lose his temper."

"I know how he would talk exactly," I returned. "He has a kind of loving banter with him that is irresistible to any man with a good heart. I am very glad to hear there is anything like communion begun between them. Weir will get good from him."

"My man-of-all-work is going to leave me. I wonder if the old man would take his place."

"I do not know whether he is fit for it. But of one thing you may be sure—if Old Rogers does not honestly believe he is fit for it, he will not take it. And he will tell you why too."

"Of that, however, I think I may be a better judge than he. There is nothing to which a good sailor cannot turn his hand, whatever he may think himself. It is not like a routine trade. Things are never twice the same at sea. The sailor has a thousand chances of using his judgment—if he has any to use—and that Old Rogers has in no common degree, so I should have no fear of him. If he won't let me steer him, you must put your hand to the tiller for me."

"I will do what I can," I answered, "for nothing would please me more than to see him in your service. It would be much better for him, and his wife too, than living by uncertain jobs as he does now."

(The result was that Old Rogers consented to try for a month. But when the end of the month came, nothing was said on either side, and the old man remained. And I could see several little new comforts about the cottage, in consequence of the regularity of his wages.)

At length I brought my conversation with Dr. Duncan around to my interview with Catharine Weir.

"Can you understand," I said, "a woman finding it so hard to forgive her own father?"

"Are you sure it is her father?"

"Surely she has not this feeling toward more than one. That she has it toward her father, I know."

"I don't know," he answered. "I have known resentment preponderate over every other feeling and passion—in the mind of a woman too. I once heard of a good woman who cherished this feeling against a good man because of some distrustful words he had once addressed to her. She had lived to a great age, and was expressing to her clergyman her desire that God would take her away—she had been waiting a long time. The clergyman, a very shrewd as well as devout man, and not without a touch of humor, said, 'Perhaps God doesn't mean to let you die till you've forgiven Mr. Maxwell." She was as if struck with a flash of thought, sat silent during the rest of his visit. When the clergyman called the next day, he found Mr.Maxwell and her talking together very quietly over a cup of tea. And she hadn't long to wait after that, I

127

was told, but was gathered to her fathers—or went home to her children, whichever is the better phrase."

"I wish I had your experience, Dr. Duncan," I said.

"I have not had so much experience as a general practitioner, because I have been so long at sea. But I am satisfied that until a medical man knows a good deal more about his patient than most medical men give themselves the trouble to find out, his prescriptions will partake a good deal more than necessary of haphazard. As to this question of obstinate resentment, I know one case in which it is the ruling presence of a woman's life—the very light that is in her is resentment."

"Tell me something about her."

"I will. But even to you I will mention no names. I was called to attend a lady at a house where I had never yet been."

"Was it in—?" I began, but checked myself. Dr. Duncan smiled and went on without remark. I could see that he told his story with great care, lest he should let anything slip that might give a clue to the place or people.

"I was led up into an old-fashioned, richly furnished room. A great wood fire burned on the hearth. The bed was surrounded with heavy dark curtains. In the bed lay one of the loveliest young creatures I had ever seen, and, one on each side, stood two of the most dreadful-looking women I have ever beheld. Still as death they stood, while I examined my patient, with moveless faces, one as white as the other. One was evidently mistress, and the other the servant. The latter looked more self-contained than the former, but less determined and possibly more cruel. That both could be unkind was plain enough. There was trouble and signs of inward conflict in the eyes of the mistress. The maid gave no sign of any inside to her at all, but stood watching her mistress. A child's toy was lying in the corner of the room.

"I found the lady very weak and very feverish—a quick, feeble pulse, and a restlessness in her eye which I felt contained the secret of her disorder. She kept glancing toward the door, which would not open for all her looking, and I heard her once murmur to herself, 'He won't come!' I prescribed for her as far as I could venture, but begged a word with her mother. She went with me into an adjoining room.

" 'The lady is longing for something,' I said, not wishing to be so definite as I could have been.

"The mother made no reply. I saw her lips shut yet closer than

128

she had before.

" 'She is your daughter, is she not?'

" 'Yes,' very decidedly.

" 'Could you not find out what she wishes?'

" 'Perhaps I could guess.'

" 'I do not think I can do her any good till she has what she wants.'

" 'Is that your mode of prescribing, Doctor?' she said, tartly.

" 'Yes, certainly,' I answered, 'in the present case. Is she married?'

" 'Yes.'

" 'Has she any children?'

" 'One daughter.'

" 'Let her see her, then.'

" 'She does not care to see her.'

" 'Where is her husband?'

" 'Excuse me, Doctor. I did not send for you to ask questions, but to give advice.'

" 'And I came to ask questions, in order that I may give advice. Do you think a human being is like a clock that can be taken to pieces, cleaned, and put together again?'

" 'My daughter's condition is not a fit subject for jesting.'

" 'Certainly not. Send for her husband or the undertaker, whichever you please,' I said, forgetting my manners and my temper together, for I was more irritable then than I am now, and there was something so repulsive about the woman that I felt as if I was talking to an evil creature that, for her own ends, was tormenting the dying lady.

" 'I understood you were a gentleman of experience and breeding.'

" 'I am not in question, Madam. It is your daughter. She must see her husband if it be possible.'

" 'It is not possible.'

" 'Why?'

" 'I say it is not possible, and that is enough. Good morning.'

"I could say no more at that time. I called the next day. She was just the same, only that I knew she wanted to speak to me, and dared not because of the presence of the two women. Her troubled eyes searched mine for pity and help, and I could not tell what to do for her. There are, indeed, strongholds of injustice and wrong into which no law can enter to help.

"One afternoon, about a week after my first visit, I was sitting by her bedside, wondering what could be done to get her out of the clutches of these tormentors who were consuming her in the slow fire of her own affections. I heard a faint noise, a rapid foot in the house so quiet before—heard doors open and shut, then a dull sound of conflict of some sort. Presently a quick step came up the oak stair. The face of my patient flushed, and her eyes gleamed as if her soul would come out of them. Weak as she was, she sat up in bed, and the two women darted from the room.

" 'My husband!' said the girl, for indeed she was little more in age. 'They will murder him.'

"I heard a cry, and what sounded like an inarticulate imprecation, but both from a woman's voice. Then a young man, as fine a fellow as I ever saw—palefaced, dressed like a gamekeeper but evidently a gentleman—walked quietly into the room. The two women followed in fierce wrath, as red as he was white. He came round the bed, and she fell into his embrace.

"I had gone to the mother. 'Let us have no scene now,' I said, 'or her blood will be on your head.'

"She took no notice of what I said, but stood silently glaring, not gazing, at the pair. I feared an outburst and had resolved, if it came, to carry her at once from the room.

"But in a moment more the young man lifted up his wife's head. Seeing the look of terror in his face, I hastened to him, and lifting her from him, laid her down, dead. Disease of the heart, I believe.

"The mother burst into a shriek—not of horror or grief or remorse, but of deadly hatred. 'Look at your work!' she cried to him as he stood gazing in stupor on the face of the girl. 'You said she was yours, not mine. Take her. You may have her now you have killed her.'

" 'He may have killed her, but you have murdered her, Madam,' I said, as I took the man by the arm, and led him away, yielding like a child. But the moment I got him out of the house, he gave a groan and broke away from me. I heard the gallop of a horse, and saw him tearing away at full speed along the London road. I never heard more of him or of the story."

(I could hardly doubt whose was the story I had heard. Things which seem as if they could not happen in a civilized country and a polished age, are proved as possible as ever where the heart is unloving, the feelings unrefined, self the center, and God nowhere in the man or woman's vision. The terrible things that one reads in old histories or in modern newspapers were done by human beings, not by demons.

(I did not let my friend know that I knew what he concealed, and indeed knew all the story:

(Dorothy—*the gift of God*, a wonderful name, to be so treated, faring in this, however, like many other of God's gifts—Dorothy Oldcastle was the eldest daughter of Jeremy and Sibyl Oldcastle, and the sister, therefore, of Ethelwyn. Her father, an easygoing man entirely under the dominion of his wife, died when Dorothy was about fifteen. Her mother sent her to school, with especial recommendation to the care of a clergyman in the neighborhood, though the mother paid no attention to what our Lord or His apostles said, nor indeed seemed to care to ask herself if what she did was right.

(Dorothy was there three or four years. She and the clergyman's son fell in love with each other. The mother heard of it and sent for her home. She had other views for her. Of course, in such eyes, a daughter's fancy was a thing to be sneered at. But she found, to her fierce disdain, that she had not been able to keep all her beloved obstinacy to herself—she had transmitted a portion of it to her daughter. But in the daughter it was combined with noble qualities and, ceasing to be the evil thing it was in her mother, became an honorable firmness, rendering her able to withstand her mother's stormy importunities. Thus Nature had begun to right herself—the right in the daughter turning to meet and defy the wrong in the mother—and that in the same strength of character which the mother had misused for evil and selfish ends. And thus the bad breed was broken. She was and would be true to her love. The consequent scenes were dreadful. The spirit, but not the will of the girl, was all but broken. She felt that she could not sustain the strife long.

(The young man had procured a good appointment in India, whither he must sail within a month. The end was that Dorothy left her mother's house. Mr. Gladwyn was waiting for her near, and conducted her to his father who had constantly refused to aid Mrs. Oldcastle by interfering in the matter. They were married the next day by the clergyman of a neighboring parish. But almost immediately she was taken so ill that it was impossible for her to accompany her husband and she was compelled to remain behind, hoping to join him the following year.

(Before the time arrived, she gave birth to my little friend Judy, and her departure was again delayed, probably by the early stages of the disease of which she died. Then, just as she was about to set sail for India, news arrived that Mr. Gladwyn had had a sunstroke, and would come home as soon as he was able. So, instead of going to join him, she must wait where she was.

(His mother had been dead for some time. His father was found dead in his chair soon after the news of the illness of his son, and so the poor young creature was left alone with her child, without money, and in weak health. The old man had left nothing behind him but his furniture and books, and nothing could be done in arranging his affairs till the arrival of his son. Mrs. Oldcastle wrote, offering her daughter all that she required in her old home.

(She had not been more than a few days in the house before her mother began to tyrannize over her as in old times, and although Mrs. Gladwyn's health was evidently failing in consequence, Mrs. Oldcastle either did not see the cause, or could not restrain her evil impulses. At length the news arrived of Mr. Gladwyn's departure for home. Perhaps then, for the first time, the temptation entered the mother's mind to take her revenge, by making her daughter's illness a pretext for refusing him admission to her presence. She told her she should not see him till she was better; persisted in her resolution after his arrival; and effected, by the help of Sarah, that he should not gain admittance to the house. It was only by the connivance of Ethelwyn, then a girl about fifteen, that he was admitted by the underground entrance.

(What a horror of darkness seemed to hang over that family! What deeds of wickedness! But the horror came from within—selfishness, and fierceness of temper were its source—no unhappy doom. The worship of one's own will fumes out around the being an atmosphere of evil, an altogether abnormal condition of the moral firmament, out of which will break the very flames of hell.)

I had very little time for the privacy of the church that night. Dark as it was, however, I went in before I went home. I groped my way into the pulpit, and sat down in the darkness and thought. The words of Dr. Duncan had opened up a good deal to me. Yet my personal interest in his story did not make me forget poor Catharine Weir and the terrible sore in her heart. And I saw that of herself she would not, could not, forgive to all eternity—that all the pains of hell could not make her forgive—for it was a divine glory to forgive and must come from God. And thinking of Mrs.

Oldcastle, I saw that in ourselves we could be sure of no safety, not from the worst and vilest sins. Only by being filled with a higher spirit than our own are we, or can we be, safe from this eternal death of our being. This spirit was fighting the evil spirit in Catharine Weir—how was I to urge her to give ear to the good? If will would but side with God, the forces of self, deserted by their leader, must soon quit the field, and the woman—the kingdom within her no longer torn by conflicting forces—would sit quiet at the feet of the Master. Might she not be roused to utter one feeble cry to God for help? That would be one step toward the forgiveness of others. To ask something for herself would be a great advance in such a proud nature as hers, and to ask good heartily is the very next step to giving good heartily.

Many thoughts such as these passed through my mind, chiefly associated with her, for I could not think how to think about Mrs. Oldcastle yet. And I kept lifting up my heart to the God who had cared to make me, and then drew me to be a preacher to my fellows, and had surely something to give me to say to them. Might not my humble ignorance work His will, though my wrath could not work His righteousness? And I descended from the pulpit thinking with myself, "Let Him do as He will. Here I am. I will say what I see. Let Him make it good."

SIXTEEN

THE ORGAN

The next morning I spoke about the words of our Lord:

"If ye then, being evil, know how to give good gifts to your children, how much more shall your Heavenly Father give the Holy Spirit to them that ask Him!"

When I rose in the reading desk, I saw Catharine Weir and Mrs. Oldcastle and Judy, all looking me in the face. To my surprise and discomposure, Miss Oldcastle was there for the first time. And by her side was the gentleman whom the day before I had encountered on horseback. He sat carelessly, easily, contentedly—indifferently. I could not help seeing that he was always behind the rest of the congregation, as if he had no idea of what was coming next, or did not care to conform.

Gladly would I have shunned the necessity of preaching that was laid upon me. "But," I said to myself, "shall the work given me to do fail because of my perturbation of spirit? No harm is done, though I suffer, but much harm if one tone fails of its force because I suffer." I therefore prayed God to help me, and looking to Him for aid, I cast my care upon Him, kept my thoughts strenuously away from that which discomposed me, and never turned my eyes toward the Oldcastle Hall pew from the moment I entered the pulpit. Partly, I presume, from the freedom given by the sense of irresponsibility for the result, I being weak and God strong, I preached, I think, a better sermon than I had ever preached before. But when I got into the vestry I found that I could scarcely stand for trembling. I must have looked ill, for my attendant got me a glass of wine without even asking, although it was not my custom to take any there.

I recovered in a few moments from my weakness but, altogether disinclined to face any of my congregation, I went out at my vestry door and home through the shrubbery, a path I seldom used because it had a separatist look about it. When I got to my study, I threw myself on a couch, and fell fast asleep. How often in trouble have I had to thank God for sleep as one of His best gifts! And how often, when I have awaked refreshed and calm, have I thought of poor Sir Philip Sidney who, dying slowly and patiently in the prime of life and health, was sorely troubled in his mind to know how he had offended God because, having prayed earnestly for sleep, no sleep came in answer to his cry!

I woke just in time for my afternoon service, and the peace in my heart was a marvel and a delight. I felt almost as if I were walking in a blessed dream from a world of serener air than ours.

I found, after I was already in the reading desk, that I was a few minutes early. With bowed head, I was simply living in the consciousness of the presence of a supreme quiet, when the first low notes of the organ broke upon my stillness with the sense of a deeper delight. Never before had I felt the triumph of contemplation in Handel's rendering of "I Know That My Redeemer Liveth." And through it all ran a cold silvery quiver of sadness, like the light in the east after the sun is gone down, which would have been pain but for the golden glow of the west. Before the music ceased, it crossed my mind that I had never before heard that organ utter the language of Handel. But I had no time to think more about it just then, for I rose to read the words of our Lord, "I will arise and go to My Father."

There was no one in the Hall pew. Indeed, it was a rare occurrence if anyone was in that pew in the afternoon.

But, for all the quietness of my mind during that evening service, I fell ill before I went to bed, and awoke in the morning with a headache which increased along with other signs, until I thought it better to send for Dr. Duncan. I am not so much an imbecile as to suppose that a history of the following six weeks would be interesting. I suffered that long from low fever, and several more weeks passed during which I was unable to meet my flock. Thanks to the care of Mr. Brownrigg, a clever young man in priest's orders at Addicehead kindly undertook my parish duties for me, and thus relieved me of all anxiety.

135

SEVENTEEN

JUDY'S NEWS

I have reason to fear that during my illness, when I was light-headed from fever, I may have talked a good deal of nonsense about Miss Oldcastle. I remember that I was haunted with visions of magnificent conventual ruins which I had discovered and had wandered through at my own lonely will. Within was a labyrinth of passages in the walls, and long corridors and sudden galleries. Through these I was ever wandering, ever discovering new rooms, new galleries, new marvels of architecture, yet ever disappointed and ever dissatisfied, because I knew that in one room somewhere in the forgotten mysteries of the pile sat Ethelwyn reading, never lifting those sea-blue eyes of hers from the great volume on her knee, reading every word, slowly turning leaf after leaf. I knew that she would sit there reading till every leaf in the huge volume was turned, and she came to the last and read it from top to bottom, down to the *finis* and the urn with a weeping willow over it, when she would close the book with a sigh, lay it down on the floor, rise and walk slowly away forever. I knew that if I did not find her before that terrible last page was read, I should never find her at all, but have to go wandering alone all my life through those dreary galleries and corridors, with only one hope left—that I might yet, before I died, find the "palace chamber far apart," and see the and forsaken volume lying on the floor where she had left it, and the chair beside it on which she had sat so long waiting for someone in vain.

And perhaps to words spoken under these impressions may partly be attributed the fact (which I knew nothing of till long

136

afterward) that the people of the village began to couple my name with that of Miss Oldcastle.

When all this vanished from me in the returning wave of health that spread through my weary brain, I was yet left anxious and thoughtful. There was no one from whom I could ask information about the family at the Hall, so that I was just driven to the best thing—to try to cast my care upon Him who cared for my care. How often do we look upon God as our last and feeblest resource! We go to Him because we have nowhere else to go. And then we learn that the storms of life have driven us not upon the rocks but into the desired haven.

One day when I was sitting reading in my study, who should be announced but my friend Judy!

"O dear Mr. Walton, I am so sorry! I haven't had a chance of coming to see you before, though we've always managed—I mean Auntie and I—to hear about you. I would have come to nurse you, but it was no use thinking of it."

I smiled as I thanked her.

"Ah! You think, because I'm such a tomboy, that I couldn't nurse you? I only wish I had had a chance of letting you see. I am so sorry for you!"

"But I'm nearly well now, Judy, and I have been taken good care of. But now I want to hear how everybody is at the Hall."

"What, Grannie and the Wolf and all?"

"As many as you please to tell me about."

"Well, Grannie is gracious to everybody but Auntie."

"Why isn't she gracious to Auntie?"

"I don't know. I only guess."

"Is your visitor gone?"

"Yes, long ago. Do you know, I think Grannie wants Auntie to marry him, and Auntie doesn't quite like it. But he's very nice. He's so funny. He'll be back again soon, I dare say. I don't quite like him—not so well as you by a whole half, Mr. Walton. I wish you would marry Auntie, but that would never do. It would drive Grannie out of her wits."

To stop her and hide some confusion, I said, "Now tell me about the rest of them."

"Sarah comes next. She's as white and as wolfy as ever. Mr. Walton, I hate that woman. She walks like a cat. I am sure she is bad."

"Did you ever think, Judy, what an awful thing it is to be bad?

If you did, I think you would be so sorry for her, you could not hate her."

At the same time, knowing what I knew, and remembering that impressions can date from farther back than the conscious memory can reach, I was not surprised to hear that Judy hated Sarah, though I could not believe that in such a child the hatred was of the most deadly description.

"I am afraid I must go on hating in the meantime," said Judy. "I wish someone would marry Auntie and turn Sarah away. But that couldn't be, so long as Grannie lives."

"How is Mr. Stoddart?"

"That's one of the things Auntie said I was to be sure to tell you."

"Then your aunt knew you were coming to see me?"

"Oh, yes, I told her. Not Grannie, you know. You mustn't let it out."

"I shall be careful. How is Mr. Stoddart, then?"

"Not well at all. He was taken ill before you, and has been in bed and by the fireside ever since. Auntie doesn't know what to do with him, he is so out of spirits."

"If tomorrow is fine, I shall go and see him."

"Thank you. I believe that's just what Auntie wanted. He won't like it at first, I dare say. But he'll come to, and you'll do him good. You do everybody good you come near."

"I wish that were true, Judy. I fear it is not. What good did I ever do you?"

"Do me?" she exclaimed, half angry at the question. "Don't you know I have been an altered character ever since I knew you?" And here she laughed, leaving me in absolute ignorance of how to interpret her. But presently her eyes grew clearer, and I could see the slow film of a tear gathering. "Mr. Walton," she said, "I have been trying not to be selfish. You have done me that much good."

"I am very glad, Judy. Don't forget who can do you all good. There is One who can not only show you what is right, but make you able to do and be what is right."

Judy did not answer, but sat looking fixedly at the carpet. She was thinking though, I saw.

"Who has played the organ, Judy, since your uncle was taken ill?" I asked at length.

"Why, Auntie, to be sure. Didn't you hear?"

"No," I answered, turning almost sick at the idea of having been away while she was giving voice and expression to the dear asthmatic old pipes. Think of her there, and me here!

"Then," I said to myself, "it must have been she that played "I Know That My Redeemer Liveth!" And, instead of thanking God for that, here I am murmuring that He did not give me more! And this child has just been telling me that I have taught her to try not to be selfish."

"When was your uncle taken ill?"

"I don't exactly remember. But you will come and see him tomorrow? And then we shall see you too, for we are always in and out of his room just now."

"I will come if Dr. Duncan will let me. Perhaps he will take me in his carriage."

"No, no. Don't you come with him. Uncle can't bear doctors. He never was ill in his life before, and he behaves to Dr. Duncan just as if he had made him ill. I wish I could send the carriage for you. But I can't, you know."

"Never mind, Judy. I shall manage somehow. What is the name of the gentleman who was staying with you?"

"Don't you know? Captain George Everard. He would change his name to Oldcastle, you know."

What a foolish pain, like a spear thrust, they sent through me—those words spoken in such a taken-for-granted way!

"He's a relation, on Grannie's side mostly, I believe. But I never could understand the explanation. All the husbands and wives in our family, for a hundred and fifty years, have been more or less cousins, or half-cousins, or second or third cousins. Captain Everard has what Grannie calls a neat little property somewhere in Northumberland. His second brother is dead, and the eldest is something worse for the wear, as Grannie says, so that the captain comes just within sight of the coronet of an old uncle who ought to have been dead long ago. Just the match for Auntie!"

"But you say Auntie doesn't like him."

"Oh, but you know that doesn't matter," returned Judy, with bitterness. "What will Grannie care for that? It's nothing to anybody but Auntie, and she must get used to it. Nobody makes anything of her."

"How were you able to get here today?" I asked, as she rose to go.

"Grannie is in London, and the wolf is with her. Auntie

wouldn't leave Uncle."

"They have been a good deal in London of late, have they not?"

"Yes. They say it's about money of Auntie's. But I don't understand. I think it's that Grannie wants to make the captain marry her, for they sometimes see him when they go to London."

It was only after she had gone that I thought how astounding it would have been to me to hear a girl of her age show such an acquaintance with worldliness and scheming, had I not been personally so much concerned about one of the objects of her remarks. It was a satisfaction to think that the aunt had such a friend and ally in her wild niece. Evidently she had inherited her father's fearlessness, and if only it should turn out that she had likewise inherited her mother's firmness, she might render the best possible service to her aunt.

EIGHTEEN

THE INVALID

The following day being very fine, I walked to Oldcastle Hall, but much slower than I was willing. I found to my relief that Mrs. Oldcastle had not yet returned. I was shown at once to Mr. Stoddart's library, where I found the two ladies in attendance upon him. He was seated by a splendid fire in the most luxurious of easy chairs, with his furred feet buried in the long hair of the hearthrug. He looked worn and peevish, and all the placidity of his countenance had vanished. The smooth expanse of forehead was drawn into fifty wrinkles, like a sea over which the fretting wind has been blowing. Nor was it only suffering that his face expressed. He looked like a man who strongly suspected that he was ill-used.

"You are well off, Mr. Stoddart," I said, "to have two such nurses."

"They are very kind," sighed the patient.

Aunt and niece rose and left the room quietly.

"Do you suffer much, Mr. Stoddart?"

"Much weariness worse than pain. I could welcome death."

"I do not think, from what Dr. Duncan says of you, that there is reason to apprehend more than a lingering illness," I said, to try him, I confess.

"I hope not, indeed," he exclaimed angrily, sitting up in his chair. "What right has Dr. Duncan to talk of me so?"

"To a friend, you know," I returned, apologetically, "who is much interested in your welfare."

"Yes, of course. So is the doctor. A sick man belongs to you both by prescription."

Satisfied that, ill as he was, he might be better if he would, I asked, "Do you remember how Ligarius, in *Julius Caesar* discards his sickness?"

" 'I am not sick, if Brutus have in hand any exploit worthy the name of honor.' "

"I want to be well because I don't like to be ill. But what there is in this foggy, swampy world worth being well for, I'm sure I haven't found out yet."

"If you have not, it must be because you have never tried to find out. But I'm not going to attack you when you are not able to defend yourself. We shall find a better time for that. But can't I do something for you? Would you like me to read to you for half an hour?"

"No, thank you. The girls tire me out with reading to me. I hate the very sound of their voices."

"I have today's *Times* in my pocket."

"I've heard all the news already."

"Then I think I shall only bore you if I stay."

He made no answer. I rose. He returned my "Good morning" as if there was nothing good in the world, least of all this same morning.

I found the ladies in the outer room. Judy was on her knees on the floor occupied with a long row of books. And then I learned the secret—how Mr. Stoddart reached the volumes arranged in the ceiling beams. Judy rose from the floor, and proceeded to put in motion a mechanical arrangement concealed in one of the bookshelves along the wall. There were strong cords reaching from the ceiling, and attached to the shelf, or rather long box (open sideways), which contained the books.

"Do take care, Judy," said Ethelwyn. "You know it is very venturous of you to let that shelf down, when Uncle is as jealous of his books as a hen of her chickens. I oughtn't to have let you touch the cords."

"You couldn't help it, Auntie dear, for I had the shelf halfway down before you saw me," returned Judy, proceeding to raise the books to their usual position under the ceiling.

But in another moment, either from Judy's awkwardness or from the gradual decay and final fracture of some cord, down came the whole shelf with a thundering noise, and the books were scattered about the floor. The door of the inner room opened and Mr. Stoddart appeared. His brow was already flushed, but when he saw the condition of his books, he broke out in a passion to which he could not have given way but for the weak state of his health.

"How *dare* you?" he said, with terrible emphasis on the word *dare*. "Judy, I beg you will not again show yourself in my apartment till I send for you."

"And then," said Judy, leaving the room, "I am not in the least likely to be otherwise engaged."

"I am very sorry, Uncle," began Miss Oldcastle.

But Mr. Stoddart had already retreated and banged the door behind him. So Miss Oldcastle and I were left standing together amid the ruins. She glanced at me with a distressed look. I smiled. She smiled in return.

"He will be sorry when he comes to himself," I said, "so we must take his repentance now, and think nothing more of the matter than if he had already said he was sorry. Besides, when books are in the case, I, for one, must not be too hard on my unfortunate neighbor."

"Thank you, Mr. Walton, for taking my uncle's part. He has been very good to me, and dear Judy is provoking sometimes. I am afraid I help to spoil her, but you would hardly believe how good she really is, and what a comfort she is to me."

"I think I understand Judy," I replied, "and I shall be mistaken if she does not turn out a very fine woman. The marvel to me is that, with all the various influences among which she is placed here, she is not seriously spoiled after all. I have the greatest regard for, and confidence in, my friend Judy."

Ethelwyn—Miss Oldcastle, I should say—gave me such a pleased look that I was well recompensed for my defense of Judy.

"Will you come with me," she said, "for our talk may continue to annoy Mr. Stoddart."

"I am at your service," I returned, and followed her from the room.

"Are you still as fond of the old quarry as you used to be, Miss Oldcastle?" I said, as we caught a glimpse of it from the window of a long passage.

"I am. I go there most days. I have not been today, though. Would you like to go down?"

"Very much," I said.

"Ah! I forgot, though. You must not go: it is not a fit place for an invalid."

143

"I cannot call myself an invalid now."

"Your face, I am sorry to say, contradicts your words." And she looked so kindly at me that I almost broke into thanks for the mere look. "And indeed," she went on, "it is too damp down there, not to speak of the stairs."

By this time we had reached the little room in which I was received the first time I visited the Hall. There we found Judy.

"If you are not too tired already, I should like to show you my little study. It has, I think, a better view than any other room in the house," said Miss Oldcastle.

"I shall be delighted," I replied.

"Come, Judy," said her aunt.

"You don't want me, I am sure, Auntie."

"I do, Judy, really. You mustn't be cross to us because Uncle has been cross to you. Uncle is not well, you know, and isn't a bit like himself. And you know you should not have meddled with his machinery."

And Miss Oldcastle put her arm round Judy and kissed her, whereupon Judy jumped from her seat, threw her book down, and ran to one of the several doors that opened from the room. This disclosed a little staircase, almost like a ladder, that wound about up to a charming little room, whose window looked down upon the Bishop's Basin, glimmering slaty through the tops of the trees between. It was paneled in dark oak, like the room below, but with more carving. Just opposite the window was a small space of brightness formed by the backs of nicely bound books. Seeing that these attracted my eye, Miss Oldcastle said, "Those are almost all gifts from my uncle. He is really very kind. You will not think of him as you have seen him today?"

"Indeed I will not," I replied.

"Do sit down," said Miss Oldcastle. "You have been very ill, and I could do nothing for you who have been so kind to me." She spoke as if she had wanted to say this.

"I only wish I had a chance of doing anything for you," I said, as I took a chair near the window. "But if I had done all I ever could hope to do, you have repaid me long ago, I think."

"How? I do not know what you mean, Mr. Walton. I have never done you the least service."

"Tell me first, did you play the organ in church that afternoon when—after—before I was taken ill—I mean the same day you had—a friend with you in the pew in the morning?"

144

I dare say my voice was as irregular as my construction. I ventured just one glance. Her face was flushed. But she answered me at once, "I did."

"Then I am in your debt more than you know or I can tell you."

"Why, if that is all, I have played the organ every Sunday since Uncle was taken ill," she said, smiling.

"I know that now, but I did not know it. It is only for what I heard that I mean now to acknowledge my obligation. Tell me, Miss Oldcastle, what is the most precious gift one person can give another?"

She hesitated; and I, fearing to embarrass her, answered for her.

"It must be something imperishable in its own nature. If, instead of a gem, or even of a flower, we could cast the gift of a lovely thought into the heart of a friend, that would be giving as the angels, I suppose, must give. But you did more and better for me than that. I had been troubled all the morning, and you made me know that 'my Redeemer liveth.' I did not know you were playing, mind, though I felt a difference. You gave me more trust in God, and what other gift so great could one give? I think that last impression, just as I was taken ill, must have helped me through my illness. Often, when I was most oppressed, that song would rise up in the troubled air of my mind, sung by a voice which, though I never heard you sing, I never questioned to be yours."

She turned her face toward me: those sea-blue eyes were full of tears.

"I was troubled myself," she said, with a faltering voice, "when I sang—I mean played—that. I am so glad it did somebody good! I fear it did not do me much. I will sing it to you now, if you like."

And she rose to get the music. But that instant Judy, who had left the room, bounded into it with the exclamation, "Auntie, Auntie, here's Grannie!"

Miss Oldcastle turned pale. I confess I felt embarrassed, as if I had been caught in something underhand.

"Is she come in?" asked Miss Oldcastle, trying to speak with indifference.

"She is just at the door—must be getting out of the fly now. What shall we do?"

"What do you mean, Judy?" said her aunt.

"Well, you know, Auntie, as well as I do, that Grannie will look as black as a thundercloud to find Mr. Walton here, and if she doesn't speak as loud, it will only be because she can't. I don't care for myself, but you know on whose head the storm will fall. Do, dear Mr. Walton, come down the back stairs. Then she won't be a bit the wiser. I'll manage it all."

Here was a dilemma for me—either to bring suffering on her, to save whom I would have borne any pain, or to creep out of the house as if I were and ought to be ashamed of myself. Miss Oldcastle, however, did not leave it to me to settle the matter.

"Judy, for shame to propose such a thing to Mr. Walton! I am very sorry that he may chance to have an unpleasant meeting with Mamma, but we can't help it. Come, Judy, we will show Mr. Walton out together."

"It wasn't for Mr. Walton's sake," returned Judy, pouting. "You are very troublesome, Auntie. Mr. Walton, she is so hard to take care of! And she's worse since you came. I shall have to give her up someday. Do be generous, Mr. Walton, and take my side— that is, Auntie's."

"I am afraid, Judy, I must thank your aunt for taking the part of my duty against my inclination. But this kindness, at least," I said to Miss Oldcastle, "I can never hope to return."

It was a stupid speech, but I could not be annoyed that I had made it.

"All obligations are not burdens to be got rid of, are they?" she replied, with a sweet smile on her pale, troubled face. I was more moved for her, deliberately handing her over to the torture for the truth's sake, than I care to confess.

Miss Oldcastle led the way down the stairs; I followed, and Judy brought up the rear. The affair was not so bad as it might have been. I insisted on going out alone and met Mrs. Oldcastle in the hall only. She held out no hand to greet me. I bowed, and said I was sorry to find Mr. Stoddart so far from well.

"I fear he is far from well," she returned, "certainly, in my opinion, too ill to receive visitors."

So saying, she bowed and passed on. I turned and walked out, not ill-pleased with my visit.

From that day I recovered rapidly, and the next Sunday had the pleasure of preaching to my flock. Mr. Aikin, the gentleman already mentioned as doing duty for me, read prayers. I took for my subject one of our Lord's miracles of healing and tried to show my

146

people that all healing, and all kinds of healing, come as certainly and only from His hand as those instances in which He put forth His bodily hand and touched the diseased and told them to be whole.

And as they left the church the organ played, " 'Comfort ye, comfort ye My people,' saith your God."

I tried hard to prevent my new feelings from so filling my mind as to make me fail of my duty toward my flock. I said to myself, "Let me be the more gentle, the more honorable, the more tender toward these my brothers and sisters, for they are her brothers and sisters too." I wanted to do my work the better that I loved her.

Thus week after week passed, with little that I can remember worthy of record. I seldom saw Miss Oldcastle, and during this period never alone.

I could not venture more until she had seen more of me, and how to enjoy her society while her mother was so unfriendly, I did not know. I feared that to call oftener might only prevent me from seeing her at all, and I could not tell how far such measures might expedite the event I most dreaded, or add to the discomfort to which Miss Oldcastle was already so much exposed. Meantime I heard nothing of Captain Everard, and the comfort that flowed from such a negative source was yet of a very positive character. I was in some measure deterred from making further advances by the thought that her favor for Captain Everard might be greater than Judy had represented it. I had always shrunk from rivalry of every kind—it was, somehow, contrary to my nature. Besides, Miss Oldcastle was likely to be rich someday—apparently had money of her own even now—and I writhed at the thought of being supposed to marry for money. "Ah! you see!" they would say. "That's the way with the clergy! They talk about poverty and faith, pretending to despise riches and to trust in God, but just put money in their way, and what chance will a poor girl have beside a rich one! It's all very well in the pulpit. It's their business to talk so. But does one of them believe what he says or at least act upon it?"

I mention this only as a repressing influence, to which I certainly should not have been such a fool as to yield, had I seen the way otherwise clear. For a man, by showing how to use money, or rather by simply using money aright, may do more good than by refusing to possess it if it comes to him in an entirely honorable way. But I felt sure—(if I should be so blessed as to marry Miss

Oldcastle)—that the poor of my own people would be those most likely to understand my position and feelings, and least likely to impute to me worldly motives.

Ethelwyn played the organ still, but I never made any attempt to see her as she came in or went from the organ loft. She seemed, by some intuition, to know the music I liked best, and great help she often gave me by so uplifting my heart upon the billows of the organ harmony.

So the time went on. I called once or twice upon Mr. Stoddart, and found him, as I thought, better. But he would not allow that he was. Dr. Duncan said he was better, and would be better still if he would only believe it and exert himself.

NINETEEN

MOOD AND WILL

Winter came apace, with its fogs, and dripping boughs, and sodden paths, and rotting leaves, and rains, and skies of weary gray, but also with its fierce red suns, and delicate ice over prisoned waters, and white chaotic snowstorms. And when the hard frost came, it brought Mr. Stoddart to my door.

He entered my room with something of the countenance Naaman must have borne after his flesh had come again like the flesh of a little child. He did not look ashamed, but his pale face looked humbled and distressed. Its somewhat self-satisfied placidity had vanished, and instead of the usual diffused geniality, it now showed traces of feeling and plain signs of suffering. I seated him comfortably by the fire and began to chat.

"The cold weather, which makes so many invalids creep into bed, seems to have brought you out into the air, Mr. Stoddart," I said.

"I feel just as if I were coming out of a winter. Don't you think illness is a kind of human winter?"

"Certainly, more or less stormy. With some, a winter of snow and hail and piercing winds; with others, of black frosts and creeping fogs, with now and then a glimmer of the sun."

"The last is more like mine. I feel as if I had been in a wet hole in the earth. Mr. Walton, I will explain myself. I have come to tell you how sorry and ashamed I am that I behaved so badly to you every time you came to see me."

"Oh, nonsense!" I said. "It was your illness, not you."

"At least, my dear sir, the facts of my behavior did not really represent my feelings toward you."

"I know that as well as you do. Don't say another word about it. You had the best excuse of being cross. I should have had none for being offended."

"It was only the outside of me."

"Yes, yes, I acknowledge it heartily."

"But that does not settle the matter between me and myself, Mr. Walton, although, by your goodness, it settles it between me and you. It is humiliating to think that illness should so completely overcrow me that I am no more myself—lose my hold, in fact, of what I call me—so that I am almost driven to doubt my personal identity.

"I have labored much to withdraw my mind from the influence of money and ambition and pleasure, and to turn it to the contemplation of spiritual things. Yet on the first attack of a depressing illness, I ceased to be a gentleman, I was rude to ladies who did their best and kindest to serve me, and I talked to the friend who came to cheer and comfort me as if he were an idle vagrant. I am ashamed that it should be possible for me to behave so and am humiliated to have no assurance that I should not again behave in the same manner, should my illness return."

"I understand perfectly what you mean, for I fancy I know a little more of illness than you do. Shall I tell you where the fault of your self-training lies?"

"That is just what I want. The things which it pleased me to contemplate, when I was well, gave me no pleasure when I was ill. Nothing seemed the same."

"If we were always in a right mood, there would be no room for the exercises of the will: we should go by mood and inclination only. Where you have been wrong is that you influence your feelings only by thought and argument with yourself, and not also by contact with your fellows. Besides myself and the two ladies, you have hardly a friend in this neighborhood. One friend cannot afford you half enough experience to teach you the relations of life and human needs. At best, under such circumstances, you can only have right theories; practice for realizing them in yourself is nowhere—'but if a man love not his brother whom he hath seen, how can he love God whom he hath not seen?' To love our neighbor is a great help toward loving God. How this love is to come about without relations, I do not see. And how without this love we are to bear up against the thousand irritations of our unavoidable human relations, I cannot tell either."

"But," returned Mr. Stoddart, "I have true regard for you, and some friendly communication with you. If human contact were what is required in my case, how should I fail just with respect to the only man with whom I hold such?"

"Because the relations in which you stood with me were those of the individual, not of the race. You like me because I am fortunate enough to please you—to be a gentleman, I hope—to be a man of some education, and capable of understanding what you tell me of your plans and pursuits. But you do not feel any relation to me on the ground of my humanity—that God made me and therefore I am your brother. It is not because we grow out of the same stem, but merely because my leaf is a little like your own that you draw to me. Disturb your liking, and your love vanishes."

"You are severe."

"I don't mean really vanishes, but disappears for the time. Yet you will confess you have to wait till it comes back again of itself."

"Yes, I confess. To my sorrow, I find it so."

"Let me tell you the truth, Mr. Stoddart. You seem to me to have been only a dilettante or amateur in spiritual matters. Do not imagine I mean hypocrite. Very far from it. The word *amateur* itself suggests a real interest, though it may be superficial. But in relations one must be *all* there. You have taken much interest in unusual forms of theory, and in mystical speculations, to which in themselves I make no objection. But to be content with those, instead of knowing God Himself, or to substitute a general amateur friendship toward the race for the love of your neighbor, is a mockery which will always manifest itself to an honest mind like yours in such failure and disappointment in your own character as you are now lamenting, if not in some mode far more alarming, because gross and terrible."

"Am I to understand you, then, that relations with one's neighbors ought to take the place of meditation?"

"By no means. They ought to go side by side, if you would have at once a healthy mind to judge, and the means of either verifying your speculations or discovering their falsehood."

"But where am I to find such friends besides yourself with whom to hold spiritual communion?"

"It is the communion of spiritual deeds—deeds of justice, of mercy, of humility, the kind word, the cup of cold water, the visitation in sickness, the lending of money—not spiritual conference or talk. The latter will come of itself where it is natural. You would soon find that it is not only to those whose spiritual windows are of the same shape as your own that you are neighbor; there is one poor man in my congregation who knows more, *practically*, of spirituality of mind than any of us. Perhaps you could not teach him much, but he could teach you. At all events, our neighbors are just those round about us. And the most ignorant man in a little place like Marshmallows, one like you ought to know and understand, and have some good influence upon. He is your brother whom you are bound to care for and elevate—not socially but in himself—if it be possible. Never was there a more injurious mistake than to say it is the business of only the clergy to care for souls."

"But that would leave me no time for myself."

"Would that be no time for yourself spent in leading a noble, Christian life? In verifying the words of our Lord by doing them? In building your house on the rock of action instead of the sands of theory? You would find health radiating into your own bosom, healing sympathies springing up in the most barren acquaintance, channels opening for the inrush of truth into your own mind, and opportunities afforded for the exercise of that self-discipline, the lack of which led to the failures which you now bemoan. Some of your speculations would fall into the background simply because the truth, showing itself grandly true, had so filled and occupied your mind that it left no room for anxiety about such questions. Nothing so much as humble ministrations to your neighbors will help you to that perfect love of God which casteth out fear. Nothing but the love of God—that God revealed in Christ—will make you able to love your neighbor aright. And the Spirit of God will by these loves strengthen you to believe in the light even in the midst of darkness; to hold the resolution formed in health when sickness has altered the appearance of everything around you; and to feel tenderly toward your fellow, even when you yourself are dejected or in pain. But, I fear I have transgressed the bounds of all propriety. I can only say I have spoken in proportion to my feeling of its weight and truth."

"I thank you heartily," returned Mr. Stoddart, rising. "I promise you to think over what you have been saying. I hope to be in the organ loft next Sunday."

So he was. And Miss Oldcastle was in the pew with her mother. Nor did she go anymore to Addicehead to church.

TWENTY

THE DEVIL IN THOMAS WEIR

As the winter went on, it was sad to look on the slow decline of Catharine Weir. It seemed as if the dead season was dragging her to its bosom, to lay her among the leaves of past summers. She was still to be found in the shop, or appeared in it as often as the bell rang to announce a customer, but she was terribly worn, and her step indicated much weakness. Nor had the signs of restless trouble diminished. There was the same dry, fierce fire in her eyes, the same forceful compression of her lips, the same evidences of brooding over some absorbing thought or feeling. She seemed to me, and to Dr. Duncan as well, to be dying of resentment. Would nobody do anything for her? Would not her father help her? He was grown more gentle now, as Christian principles and feelings had begun to rise and operate in him. And surely the influence of his son must by this time have done something not only to soften his character generally, but to appease the anger he had cherished toward the one ewe-lamb, against which—having wandered away into the desert place—he had closed and barred the door of the sheepfold. I would go and see him, and see what could be done for her.

(When I thought of a thing and had concluded it might do, I seldom put off the consequent action. I found I was wrong sometimes, and that the particular action did no good; but thus movement was kept up in my operative nature, preventing it from sinking toward inactivity. Besides, to find out what will *not* do is a step toward finding out what will do, and an unsuccessful attempt may set something in motion that will help.)

A red, rayless sun was looking through the frosty fog of the winter morning as I walked across the bridge to find Thomas Weir in his workshop. The poplars stood all along the dark, cold river like goblin sentinels, with black heads upon which the long hair stood on end. Nature looked like a life out of which the love had vanished. I turned from it and hastened on.

Tom was busy working with a spokeshave at the spoke of a cartwheel. How curiously the smallest visual fact will sometimes keep its place in the memory, when it cannot, with all earnestness of endeavor, recall a far more important fact!

"A cold morning, Thomas," I called from the door.

"I can always keep myself warm, Sir."

"What are you doing, Tom?" I said, going up to him first.

"A little job for myself, Sir. I'm making a few bookshelves."

"I want to have a little talk with your father. Just let me have half an hour."

"Yes, Sir, certainly."

I went to the other end of the shop for, curiously, although father and son were on the best of terms, they always worked as far from each other as the shop would permit, and it was a very large room.

"It is not easy always to keep warm through and through, Thomas," I said.

I suppose my tone revealed to his quick perceptions that "more was meant than met the ear." He looked up from his work, his tool filled with an uncompleted shaving.

"And when the heart gets cold," I went on, "it is not easily warmed again. The fire's hard to light there, Thomas."

Still he looked at me, stopped over his work, apparently with a presentiment of what was coming.

I continued, "I fear there is no way of lighting it again, except the blacksmith's way."

"Hammering the iron till it is red-hot, you mean, Sir?"

"I do. When a man's heart has grown cold, the blows of affliction must fall thick and heavy before the fire can light it. When did you last see your daughter Catharine, Thomas?"

His head dropped, and he began to work as if for bare life. Not a word came from the form now bent over his tool, as if he had never lifted himself up since he first began in the morning. I could just see that his face was deadly pale, and his lips compressed like those of one of the violent who take the kingdom of heaven by force. He went on working till the silence became so lengthened that it seemed settled into the endless. I felt embarrassed. To break a silence is sometimes as hard as to break a spell. What Thomas would have done or said if he had not had this safety valve of bodily exertion, I cannot even imagine.

"Thomas," I said, at length, laying my hand on his shoulder, "you are not going to part company with me, I hope?"

"You drive a man too far, Sir, and I don't know that I oughtn't to be ashamed of it. But you don't know where to stop. A man must be at peace somewhen."

"The question is, Thomas, whether I would be driving you on or back. You and I too must go on or back. I want to go on, myself, and to make you go on too. I don't want to be parted from you now or then."

"That's all very well, Sir, and very kind, I don't doubt. But, as I said afore, a man must be at peace somewhen."

"Peace! I trust in God we shall both have it one day, some-when, as you say. Have you this peace so plentifully now that you are satisfied? You will never get it but by going on."

"I do not think there is any good in stirring a puddle. Let bygones be bygones. You make a mistake, Sir, in rousing an anger which I would willingly let sleep."

"Better a wakeful anger and a wakeful conscience with it, than an anger sunk into indifference and a sleeping dog of conscience that will not bark. To have ceased to be angry is not one step nearer to your daughter. Better strike her, abuse her, with the chance of a kiss to follow. Ah! Thomas, you are like Jonah with his gourd."

"I don't see what that has to do with it."

"I will tell you. You are fierce in wrath at the disgrace to your family. Your pride is up in arms. You don't care for the misery of your daughter who, the more wrong she has done, is the more to be pitied by a father's heart. The wrong your daughter has done you care nothing about, or you would have taken her to your arms years ago, in the hope that the fervor of your love would drive the devil out of her and make her repent. I say it is not the wrong but the disgrace you care for. The gourd of your pride is withered, and yet you will water it with your daughter's misery."

"Go out of my shop," he cried, "or I may say what I should be sorry for."

I turned at once and left him. I found young Tom round the

corner, leaning against the wall, reading his Virgil.

"Don't speak to your father for awhile, Tom," I said. "I've put him out of temper. He will be best left alone."

He looked frightened.

"There's no harm done, Tom, my boy. I've been talking to him about your sister. He must have time to think over what I have said to him. Be as attentive to him as you can."

"I will, Sir."

I had called up all the man's old misery, set the wound bleeding again. Shame was once more wide awake and tearing at his heart. That his daughter should have done so! For she had been his pride. She had been the belle of the village, had been apprenticed to a dressmaker in Addicehead and had, after a year and a half, returned with child. The fact of Addicehead being a garrison town had something to do with her fate. In springtime, when flowers were loveliest and hope was strongest for summer, her life was changed into a dreary, windswept, rain-sodden moor. The man who can accept such a sacrifice from a woman—much less will it from her—is as contemptible as the pharisee who, with his long prayers, devours the widow's house. He leaves her desolate while he walks off free.

But Catharine never would utter a word to reveal the name or condition of him by whom she had been wronged. To his child, as long as he drew his life from her, she behaved with strange alternations of dislike and passionate affection, after which season the latter began to diminish in violence, and the former to become more fixed. By the time I had made their acquaintance, her feelings seemed to have settled into what would have been indifference, but for the constant reminder of her shame and wrong which his very presence was.

The child had been born under her father's roof. What a wretched time it must have been for both her and her father until she left his house!

TWENTY-ONE

THE DEVIL IN
CATHARINE WEIR

About this time my father was taken ill, and several journeys to London followed. I had a half sister, about half my own age, whose anxiety during my father's illness rendered my visits more frequent than perhaps they would have been. But my sister was right in her anxiety: my father grew worse, and in December he died. I will not eulogize one so dear to me. That he was no common man will appear from his unconventionality and justice in leaving his property to my sister, saying in his will that he had done all I could require of him in giving me a good education and that men having means in their power which women had not, it was unjust to the latter to make them (without a choice) dependent upon the former. After the funeral, my sister begged me to take her with me. So, after arranging affairs, we set out and reached Marshmallows on New Year's Day.

My sister being so much younger than myself, her presence in my house made very little change in my habits. She came into my ways without any difficulty, and soon I began to find her of considerable service among the poor and sick of my flock, the latter class being more numerous this winter, on account of the greater severity of the weather.

I now began to note a change in the habits of Catharine Weir. As far as I remember, I had never up to this time seen her out of her own house, except in church, at which she had been a regular attendant for many weeks. Now, however, I began to meet her when and where I least expected—I do not say often, but so often

157

as to make me believe she wandered about frequently. It was always at night, however, and always in stormy weather. The marvel was not that a sick woman could be there—for a sick woman may be able to do anything—but that she could do so more than once. At the same time, I began to miss her from church.

I had naturally a predilection for rough weather. I think I enjoyed fighting with a storm in winter nearly as much as lying on the grass under a beech tree in summer. There is a pleasure of its own in conflict, and I have always experienced a certain indescribable exaltation even in struggling with a well-set, thoroughly roused storm of wind and snow or rain. I was now quite well, and had no reason to fear bad consequences from the indulgence of this surely innocent form of the love of strife.

One January afternoon, just as twilight was folding her gray cloak about her, I felt as if the elements were calling me, and I rose to obey the summons. My sister was, by this time, so accustomed to my going out in all weathers that she troubled me with no expostulation. My spirits began to rise the moment I was in the wind. Keen and cold and unsparing, it swept through the leafless branches around me with a different hiss for every tree that bent and swayed and tossed in its torrent. I made my way to the gate and out upon the road and then, turning to the right, away from the village. I sought a kind of common, open and treeless, the nearest approach to a wind-swept moor in the county.

I had walked with my head bent low against the blast for the better part of a mile, fighting for every step of the way. I came to a deep-cut opening at right angles from the road, whence at some time or other a large quantity of sand had been carted. I turned into it to recover my breath, and to listen to the wind in its fierce rush over the common. I was startled by such a moan as seemed about to break into a storm of passionate cries, but was followed by the words, "O God! I cannot bear it longer! Hast Thou no help for me?"

I knew that Catharine Weir was beside me, though I could not see where she was. In a moment more, however, I thought I could distinguish her figure crouching in an attitude of abandoned despair, the body bent forward over the drawn-up knees, and the face thus hidden even from the darkness. I resolved to make an attempt to probe the evil to its root, though I had but little hope of doing any good. I went near her with the words, "God has, indeed, help for His own offspring. Has He not suffered that He might help? But you have not yet forgiven."

When I began to speak she gave a slight start—she was far too miserable to be terrified at anything. Before I had finished, she stood erect on her feet, facing me, with the whiteness of her face glimmering through the blackness of the night.

"I ask Him for peace," she said, "and He sends me more torment."

"If we had what we asked for always, we should too often find it was not what we wanted, after all."

"You will not leave me alone," she said. "It is too bad."

Poor woman! It was well for her she could pray to God in her trouble, for she could scarcely endure a word from her fellowman. Despairing before God, she was fierce as a tigress to her fellow-sinner who would stretch a hand to help her out of the mire, and set her beside him on the rock which he felt firm under his own feet.

"I will not leave you alone, Catharine," I said. "Scorn my interference as you will. I have yet to give an account of you—and I have to fear lest my Master should require your blood at my hands. I did not follow you here, but I have found you here, and I must speak."

All this time the wind was roaring overhead. But in the hollow was stillness, and I was so near that I could hear every word she spoke in her low, compressed tone.

"Have you a right to persecute me," she said, "because I am unhappy?"

"I have a right and more—a duty to aid your better self against your worse. You, I fear, are siding with your worse self."

"You judge me hard. I have had wrongs that—"

And here she stopped in a way that let me know she could say no more.

"That you have had wrongs, and bitter wrongs, I do not for a moment doubt. And him who has done you most wrong you will not forgive."

"No."

"No, not even for the sake of Him who, hanging on the tree—after all the bitterness of blows and whipping and derision and rudest gestures and taunts, even when the faintness of death was upon Him—cried to His Father to forgive their cruelty? He asks you to forgive the man who wronged you, and you will not—not even for Him? O, Catharine, Catharine!"

"It is very easy to talk, Mr. Walton," she returned, with forced but cool scorn.

"Tell me then," I said, "have *you* nothing to repent of? Have *you* done no wrong in this miserable matter?"

"I do not understand you, Sir," she said, freezingly.

"Catharine Weir," I said, "did not God give you a house to keep fair and pure for Him? Did you keep it such?"

"He told me lies," she cried fiercely, with a cry that seemed to pierce the storm and rise toward the everlasting justice. "He lied and I trusted. For his sake I sinned, and he threw me from him."

"You gave him what was not yours to give. What right had you to cast your pearl before a swine? But dare you say it was all for his sake you did it? Was it all self-denial? Was there no self-indulgence?"

She made a broken gesture of lifting her hands to her head, let them drop by her side, and said nothing.

"You knew you were doing wrong. You felt it even more than he did, for God made you with a more delicate sense of purity, with a womanly foreboding of disgrace to help you to hold your cup of honor steady, which yet you dropped on the ground. Do not seek refuge in the cant about a woman's weakness. A woman is just as strong as she will be. And now, instead of humbling yourself before your Father in heaven, whom you have wronged more even than your father on earth, you rage over your injuries and cherish hatred against him who wronged you. But I will go yet further and show you, in God's name, that you wronged your seducer, for you were his keeper, as he was yours. What if he had found a noble-hearted girl, who also trusted him entirely just until she knew she ought not to listen to him a moment longer—who, when his love showed itself less than human, caring but for itself, rose in the royalty of her maidenhood, and looked him in the face—would he not have been ashamed before her and so before himself, seeing in the glass of her dignity his own contemptibleness? But instead of such a woman, he found you who let him do as he would. No redemption for him in you. And now he walks the earth the worse for you, defiled by your spoil, glorying in his poor victory over you, despising all women for your sake, unrepentant and proud, ruining others the easier that he has already ruined you."

"He does! He does!" she shrieked. "But I will have my revenge. I can and I will!"

And, darting past me, she rushed out into the storm. Her dim shape went down the wind before me into the darkness. I followed in the same direction, fast and faster, for the wind was behind me, and a vague fear which ever grew in my heart urged me to overtake her. What had I done? To what had I driven her? All I had said was true, and I had spoken from motives which I could not condemn. Poor sister," I thought, "was it for me thus to reproach thee who hadst suffered already so fiercely? If the Spirit speaking in thy heart could not win thee, how should my words of hard accusation, true though they were, every one of them, rouse in thee anything but the wrath that springs from shame? Should I not have tried again, and yet again, to waken thy love? And then a sweet and healing shame, like that of her who bathed the Master's feet with her tears, would have bred fresh love, and no wrath."

But I answered myself that my heart had not been the less tender toward her for that I had tried to humble her, for it was that she might slip from under the net of her pride. Even when my tongue spoke the hardest things I could find, my heart was yearning over her.

The wind fell a little as we came near the village, and the rain began to come down in torrents. Suddenly, her strength giving way, she fell to the earth with a cry. I was beside her in a moment. She was insensible. I did what I could for her, and in a few minutes she began to come to.

"Where am I? Who is it?" she asked listlessly.

When she found who I was, she made a great effort to rise and succeeded.

"You must take my arm," I said, "and I will help you to the vicarage."

"I will go home," she answered.

"Lean on me now, at least, for you must get somewhere."

"What does it matter?" she said, in a tone of despair that went to my very heart.

A wild half cry, half sob followed, and then she took my arm and said nothing more. Nor did I trouble her with any words, except, when we reached the gate, to beg her to come into the vicarage instead of going home. But she would not listen to me, and so I took her home.

She pulled the key of the shop from her pocket. Her hand trembled so that I took it from her and opened the door. A candle was flickering on the counter, and stretched out there lay little Gerard, fast asleep.

"Ah! little darling!" I said in my heart, "this is not much like painting the sky yet. But who knows?" And as I uttered the commonplace question in my mind, in my mind it was suddenly changed for the answer was, "God."

I lifted the little fellow in my arms. He had fallen asleep weeping, and his face was dirty and streaked with the channels of his tears. Catharine stood with the candle in her hand, waiting for me to go. But, without heeding her, I bore my child to the door that led to their dwelling. I had never been up those stairs before and, therefore, knew nothing of the way. But, without offering any opposition, his mother followed and lighted my way. What a sad face of suffering and strife it was upon which that dim light fell! She set the candle down upon the table of a small room at the top of the stairs, which might have been comfortable enough but that it was neglected and disordered. I saw that her child did not sleep with her, for his crib stood in a corner of their sitting room.

I sat down on a haircloth couch and proceeded to undress little Gerard, trying not to wake him. In this I was almost successful. Catharine stood staring at me without saying a word. She looked dazed, perhaps from the effects of her fall, but she did bring me his nightgown. Just as I had finished putting it on, and was rising to lay him in his crib, he opened his eyes and looked at me. Then he gave a hurried look round for his mother, and threw his arms about my neck and kissed me. I laid him down, and the same moment he was fast asleep. In the morning it would not be even a dream to him.

"Now," I thought, "you are safe for the night, poor fatherless child. Even your mother's hardness will not make you sad now. Perhaps the Heavenly Father will send you loving dreams."

I turned to Catharine and bade her good-night. Instead of returning my leave-taking, she said, "Do not fancy you will get the better of me, Mr. Walton, by being kind to that boy. I will have my revenge, and I know how. I am only waiting my time. When he is just going to drink, I will dash it from his hand. I will. At the altar I will."

Her eyes were flashing almost with madness, and she made fierce gestures with her arm. I saw that argument was useless.

"You loved him once, Catharine," I said. "Love him again. Love him better. Forgive him. Revenge is far worse than anything

162

you have done yet."

"What do I care? Why should I care?" And she laughed terribly.

I made haste to leave the room and the house. I lingered outside, however, for nearly an hour, lest she should do something altogether insane. But at length I saw the candle appear in the shop, which was some relief to my anxiety. Reflecting that her one consuming thought of revenge was some security for her conduct otherwise, I went home.

That night my own troubles seemed small to me, and I did not brood over them at all. My mind was filled with the idea of the sad misery which that poor woman was, and I prayed for her as a desolate human world whose sun had deserted the heavens, whose fair fields, rivers, and groves were hardening into the frost of death. "If I am sorrowful," I said, "God lives, nonetheless. And His will is better than mine, yea, is my hidden and perfected will. In Him is my life. His will be done. What, then, is my trouble compared to hers? I will not sink into it and be selfish."

In the morning my first business was to inquire after her. I found her in the shop, looking very ill, and obstinately reserved. Gerard sat in a corner, looking as far from happy as a child of his years could look. As I left the shop, he crept out with me.

"Gerard, come back," cried his mother.

"I will not take him away," I said.

The boy looked up in my face, as if he wanted to whisper to me, and I stooped to listen.

"I dreamed last night," said the boy, "that a big angel with white wings came and took me out of my bed, and carried me high, high up—so high that I could not dream anymore."

"We shall be carried up so high one day, Gerard, my boy, that we shall not want to dream anymore, for we shall be carried up to God Himself. But, until then, you should go back to your mother."

He obeyed at once, and I went on through the village.

TWENTY-TWO

THE DEVIL IN THE VICAR

I wanted just to pass the gate and look up the road toward Old-castle Hall. I thought to see nothing but the empty road between the leafless trees, lying there like a dead stream that would not bear me on to the "sunny pleasure dome with caves of ice" that lay beyond. But just as I reached the gate, Miss Oldcastle came out of the lodge, where I learned afterward the woman who kept the gate was ill.

When she saw me she stopped, and I entered hurriedly and addressed her. But I could say nothing better than the merest commonplaces, for her old manner, a certain coldness shadowed with haughtiness, had returned. This was somehow blended with the sweetness in her face and the gentleness of her manners—there the opposites were, and I could feel them both. There was likewise a certain drawing of herself away from me which checked the smallest advance on my part, so that I bade her good-morning and went away, feeling like "a man forbid"—as if I had done her some wrong and she had chidden me for it. What a stone lay in my breast! I could hardly breathe for it. What could have caused her to change her manner toward me? I had made no advance and could not have offended her. But there I stood enchanted, and there she floated away between the trees, till she turned the slow sweep and I, breathing deep as she vanished from my sight, turned likewise and walked back the dreary way to the village. And now I knew that I had never been more miserable in my life before—and I knew too that I had never loved her as I did now.

But I would continue to try to do my work as if nothing had

164

happened. So I went on to fulfill the plan with which I had left home, including, as it did, a visit to Thomas Weir, whom I had not seen in his shop since he had ordered me out of it. This was more accidental than intentional. I was pleased to find that my words had had force enough to rouse his wrath. Anything rather than indifference! That the heart of the honest man would in the end right me, I could not doubt. In the meantime I would see whether a friendly call might not improve the state of affairs. Till he yielded to the voice within him, however, I could not expect that our relation to each other would be restored. As long as he resisted his conscience, and knew that I sided with his conscience, it was impossible that he should regard me with peaceful eyes.

I found him busy, as usual, for he was one of the most diligent men I have ever known. But his face was gloomy, and I thought or fancied that the old scorn had begun once more to usurp the expression of it. Young Tom was not in the shop.

"It is a long time since I saw you, now, Thomas."

"I can hardly wonder at that," he returned, as if he were trying to do me justice; but his eyes dropped, and he resumed his work and said no more. I thought it better to make no reference to the past.

"How is Tom?" I asked.

"Well enough," he returned. Then, with a smile of peevishness not unmingled with contempt, he added, "He's getting too uppish for me. I don't think the Latin agrees with him."

I could not help suspecting at once how the matter stood, namely, that the father, unhappy in his conduct to his daughter, and unable to make up his mind to do right with regard to her, had been behaving captiously and unjustly to his son, and so had rendered himself more miserable than ever.

"Perhaps he finds it too much for him without me," I said, evasively, "but I called today partly to inform him that I am quite ready now to recommence our readings together, after which I hope you will find the Latin agrees with him better."

"I wish you would let him alone, Sir—I mean, take no more trouble about him. You see I can't do as you want me. I wasn't made to go another man's way, and so it's very hard—more than I can bear—to be under so much obligation to you."

"But you mistake me altogether, Thomas. It is for the lad's own sake that I want to go on reading with him, and hope you won't interfere between him and any use I can be of to him. I assure you, to have you go my way instead of your own is the last thing I could wish, though I confess I do wish very much that you would choose the right way for your own way."

He made me no answer but maintained a sullen silence.

"Thomas," I said, at length, "I had thought you were breaking every bond of Satan that withheld you from entering into the kingdom of heaven. But I fear he has strengthened his bands, and holds you now as much a captive as ever. It is not even your own way you are walking in, but his."

"It's no use your trying to frighten me. I don't believe in the devil."

"It is God I want you to believe in, and I am not going to dispute with you about whether there is a devil. In a matter of life and death, we have no time for settling every disputed point."

"Life or death! What do you mean?"

"I mean that whether you believe there is a devil or not, you *know* there is an evil power in your mind dragging you down. I am not speaking in generalities. I mean *now*, and you know as to what I mean it. And if you yield to it, that evil power will drag you down to death. It is a matter of life or death, not of theory about the devil."

"Well, I always did say that if you once give a priest an inch, he'll take an ell, and I am sorry I forgot it for once."

Having said this, he shut up his mouth in a manner that indicated plainly enough he would not open it again for some time. This, more than his speech, irritated me, and with a mere "Good morning," I walked out of the shop.

No sooner was I in the open air than I knew that I too—I as well as poor Thomas Weir—was under a spell; knew that I had gone to him before I had recovered sufficiently from the mingled disappointment and mortification of my interview with Miss Oldcastle; that while I spoke to him I was not speaking with a whole heart; that I had been discharging a duty as if I had been discharging a musket; that, although I had spoken the truth, I had spoken it ungraciously and selfishly.

I could not bear it. I turned and went back into the shop.

"Thomas, my friend," I said, holding out my hand, "I beg your pardon. I was wrong. I spoke to you as I ought not. I was troubled in my own mind, and that made me lose my temper and be rude to you, who are far more troubled than I. Forgive me!"

He did not take my hand at first, but stared at me as if he supposed that I was backing up what I had said last with more of the same sort. But by the time I had finished he saw what I meant. His countenance altered, and he looked as if the evil spirit were about to depart from him. He held out his hand, gave mine a great grasp, dropped his head, went on with his work without a word.

I went out of the shop once more, but in a greatly altered mood.

On the way home, I tried to find out how it was that I had that morning failed so signally. I had little virtue in keeping my temper, because it was naturally very even. Therefore, I had the more shame in losing it. I had borne all my uneasiness about Miss Oldcastle without, as far as I knew, transgressing in this fashion till this very morning.

Till this morning I had experienced no personal mortification with respect to Miss Oldcastle. It was not the mere disappointment of having no more talk with her—for the sight of her was a blessing I had not in the least expected—but the fact that she had repelled or seemed to repel me. And thus I found that self was at the root of the wrong I had done. I ought to have been as tender as a mother over her wounded child. Something was wrong when one whose special business it was to serve his people, in the name of Him who was full of grace and truth, made them suffer because of his own inward pain.

No sooner had I settled this in my mind than my trouble returned with a sudden pang. Had I actually seen her that morning, and spoken to her, and left her with a pain in my heart? What if that face of hers was doomed ever to bring with it such a pain—to be ever to me no more than a lovely vision radiating grief? If so, I would endure in silence and as patiently as I could, trying to make up for the lack of brightness in my own fate by causing more brightness in the fate of others.

That moment I felt a little hand poke itself into mine. I looked down, and there was Gerard Weir looking up in my face. I found myself in the midst of the children coming out of school, for it was Saturday, and a half holiday. He smiled up in my face, and I smiled in his. And so, hand in hand, we went on to the vicarage where I gave him up to my sister. But I cannot convey any notion of the quietness that entered my heart with the grasp of that childish hand. I think it was the faith of the boy in me that comforted me; but I could not help thinking of the words of our Lord about receiving a child in His name, and so receiving Him. By the time we reached the vicarage my heart was very quiet. As the little child held my hand, so I seemed to be holding God's hand. A sense of heart-security, as well as soul-safety, awoke in me, and I said to myself, "Surely He will take care of my heart as well as of my mind and my conscience." For one blessed moment I seemed to be at the very center of things, and I thought I then knew something of what the Apostle Paul meant when he said, "Your life is hid with Christ in God."

I had not had my usual ramble this morning and was otherwise ill-prepared for Sunday, so I went early into the church. But, finding that the sexton's wife had not yet finished lighting the stove, I sat down to wait by my own fire in the vestry.

I was very particular in having the church well warmed before Sunday. I think some persons must neglect this on principle, because warmth may make a weary creature go to sleep here and there about the place—as if any healing doctrine could enter the soul while it is on the rack of the frost. The clergy should see—for it is their business—that their people have no occasion to think of their bodies at all while they are in church. They have enough ado to think of the truth. When our Lord was feeding even their bodies, He made them all sit down on the grass. It is worth noticing that there was much grass in the place—a rare thing, I should think, in those countries—and therefore, perhaps, it was chosen by Him for their comfort in feeding their souls and bodies both. One of the reasons why some churches are the least likely places for anything good to be found is that they are as wretchedly cold to the body as they are to the soul—too cold every way for anything to grow in them. Edelweiss, "noblewhite," as they call a plant growing under the snow on some of the Alps, could not survive the winter in such churches. There is small welcome in a cold house, and the clergyman, who is the steward, should look to it. It is for him to give his Master's friends a welcome to his Master's house, for the welcome of a servant is precious, and nowadays very rare.

I went into the old church, which looked as if it were quietly waiting for its people. As if, having gathered a soul of its own out of the generations that have worshiped here for so long, it had feeling enough to grow hungry for a psalm before the end of the week.

To my amazement and delight the old organ woke up and began to think aloud. It began to sigh out the "Agnes Dei" of Mozart's *Twelfth Mass* upon the air of the still church. How could it be? I know now, and I guessed then, though I took no step to verify my conjecture, for I felt that I was upon my honor. I sat in one of the pews and listened till the old organ sobbed itself into silence. Then I heard the steps of the sexton's wife vanish from the church, heard her lock the door, and I knew I was alone in the ancient pile, with the twilight growing thick about me; and I felt like Sir Galahad when, after the "rolling organ harmony," he heard "wings flutter, voices hover clear."

I lingered on long in the dark church and there I made my sermon for the next morning. Its original germ, its concentrated essence of sermon, was in these four verses:

> Had I the grace to win the grace
> Of some old man complete in lore,
> My face would worship at his face,
> Like childhood seated on the floor.
>
> Had I the grace to win the grace
> Of childhood, loving, shy, apart,
> The child should find a nearer place.
> And teach me resting on my heart.
>
> Had I the grace to win the grace
> Of maiden living all above,
> My soul would trample down the base,
> That she might have a man to love.
>
> A grace I have no grace to win
> Knocks now at my half-open door:
> Ah, Lord of glory, come Thou in,
> Thy grace divine is all and more.

I told my people that God had created all our worships, reverences, tendernesses, loves. That they had come out of His heart and were put into us because they were in Him first. That all we could imagine of the wise, the lovely, the beautiful, was in Him, only infinitely more than we could imagine or understand. That in Him was all the wise teaching of the best man and more; all the grace, gentleness, and truth of the best child and more; all the tenderness and devotion of the truest woman and more. Therefore, we must be all God's, and all our aspirations, all our worships, all our honors, all our loves, must center in Him.

TWENTY-THREE

AN ANGEL UNAWARES

I resolved on Monday to have the long country walk I had been disappointed of on Saturday. It was such a day as seems impossible to describe except in negatives. It was not stormy, it was not rainy, it was not sunshiny, it was not snowy, it was not frosty, it was not foggy, it was not clear—it was nothing but cloudy and quiet and cold, and generally ungenial, with just a puff of wind now and then. It was an exact representation of my own mind and heart. The summer was thousands of miles off on the other side of the globe. Ethelwyn seemed millions of miles away. The summer might come back but she never would come nearer. The whole of life appeared faint and foggy. I seemed to have done no good. I had driven Catharine Weir to the verge of suicide, while at the same time I could not restrain her from the contemplation of some dire revenge. I had lost the man upon whom I had most reckoned as a seal of my ministry, namely, Thomas Weir. True, there was Old Rogers, but Old Rogers was just as good before I found him. I could not dream of having made him any better. And so I went on brooding over all the disappointing portions of my labor, all the time thinking about myself instead of God and the work that lay for me to do in the days to come.

"Nobody," I said, "but Old Rogers understands me. Nobody would care, as far as my teaching goes, if another man took my place from next Sunday forward." And for Miss Oldcastle, her playing "Agnus Dei"—even if she intended that I should hear it—indicated at most that she thought she had gone too far and been unkind that morning, or perhaps was afraid lest she should be

170

accountable for any failure I might make in my Sunday duties, and therefore felt bound to do something to restore me.

Unconsciously choosing the dreariest path, I wandered up the side of the slow black river, caring for nothing. The first miserable afternoon at Marshmallows looked now as if it had been the whole of my coming relation to the place seen through a reversed telescope. And here I was in it now.

When I came to the bridge I wanted to cross—a wooden one—I found that the approach to it had been partly undermined and carried away; for here the river had overflowed its banks in one of the late storms, and all about the place was still very wet and swampy. I could therefore get no farther in my gloomy walk, and so turned back upon my steps. Scarcely had I done so when I saw a man coming toward me upon the river walk. I could not mistake him at any distance—Old Rogers.

"Well, Old Rogers," I said, trying to speak cheerfully, "you cannot get much farther this way, without wading a bit, at least."

"I don't want to go no farther now, Sir. I came to find you. I told Master I wanted to leave for an hour or so. He allus lets me do just as I like."

"But how did you know where to find me?"

"I saw you come this way. You passed me right on the bridge, and didn't see me, Sir. So says I to myself, 'Old Rogers, summat's amiss wi' Parson today. He never went by me like that afore. This won't do. You just go and see.' So I went home and told Master, and here I be, Sir. And I hope you're noways offended with the liberty of me."

"Did I really pass you on the bridge?" I said, unable to understand it.

"That you did, Sir. I knowed Parson must be a goodish bit in his own in'ards afore he would do that."

"I needn't tell you that I didn't see you."

"I could tell you that, Sir. I hope there's nothing gone main wrong, Sir. Miss is well, Sir?"

"Quite well, I thank you. No, my dear fellow, nothing's gone main wrong, as you say. Some of my running tackle got jammed a bit, that's all. I'm a little out of spirits, I believe."

"Well, Sir, don't think I want to get aboard your ship, except you fling me a rope. There's a many things you mun ha' to think about that an ignorant man like me couldn't take up if you was to let 'em drop. And being a gentleman, I do believe, makes the matter worse betuxt us. And there's many a thing that no man can go talkin' about to any but only the Lord Himself. Still, you can't help us poor folks seeing when there's summat amiss, and we can't help havin' our own thoughts anymore than the sailor's jackdaw that couldn't speak. And sometimes we may be nearer the mark than you would suppose, for God has made us all of one blood, you know."

"What are you driving at, Old Rogers?" I said, with a smile, which was none the less true that I suspected he had read some of the worst trouble of my heart. For why should I mind an honorable man like him knowing what oppressed me, though I should not choose to tell it to any but one?

"I want—with the clumsy hand of a rough old tar, with a heart as soft as the pitch that makes his hand hard—to trim your sails a bit, Sir, and help you to lie a point closer to the wind. You're just not close-hauled, Sir."

"Say on, Old Rogers. I will listen with all my heart, for you have a good right to speak."

And Old Rogers spoke thus:

"Oncet upon a time we were becalmed in the South Seas—and weary work it wur, a doin' of nothin' from day to day. But when the water began to come up thick from the bottom of the water casks, it was wearier a deal. Then a thick fog came on, as white as snow a'most, and we couldn't see more than a few yards ahead or on any side of us. But the fog didn't keep the heat off—it only made it worse, and the water was fast going done. The men, some of them, were half mad with thirst. The captain took to his berth, and several of the crew to their hammocks, for it was just as hot on deck as anywhere else. The mate lay on a spare sail on the quarterdeck, groaning. I had a strong suspicion that the barque was drifting, and hove the lead again and again, but could find no bottom. Some of the men got hold of the spirits, and that didn't quench their thirst. It drove them clean mad. I had to knock one of them down myself with a capstan-bar, for he ran at the mate with his knife. At last I began to lose all hope. And still I was sure the barque was slowly drifting. My head was like to burst, and my tongue was like a lump of holystone in my mouth. Well, one morning, I had just, as I thought, lain down on the deck to breathe my last, hoping I should die, when all at once the fog lifted like the foot of a sail. I sprung to my feet. There was the blue sky overhead, but the terrible burning sun was there. A moment more, and a light air blew on my cheek, and turning my face to it as if it had been the very breath of God, I saw an island within half a mile, and the shine of water on the face of a rock on the shore. I cried out, 'Land on the weather-quarter! Fresh water in sight!' A boat was lowered, and in a few minutes we were lying, clothes and all, in a little stream that came down from the hills above.

"There's just as many good days as bad ones—as much fair weather as foul. And if a man keeps up heart, he's all the better for that, and none the worse when the evil day does come. As if there was any chance about what the days would bring forth. No, my lad," said the old sailor, assuming the dignity of his superior years under the inspiration of the truth, "neither boast, nor trust, nor hope in the morrow. Boast and trust and hope in God, for thou shalt yet praise Him, who is the health of thy countenance and thy God."

I could but hold out my hand. I had nothing to say, for he had spoken to me as an angel of God.

The old man was silent for some moments; his emotion needed time to still itself again. Nor did he return to the subject. He held out his hand once more, saying, "Good day, Sir. I must go back to my work."

"I will go back with you."

And so we walked back side by side to the village, but not a word did we speak to the other till we parted upon the bridge where we had first met. Old Rogers went to his work, and I lingered upon the bridge. I leaned upon the low parapet and looked up the stream as far as the mists would permit. Then I turned and looked down the river crawling out of sight. Then I looked to the left, and there stood my old church, quiet in the dreary day. I turned to the right and saw, as on that first afternoon, the weathercock that watched the winds over the stables at Oldcastle Hall. It caught just one glimpse of the sun through some rent in the vapors, and flung it across to me amidst the general dinginess of the hour.

TWENTY-FOUR

TWO PARISHIONERS

My parish was a large one. I have mentioned but one of the great families in it, and confined my recollections entirely to the village and its immediate neighborhood. The houses of most of the gentle-folk lay considerably apart from the church and from each other. Many of them went elsewhere to church, and I did not feel bound to visit those. Still, there were one or two families which I would have visited oftener had I had a horse. Before the winter was over I did buy a gray mare, partly to please Dr. Duncan (who urged me to do it for my health); partly because I could then do my duty better; and partly, I confess, from having been very fond of an old gray mare of my father's.

I mounted her to pay a visit to two rich maiden ladies, the Misses Jemima and Hester Crowther, who came to the services most Sundays when the weather was favorable. I had, however, called upon them only once.

I was shown with much ceremony by a butler (apparently as old as his livery of yellow and green) into the presence of the two ladies, one of whom sat in state reading a volume of the *Spectator*. She—Miss Hester—was very tall and as square as the straight long-backed chair upon which she sat. A fat asthmatic poodle lay at her feet upon the hearthrug. The other—Miss Jemima, a little, lively, gray-haired creature, who looked like a most ancient girl whom no power would ever make old—was standing upon a high chair, cooing to a cockatoo in a gilded cage. As I entered the room, the latter lady all but jumped from her perch with a merry, waver-ing laugh, and advanced to meet me.

"Jonathan, bring the cake and wine," she cried to the retreating servant.

Hester rose with a solemn stiff-backedness, which was more amusing than dignified, and extended her hand as I approached her, without moving from her place.

"We were afraid, Mr. Walton," said Jemima, "that you had forgotten we were parishioners of yours."

"That I could hardly do," I answered, "seeing you are such regular attendants at church. But I confess I have given you ground for your rebuke, Miss Jemima. I bought a horse the other day, and this is the first use I have put her to."

"We're charmed to see you. It is very good of you not to forget such uninteresting girls as we are."

"You forget, Jemima," interposed her sister, "that time is always on the wing. I should have thought we were both decidedly middle-aged, though you are the elder by I will not say how many years."

"All but ten years, Hester. I remember rocking you in your cradle scores of times. But somehow, Mr. Walton, I can't help feeling as if she were my elder sister. She is so learned, and I don't read anything but the newspapers."

"And your Bible, Jemima. Do yourself justice."

That's a matter of course, Sister. But this is not the way to entertain Mr. Walton."

"The gentlemen used to entertain the ladies when I was young, Jemima. I do not know how it may have been when you were."

"Much the same, I believe, Sister. But if you look at Mr. Walton, I think you will see that he is pretty much entertained as it is."

"I agree with Miss Hester," I said. "It is the duty of gentlemen to entertain ladies, but it is so much the kinder of ladies when they surpass their duty and condescend to entertain gentlemen."

"What can surpass duty, Mr. Walton?" asked Hester. "I confess I do not agree with your doctrines upon that point. I hope you will not think me rude, but it always seems to me that your congregation is chiefly composed of the lower classes, who may be greatly injured by such a style of preaching. I must say I think so, Mr. Walton. Only perhaps you are one of those who think a lady's opinion on such matters is worth nothing."

"On the contrary, I respect an opinion just as far as the lady or gentleman who holds it seems to me qualified to have formed it first. But you have not yet told me what you think so objectionable in my preaching."

"You always speak as if faith in Christ was something greater than duty. Now I think duty the first thing."

"I quite agree with you, Miss Hester. How can I, or any clergyman, urge a man to that which is not his duty? But tell me, is not faith in Christ a duty? Where you have mistaken me is that you think I speak of faith as higher than duty, when indeed I speak of faith as higher than any *other* duty. It is the highest duty of man. I do not say the duty he always sees clearest, or even sees at all. But when a duty becomes the highest delight of a man, the joy of his very being, he no more thinks or needs to think about it as a duty. What would you think of the love of a son who, when an appeal was made to his affections, should say, 'Oh yes, I love my mother dearly: it is my duty, of course'?"

"That sounds very plausible but still I cannot help feeling that you preach faith and not works. I do not say that you are not to preach faith, but you know that faith without works is dead."

"Now, really, Hester," interposed Miss Jemima, "I should have said that Mr. Walton was constantly preaching works. He's always telling you to do something or other. I know I always come out of the church with something on my mind, and I've got to work it off somehow before I'm comfortable."

And here Miss Jemima got up on the chair, and began to flirt with the cockatoo once more, but only in silent signs.

I cannot quite recall how this part of the conversation drew to a close. But I will tell a fact or two about the sisters which may explain their different notions of my preaching. Miss Hester scarce left the house, but spent almost the whole of her time in reading small dingy books of eighteenth-century literature. Somehow or other, respectability—in position, in morals, in religion, in conduct—was everything. The consequence was that her very nature was old-fashioned and had nothing in it of that lasting youth which is the birthright of every immortal being.

Miss Jemima, on the contrary, whose eccentricities did not lie on the side of respectability, had gone on shocking the stiff proprieties of her younger sister till she could be shocked no more. She had had a severe disappointment in youth, and had not only survived it but had saved her heart alive out of it, losing only any remnant of selfish care about herself. She now spent that love, which had before been concentrated upon one object, upon every living thing that came near her. She was very odd—with her gray hair, her clear gray eyes with wrinkled eyelids, her light step, her laugh at once girlish and cracked, darting in and out of the cottages, scolding this matron with a smile lurking in every tone, hugging that baby, boxing the ears of the other little tyrant, forgiving this one's rent, and threatening that other with awful vengeances—but it was a very lovely oddity. Their property was not large, and she knew every living thing on the place down to the dogs and pigs. And Miss Jemima, as the people always called her, was the actual queen of the neighborhood—for, though she was the very soul of kindness, she was determined to have her own way and had it.

The one lady did nothing but read, and considered that I neglected the doctrine of works as the seal of faith. The other was busy helping her neighbors from morning to night, and found little in my preaching except incentive to benevolence.

Then Miss Hester made the following further criticism on my pulpit labors:

"You are too anxious to explain everything, Mr. Walton."

What she said looks worse on paper than it sounded from her lips. She was a gentlewoman, and her tone had much to do with the impression made.

"Where can be the use of trying to make uneducated people see the grounds of everything?" she said. "It is enough that this or that is in the Bible."

"Yes, but there is just the point. What is in the Bible? Is it this or that?"

"You are their spiritual instructor: tell them what is in the Bible."

"But you have just been objecting to my mode of representing what is in the Bible."

"It will be so much worse if you add argument to convince them of what is incorrect."

"I doubt that. Falsehood will expose itself the sooner that dishonest argument is used to support it."

"You cannot expect them to judge what you tell them."

"The Bible urges us to search and understand."

"For those whose business it is, like yourself."

"Do you think, then, that the church consists of a few privileged to understand, and a great many who cannot understand and therefore need not be taught?"

"I said you had to teach them."

"But to teach is to make people understand."

"Why don't you try your friend Mrs. Oldcastle? It might do her a little good," said Miss Hester.

"I should have very little influence with Mrs. Oldcastle if I were to make the attempt. And I am not called upon to address my flock individually upon every point of character."

"I thought she was an intimate friend of yours."

"Quite the contrary. We are scarcely friendly."

"I am very glad to hear it," said Miss Jemima, who had been silent during the little controversy that her sister and I had been carrying on. "We have been quite misinformed. We thought we might have seen more of you if it had not been for her. And as very few people of her own position in society care to visit her, we thought it a pity she should be your principal friend in the parish."

"Why do they not visit her more?"

"There are strange stories about her, which it is well to leave alone. They are getting out of date too. But she is not a fit woman to be regarded as the clergyman's friend. There!" said Miss Jemima, as if she had wanted to relieve her bosom of a burden.

"I think, however, her religious opinions would correspond with your own, Mr. Walton," said Miss Hester.

"Possibly," I answered, with indifference. "I don't care much about opinion."

"Her daughter would be a nice girl, I fancy, if she weren't kept down by her mother. She looks scared, poor thing! And they say she's not quite—you know," said Miss Jemima, and gently tapped her head with a forefinger. I laughed. I thought it was not worthwhile to champion Miss Oldcastle's sanity.

"They are, and have been, a strange family as far back as I can remember, and my mother used to say the same. I am glad she comes to our church now. You mustn't let her set her cap at you, though. It wouldn't do at all. She's pretty enough too!"

"Yes," I returned, "she is rather pretty. But I don't think she looks as if she had a cap to set at anybody."

I rose to go, for I did not relish the present conversation.

I rode home slowly, brooding on the lovely marvel that out of such a rough, ungracious stem as the Oldcastle family should have sprung such a delicate, pale, winter-braved flower as Ethelwyn. I prayed that I might rescue her from that ungenial soil.

TWENTY-FIVE

SATAN CAST OUT

I was within a mile of the village, returning from my visit to the Misses Crowther. My horse, which was walking slowly along the soft side of the road, lifted her head and pricked up her ears at the sound of approaching hoofs. The riders soon came in sight—Miss Oldcastle, Judy, and Captain Everard. Miss Oldcastle I had never seen on horseback before. Judy was on a little white pony she used for galloping about the fields near the Hall. The captain was laughing and chatting gaily, now to the one, now to the other. I lifted my hat to Miss Oldcastle, without drawing bridle, and went on. The captain returned my salutation, and likewise rode on. I could just see, as they passed me, that Miss Oldcastle's pale face was flushed even to scarlet, but she only bowed and kept alongside of her companion. About twenty yards farther, I heard the clatter of Judy's pony behind me, and up she came at full gallop.

"Why didn't you stop to speak to us, Mr. Walton?" she said. "I pulled up, but you never looked at me. We shall be cross all the rest of the day because you cut us so. What have we done?"

"Nothing, Judy, that I know of," I answered, trying to speak cheerfully. "But I do not know your companion, and I was not in the humor for an introduction."

She looked hard at me with her keen gray eyes, and I felt as if the child was seeing through me. "I don't know what to make of it, Mr. Walton. You're very different, somehow, from what you used to be. There's something wrong somewhere. I only wish I could do something for you."

I felt the child's kindness, but could only say, "Thank you,

179

Judy. I am sure I should ask you if there were anything you could do for me. But you'll be left behind."

"No fear of that. My Dobbin can go much faster than their big horses. But I see you don't want me, so good-by."

She turned her pony's head as she spoke, jumped the ditch at the side of the road, and flew after them along the grass like a swallow. I likewise roused my horse and went off at a hard trot, with the vain impulse to shake off the tormenting thoughts that crowded me like gadflies. But this day was to be one of more trial still.

As I turned the corner into a street of the village, young Tom Weir was at my side. His face was pale, and he had evidently been watching for me.

"What is the matter, Tom?" I asked, in some alarm.

I could see his bare throat knot and relax, like the motion of a serpent before he could utter the words, "Kate has killed her little boy, Sir." He followed this with a stifled cry and hid his face in his hands.

"God forbid!" I exclaimed, and struck my heels in my horse's sides, nearly overturning poor Tom in my haste. "Come after me, Tom," I said, "and take the mare home."

Had I had a share, by my harsh words, in driving the woman beyond the bounds of human reason and endurance?

Before I reached the door I saw a little crowd of the villagers, mostly women and children, gathered about it. I got off my horse, and gave her to a woman to hold for Tom. With a little difficulty, I prevailed on the rest to go home, and not add to the confusion and terrors by the excitement of their presence. I entered the shop and, locking the door behind me, went up to the room above.

I found no one there. On the hearth and in the fender lay two little pools of blood. All in the house was utterly, dreadfully still. I went to the only other door, peeped in, and entered. On the bed lay the mother, white as death, but with her black eyes wide open, staring at the ceiling. On her arm lay little Gerard, just as white, except where the blood had flowed from the bandage down his deathlike face.

When Catharine caught sight of me, she showed no surprise or emotion of any kind. Her lips uttered the words, "I have done it at last. I am ready. Take me away. I shall be hanged. I don't care. I confess it. Only don't let the people stare at me."

Her lips went on moving, but I could hear no more, till suddenly she broke out in a cry of agony, "Oh! My baby! My baby!"

I heard a loud knocking at the shop door and went down to see who was there. I found Thomas Weir accompanied by Dr. Duncan. We went up together to Catharine's room. Thomas said nothing, and I found it difficult even to conjecture from his countenance what thoughts were passing through his mind.

Catharine looked from one to another of us as if she did not know the one from the other. She made no motion to rise from her bed, nor did she utter a word, although her lips would now and then move as if molding a sentence. When Dr. Duncan, after looking at the child, proceeded to take him from her, she gave him one imploring look and yielded with a moan, then began to stare hopelessly at the ceiling again. The doctor carried the child into the next room, and the grandfather followed.

"You see what you have driven me to!" cried Catharine, the moment I was left alone with her. "I hope you are satisfied."

The words went to my very soul. But when I looked at her, her eyes were wandering about over the ceiling, and I thought it better to leave her and join the others in the sitting room. The first thing I saw there was Thomas on his knees, with a basin of water, washing away the blood of his grandson from his daughter's floor. The very sight of the child had hitherto been nauseous to him, and his daughter had been beyond the reach of his forgiveness. Here was the end of it—the blood of the one shed by the hand of the other, and the father of both on his knees wiping it up. The blood flowed from a wound on the boy's head, evidently occasioned by a fall upon the fender, where the blood lay both inside and out.

In a few minutes Dr. Duncan said, "I think he'll come round."

"Will it be safe to tell his mother so?" I asked.

"I think you may."

I hastened to her room. "Your little darling is not dead, Catharine. He is coming to."

She threw herself off the bed at my feet, caught them round with her arms, and cried, "I will forgive him. I will do anything you like. I forgive George Everard. I will go and ask my father to forgive me."

I lifted her in my arms—how light she was!—and laid her again on the bed, where she lay sobbing and weeping. I went to the other room. Little Gerard opened his eyes and closed them again as I entered.

I beckoned to Thomas. "She wants to ask you to forgive her. Do not, in God's name, wait till she asks you, but go and tell her that you forgive her."

"I dare not say I forgive her," he answered. "I have more need to ask her to forgive me."

I took him by the hand and led him into her room. She feebly lifted her arms toward him. Not a word was said on either side. I left them in each other's embrace. The hard rocks had been struck with the rod, and the waters of life had flowed forth from each and had met between.

When I rejoined Dr. Duncan, I found little Gerard asleep and breathing quietly. "What do you know of this sad business, Mr. Walton?" said the doctor.

"I should like to ask the same question of you," I returned. "Young Tom told me that his sister had murdered the child. That is all I know."

"His father told me the same, and that is all I know. Do you believe it?"

"We have no evidence. We must wait till she is able to explain the thing herself."

"I believe," said Dr. Duncan, "that she struck the child, and that he fell upon the fender."

(As far as Catharine could later account, this was the truth. She could not remember with any clearness what had happened. All she remembered was that she had been more miserable than ever in her life before; that the child had come to her, as he seldom did, with some childish request or other; that she felt herself seized with intense hatred of him; and the next thing she knew was that his blood was running in a long red finger toward her. Then she knew what she had done, though not how she had done it. She remembered nothing more that happened till she lay weeping with the hope that the child would yet live. In the illness that followed, I more than once saw her shudder while she slept, dreaming what her waking memory had forgotten, and once she started awake, crying, "I have murdered him again!")

When Thomas came from his daughter's room, he looked like a man from whom the bitterness of evil had passed away. His face had that childlike expression in its paleness, and the tearfulness without tears haunted his eyes.

"She is asleep," he said.

"You and I must sit with them tonight, Thomas. You'll attend to your daughter, if she wants anything, and I know this little darling won't be frightened if he comes to himself and sees me beside him."

"God bless you, Sir," said Thomas, fervently. (And from that hour to this there has never been a coolness between us.)

"A very good arrangement," said Dr. Duncan, "only I feel as if I ought to have a share in it."

"No, no," I said. "We do not know who may want you. Besides, we are both younger than you."

"I will come over early in the morning, then, and see how you are going on."

I went home to tell my sister and arrange for the night. We carried back with us things to make the two patients comfortable. As regarded Catharine, now that she would let her fellows help her, I was anxious that she should feel that love about her which she had so long driven from her door. I wanted her to read the love of God in the love that even I could show her. And my heart still smote me for the severity with which I had spoken the truth to her.

I took my place beside Gerard, and watched through the night. The little fellow repeatedly cried out in that terror which is so often the consequence of the loss of blood, but when I laid my hand on him, he smiled without waking and lay quite still again for a while. Once or twice he woke up and looked so bewildered that I feared delirium, but a bit of jam comforted him, and he fell fast asleep again. He did not seem even to have a headache from the blow.

But when I was left alone with the child, seated in a chair by the fire—my only light—how my thoughts rushed upon the facts bearing on my own history which this day had brought before me! Horror it was to think of Miss Oldcastle as even riding with the seducer of Catharine Weir! There was torture in the thought of his touching her hand, and to think that before the summer came once more, he might be her husband! Was it fair to let her marry such a man in ignorance? Would she marry him if she knew what I knew of him? Could I speak against my rival? Blacken him even with the truth—the only defilement that can really cling? Could I, for my own dignity, do so? And was she therefore to be sacrificed in ignorance? Might not someone else do it instead of me? But, if I set it agoing, was it not precisely the same thing as if I did it myself, only more cowardly? There was but one way of doing it, and that was with the full and solemn consciousness that it was and must be a barrier between us forever. If I could give her up fully and altogether, then I might tell her the truth. But how bitter to cast away my chance!

Then came another bitter and wicked thought—my own earnestness with Catharine Weir, in urging her to forgiveness, would bear a main part in wrapping up in secrecy that evil thing which ought not to be hid. For had she not vowed to denounce the man at the very altar? Had not the revenge which I had ignorantly combatted been my best ally? And for one brief, black, wicked moment I repented that I had acted as I had. The next I was on my knees by the side of the sleeping child and repenting back again in shame and sorrow. Then came the consolation that if I suffered hereby, I suffered from doing my duty, and that was well.

Scarcely had I seated myself again by the fire when the door of the room opened softly, and Thomas appeared. "Kate wants to see you," he said.

I rose at once. "Perhaps, then, you had better stay with Gerard."

"I will, Sir, for I think she wants to speak to you alone."

I entered her chamber. A candle stood on a chest of drawers, and its light fell on her face. Her eyes glittered, but the fierceness was gone, and only the suffering remained. I drew a chair beside her and took her hand.

"I want to tell you all," she said. "He promised to marry me. I believed him. But I did very wrong. And I have been a bad mother, for I could not keep from seeing his face in Gerard's. Gerard was the name he told me to call him when I had to write to him, and so I named the little darling Gerard. How is he, Sir?"

"Doing nicely," I replied. "I do not think you need be at all uneasy about him now."

"Thank God! I forgive his father now with all my heart. I feel it easier since I saw how wicked I could be myself, and I feel it easier, too, that I have not long to live. I forgive him with all my heart, and I will take no revenge. I have never told anyone yet who he is, but I will tell you. His name is George Everard—Captain Everard. I came to know him when I was apprenticed at Addicehead. I would not tell you, Sir, if I did not know that you will not tell anyone. I saw him yesterday, and it drove me wild. But it is all over now. My heart feels so cool now. Do you think God will forgive me?"

Without one word of my own, I took out my pocket Testament

and read these words, "For if ye forgive men their trespasses, your Heavenly Father will also forgive you."

Then I read to her, from the seventh chapter of St. Luke, the story of the woman who was a sinner, and came to Jesus in Simon's house. When I had finished, I found that she was gently weeping, and so I left her and resumed my place by the boy. I told Thomas that he had better not go near her just yet. So we sat in silence together for a while, during which I felt so weary and benumbed that I fell asleep in my chair. I suddenly returned to consciousness at a cry from Gerard. He was fast asleep, but standing on his feet in his crib, pushing with his hands from before him, as if resisting someone, and crying, "Don't—don't. Go away! Mammy! Mr. Walton!"

I took him in my arms and kissed him and laid him down again, and he lay still.

Thomas came again into the room. "I am sorry to be so troublesome, Sir," he said, "But my poor daughter says there is one thing more she wants to say to you."

I returned at once. As soon as I entered the room she said eagerly, "I forgive him. I forgive him with all my heart—but don't let him take Gerard."

I assured her I would do my best to prevent any such attempt on his part, and making her promise to try to go to sleep, left her once more. Nor was either of the patients disturbed again during the night. Both slept, as it appeared, refreshingly.

In the morning the old doctor made his welcome appearance, and pronounced both quite as well as he had expected to find them. He sent young Tom to take my place, and my sister to take the father's. It was of no use trying to go to sleep, so I set out for a walk.

TWENTY-SIX

THE MAN AND THE CHILD

It was a fine frosty morning, which overcame in a great measure my depression. I sought the rugged common where I had met Catharine Weir in the storm and darkness. I reached the same chasm where I had sought a breathing space that night, and sat down upon a block of sand which the frost had detached from the wall above.

I found my mind relieved by the fact that I had urged Catharine to a confession. It was, however, a confession which I was not, could not be, at liberty to disclose. Disclosed by herself, it would have been the revenge from which I had warned her and, at the same time, my deliverance. I was relieved; at first by this view of the matter, because I might thus keep my own chance of same favorable turn, whereas, if I once told Miss Oldcastle, I must give her up forever. But my love did not long remain skulking thus behind the hedge of honor. I saw that I was unworthy of loving her, for I was willing to risk her well-being for the chance of my own happiness, a risk which involved infinitely more wretchedness to her than the loss of my dearest hopes to me. It is one thing for a man not to marry the woman he loves, and quite another thing for a woman to marry a man she cannot even respect. And that I had given her up first could never be known even to her in this world.

I was sitting in the hollow when I heard the sound of horses' hoofs in the distance, and felt a foreboding of what would appear. I was only a few yards from the road upon which the sand-cleft opened, and could see a space of it sufficient to show the persons even of rapid riders. The sounds drew nearer. I could distinguish the step of a pony and the steps of two horses besides. Up they came and swept past—Miss Oldcastle upon Judy's pony, Mr. Stoddart upon her horse, with the captain upon his own. How grateful I felt to Mr. Stoddart! And the hope arose in me that he had accompanied them at Miss Oldcastle's request.

Miss Oldcastle caught a glimpse of me, and even in the moment ere she vanished, I fancied I saw the lily-white grow rosy-red. But it must have been fancy, for she could hardly have been quite pale upon horseback on such a keen morning.

I could not sit any longer. As soon as I ceased to hear the sound of their progress, I rose and walked home, much quieter in heart and mind than when I set out.

As I entered by the nearer gate of the vicarage, I saw Old Rogers enter by the farther. He did not see me, but we met at the door.

"I'm in luck," he said, "to meet you just coming home. How's poor Miss Weir today, Sir?"

"She was rather better this morning, but I greatly doubt if she will ever get up again. That's between us, you know. Come in."

"Thank you, Sir. I wanted to have a little talk with you. You don't believe what they say—that she tried to kill the poor little fellow?" he asked, as soon as the door was closed behind us.

"If she did, she was out of her mind for the moment. But I don't believe it."

And thereupon I told him what both his master and I thought about it, but I did not tell him what she had said.

"That's just what I came to myself, Sir, turning the thing over in my old head. But there's dreadful things done in the world, Sir. There's my daughter been a telling me—"

I was instantly breathless with attention. What he chose to tell me I felt at liberty to hear, though I would not have listened to Jane herself, still in her place of attendance upon Miss Oldcastle.

"—that the old lady up at the Hall there is tormenting the life out of that daughter of hers—she don't look much like hers, do she, Sir?—wanting to make her marry a man of her choosing. I saw him go past o' horseback with her yesterday, and I didn't more than half like the looks of him. He's too like a fair-spoken captain I sailed with once, what was the hardest man I ever sailed with. His own way was everything, even after he saw it wouldn't do. Now don't you think, Sir, somebody or other ought to interfere? It's as bad as murder, that, and anybody has a right to do summat to perwent it."

"I don't know what can be done, Rogers. I can't interfere."

The old man was silent. Evidently he thought I might interfere if I pleased. I could see what he was thinking. Possibly his daughter had told him something more than he chose to communicate to me. I could not help suspecting the mode in which he judged I might interfere. But I had no plain path to follow.

"Old Rogers," I said, "I can almost guess what you mean. But I am in more difficulty with regard to what you suggest than I can easily explain to you. I need not tell you, however, that I will turn the whole matter over in my mind."

"The prey ought to be taken from the lion somehow, if it please God," returned the old man, solemnly. "The poor young lady keeps up as well as she can before her mother, but Jane do say there's a power o' crying done in her own room."

Partly to hide my emotion, partly with the resolve to do something, I said, "I will call on Mr. Stoddart this evening. I may hear something from him to suggest a mode of action."

"I don't think you'll get anything worthwhile from Mr. Stoddart. He takes things a deal too easy like. He'll be this man's man and that man's man both at oncet. I beg your pardon, Sir. But he won't help us."

"That's all I can think of at present, though," I said, whereupon the man-of-war's man, with true breeding, rose at once and took a kindly leave.

I was in the storm again. She suffering, resisting, and I standing aloof! But what could I do? She had repelled me—she would repel me. She had said that the day might come when she would ask help from me, but she had made no movement. Just to do something, I would go and see Mr. Stoddart that evening. I was sure to find him alone, for he never dined with the family, and I might possibly catch a glimpse of Miss Oldcastle.

I found little Gerard so much better, though very weak, and his mother so quiet, that I might safely leave them to the care of Mary and her brother Tom. So there was something off my mind.

The heavens were glorious with stars, but I did not care for them. Let them shine—they could not shine into me. I tried to lift my eyes to Him who is above the stars, and yet how much sustaining I got from that region, I cannot tell. But somehow things did seem a little more endurable before I reached the house.

I was passing across the hall, following the "Wolf" to Mr.

Stoddart's room, when the drawing room door opened and Miss Oldcastle came half out. Seeing me, she drew back instantly. A moment after, however, I heard the sound of her dress following us. Light as was her step, every footfall seemed to be upon my heart. I did not dare to look round. Soon, however, the silken vortex of sound behind me ceased as she turned aside in some other direction. I passed on to Mr. Stoddart's room.

He received me kindly, as he always did, but his smile flickered uneasily. He seemed in some trouble, and yet pleased to see me.

"I am glad you have taken to horseback," I said. "It gives me hope that you will be my companion sometimes when I make a round of my parish. I should like you to see some of our people. You would find more in them to interest you than perhaps you would expect."

I thus tried to seem at ease, as I was far from feeling.

"I am not so fond of riding as I used to be," he said.

"Did you like the Arab horses in India?"

"Yes, after I got used to their careless ways. That horse you must have seen me on the other day is very nearly a pure Arab. He belongs to Captain Everard and carries Miss Oldcastle beautifully. I was quite sorry to take him from her, but it was her own doing. She would have me go with her. I think I have lost much firmness since I was ill."

"If the loss of firmness means the increase of kindness, I do not think you will have to lament it," I answered. "Does Captain Everard make a long stay?"

"He stays from day to day. I wish he would go. I don't know what to do. Mrs. Oldcastle and he form one party, Miss Oldcastle and Judy another, and each is trying to gain me over. I don't want to belong to either. If they would only let me alone."

"What do they want of you, Mr. Stoddart?"

"Mrs. Oldcastle wants me to use my influence with Ethelwyn to persuade her to behave differently to Captain Everard. The old lady has set her heart on their marriage, and Ethelwyn, though she dares not break with him, yet keeps him somehow at arm's length. Then Judy is always begging me to stand up for her aunt. But what's the use of my standing up for her if she won't stand up for herself? She never says a word to me about it herself. It's all Judy's doing. How am I to know what she wants?"

"I thought you said just now she asked you to ride with her?"

"So she did, but nothing more. She did not even press it, only

189

the tears came in her eyes when I refused and I could not bear that, so I went against my will. I don't want to make enemies. I am sure I don't see why she should stand out. He's a very good match in point of property, and family too."

"Perhaps she does not like him?" I forced myself to say.

"Oh! I suppose not, or she would not be so troublesome. But she could arrange all that if she were inclined to be agreeable to her friends. After all I have done for her! Well, one must not look to be repaid for anything one does for others."

And what had this man done for her, then? He had, for his own amusement, taught her Hindustan; he had given her some insight into the principles of mechanics; and he had roused in her some taste for the writings of the mystics. But for all that regarded the dignity of her humanity and her womanhood, if she had had no teaching but what he gave her, her mind would have been merely "an unweeded garden that grows to seed." And now he complained that in return for his pains she would not submit to the degradation of marrying a man she did not love, in order to leave him in the enjoyment of his own lazy and cowardly peace. Really, he was a worse man than I had thought him. Clearly he would not help to keep her in the right path, not even interfere to prevent her from being pushed into the wrong one. But perhaps he was only expressing his own discomfort, not giving his real judgment, and I might be censuring him too hardly.

"What will be the result, do you suppose?" I asked.

"I can't tell. Sooner or later she will have to give in to her mother. She might as well yield with a good grace."

"She must do what she thinks is right," I said. "And you, Mr. Stoddart, ought to help her to do what is right. You surely would not urge her to marry a man she does not love."

"Well, no, not exactly. And yet society does not object to it. It is an acknowledged arrangement, common enough."

"Society is scarcely an interpreter of the divine will. Society will honor vile things so long as the doer has money sufficient to clothe them in a grace not their own. There is God's way of doing everything in the world, up to marrying, or down to paying a bill."

"Yes, yes, I know what you would say, and I suppose you are right. I will not urge any opinion of mine. Besides, we shall have a respite soon, for he must join his regiment in a day or two."

It was some relief to hear this, and I presently took my leave. As I walked through one of the long, dimly lighted passages, I started at Judy's light touch on my arm.

"Dear Mr. Walton—" she said, and stopped, for at the same moment Sarah appeared at the end of the passage and said,

"Miss Judy, your grandmamma wants you."

Judy took her hand from my arm, and with an almost martial stride approached Sarah and stood before her defiantly.

"Sarah," she said, "you know you are telling me a lie. Grannie does not want me. You have not been in the dining room since I left it one moment ago. Do you think, you bad woman, I am going to be afraid of you? I know you better than you think. Go away directly, or I will make you."

She stamped her little foot, and Sarah turned and walked away without a word.

As valuable as propriety of demeanor is, truth of conduct is infinitely more precious. In the face of her courage and uprightness, I could not rebuke her for her want of decorum. When I joined her she put her hand in mine, and so walked with me down the stair and out at the front door.

"You will take cold, Judy, going out like that," I said.

"I am in too great a passion to take cold," she answered. "But I have no time to talk about that creeping creature. Auntie doesn't like Captain Everard, and Grannie insists that she shall have him, whether she likes him or not. Now do tell me what you think."

"I do not quite understand you, my child."

"I know Auntie would like to know what you think, but she will never ask you herself. So *I* am asking you whether a lady ought to marry a gentleman she does not like, to please her mother."

"Certainly not, Judy. It is often wicked, and at best a mistake."

"Thank you, Mr. Walton. I will tell her. She will be glad to hear that you say so, I know."

"Mind you tell her you asked me, Judy. I should not like her to think I had been interfering, you know."

"Yes, yes, I know quite well. I will take care. Thank you. He's going tomorrow. Good night."

She bounded into the house again, and I walked away down the avenue. I saw and felt the stars now, for hope had come again in my heart, and I thanked the God of hope. "Our minds are small because they are faithless," I said to myself. "If we had faith in God, our hearts would share in His greatness and peace, for we should not then be shut up in ourselves, but would walk abroad in Him." And with a light step and a light heart I went home.

TWENTY-SEVEN

OLD MRS. TOMKINS

Very severe weather came, and much sickness followed, chiefly among the poorer people who can so ill keep out the cold. Yet some of my well-to-do parishioners, including Mr. Boulderstone, were laid up likewise. I had grown quite attached to Mr. Boulderstone by this time, not because he was what is called interesting, for he was not; not because he was clever, for he was not; not because he was well-read, for he was not; not because he was possessed of influence in the parish, though he had that influence; but simply because he was true. He was what he appeared, felt what he professed, and did what he said—appearing kind, and feeling and acting kindly. Such a man is rare and precious, were he as stupid as the Welsh giant in "Jack the Giant-killer." I could never see Mr. Boulderstone a mile off but my heart felt the warmer for the sight. Even in his great pain he seemed to forget himself as he received me, and to gain comfort from my mere presence. I could not help regarding him as a child of heaven, to be treated with the more reverence that he had the less aid to his goodness from his slow understanding.

But I could not help feeling keenly the contrast when I went from his warm, comfortable, well-defended chamber to the Tomkins' cottage and found it lying open and bare to the enemy. What holes and cracks there were about the door, through which the fierce wind rushed into the room to attack the aged feet and hands and throats! There were no defenses of threefold draperies, and no soft carpet on the brick floor—only a small rug which my sister had carried them, laid down before a weak little fire that

192

seemed to despair against the cold. True, we had had the little cottage patched up. The two Thomas Weirs had been at work upon it in the first of the cold weather this winter, but it was like putting the new cloth on the old garment, for fresh places had broken out. Although Mrs. Tomkins had fought the cold well with what rags she could spare, such razor-edged winds are hard to keep out. And here she was now, lying in bed and breathing hard, like the sore-pressed garrison which had retreated to its last defense in the keep of the castle. Poor old Tomkins sat shivering over the little fire.

"Come, come, Tomkins, this won't do," I said. "Why don't you burn your coals in weather like this?" It made my heart ache to see the little heap in a box hardly bigger than the chest of tea my sister brought from London with her. I threw half of it on the fire at once.

"Deary me, Mr. Walton, you *are* wasteful, Sir. The Lord never sent His good coals to be used that way."

"He did, though, Tomkins," I answered. "And He'll send you a little more this evening, after I get home. Keep yourself warm, man. This world's cold in winter, you know."

"Indeed, Sir, I know that, and I'm like to know it worse afore long. She's going," he said, pointing toward the bed where his wife lay.

I went to her. I had seen her several times within the last few weeks, but had observed nothing to make me consider her seriously ill. I now saw at a glance that Tomkins was right: she had not long to live.

"I am sorry to see you suffering so much, Mrs. Tomkins," I said.

"I don't suffer so very much, Sir, though, to be sure, it be hard to get the breath into my body. And I do feel cold-like, Sir."

"I'm going home directly, and I'll send you down another blanket. It's much colder today than it was yesterday."

"It's not weather-cold, Sir, wi' me. It's grave-cold, Sir. Blankets won't do me no good, Sir. I can't get it out of my head how perishing cold I shall be when I'm under the mound, though I oughtn't to mind it when it's the will o' God. It's only till the resurrection, Sir."

"But it's not the will of God, Mrs. Tomkins."

"Ain't it, Sir? Sure I thought it was."

"You believe in Jesus Christ, don't you, Mrs. Tomkins?"

"That I do, Sir, with all my heart and soul."

"Well, He says that whosoever liveth and believeth in Him shall never die."

"But you know, Sir, everybody dies. I *must* die and be laid in the churchyard, Sir. And that's what I don't like."

"But I say that is all a mistake. *You* won't die. Your body will die, and be laid away out of sight, but you will be awake, alive, more alive than you are now, a great deal."

(It is a great mistake to teach children that they have souls. Then they think of their souls as of something which is not themselves. For what a man *has* cannot be himself. Hence, when they are told that their souls go to heaven, they think of their selves as lying in the grave. They ought to be taught that they have bodies, and that their bodies die while they themselves live on. Then they will not think, as old Mrs. Tomkins did, that they will be laid in the grave. We talk as if we *possessed* souls instead of *being* souls, whereas we should teach our children to think no more of their bodies when they are dead than they do of their hair when it is cut off, or of their old clothes when they have done with them.)

"But you will be with God in your Father's house, you know. And that is enough, is it not?"

"Yes, surely, Sir. But I wish you was to be there by the bedside of me when I was a dyin'. I can't help bein' summat skeered at it. It don't come nat'ral to me, like. I ha' got used to this old bed here, cold as it has been—many's the night—wi' my good man there by the side of me."

"Send for me, Mrs. Tomkins, any moment, day or night, and I'll be with you directly."

"I think, Sir, if I had a hold ov you i' the one hand, and my man there, the Lord bless him, i' the other, I could go comfortable."

"I'll come the minute you send for me—just to keep you in mind that a better friend than I am is holding you all the time, though you mayn't feel His hands."

"But I can't help thinking, Sir, that I wouldn't be troublesome. He has such a deal to look after! And I don't see how He can think of everybody, at every minute, like. I don't mean that He will let anything go wrong, but He might forget an old body like me for a minute, like."

"You would need to be as wise as He is before you could see how He does it. But you must believe more than you can understand. It would be unreasonable to think that He must forget because you can't understand how He could remember. I think it is as hard for Him to forget anything as it is for us to remember everything, for forgetting comes of weakness, and from our not being finished yet, and He is all strength and all perfection."

"Then you think, Sir, He never forgets anything?"

I knew by the trouble that gathered on the old woman's brow what kind of thought was passing through her mind, but I let her go on. She paused for one moment only, and then resumed, much interrupted by the shortness of her breathing.

"When I was brought to bed first," she said, "it was o' twins, Sir. And oh! It was *very* hard. As I said to my man after I got my head up a bit, 'Tomkins,' says I, 'you don't know what it is to have two on 'em cryin' and cryin', and you next to nothin' to give 'em, till their cryin' sticks to your brain, and ye hear 'em when they're fast asleep, one on each side o' you. Would you believe it, Sir, I wished 'em dead? Just to get the wailin' of them out o' my head, I wished 'em dead. In the courtyard o' the squire's house, where my Tomkins worked on the home-farm, there was an old draw-well. It wasn't used, and there was a lid to it, with a hole in it, through which you could put a good big stone. And Tomkins once took me to it and put a stone in, and told me to hearken. And I hearkened, but I heard nothing, as I told him so. 'But,' says he, 'hearken, Lass.' And in a little while there comes a blast o' noise from somewheres. 'What's that, Tomkins?' I said. 'That's the stone,' says he, 'a strikin' on the water down that there well.' And I turned sick at the thoughts of it. And it's down there that I wished the darlin's that God had sent me, for there they'd be quiet."

"Mothers are often a little out of their minds at such times, Mrs. Tomkins, and so were you."

"I don't know, Sir. But I must tell you another thing. The Sunday afore that, the parson had been preachin' about 'Suffer little children,' you know, Sir, 'to come unto Me.' I suppose that was what put it in my head. But I fell asleep wi' nothin' else in my head but the cries o' the infants and the sound o' the stone in the draw-well. And I dreamed that I had one o' them under each arm, cryin' dreadful, and was walkin' across the court the way to the draw-well, when all at once a man come up to me and held out his hands, and said, 'Gie me my childer.' And I was in a terrible fear. And I gave him first one and then the t'other, and he took them, and one laid its head on one shoulder of him, and t'other upon t'other, and they stopped their cryin', and fell fast asleep. And away he walked wi' them into the dark, and I saw him no more. And then I awoke cryin', and I didn't know why. And I took my twins to me, and my breasts was full, and my heart was as full o' love to them, and they hardly cried worth mentionin' again. But afore they was two years old, they both died o' the brown chytis, Sir—and I think that He took them."

"He did take them, Mrs. Tomkins, and you'll see them again soon."

"But, if He never forgets anything—"

"I didn't say that. I think He can do what He pleases. And if He pleases to forget anything, then He can forget it. And I think that is what He does with our sins—that is, after He has got them away from us, once we are clean from them altogether. It would be a dreadful thing if He forgot them before that and left them sticking fast to us and defiling us. How then should we ever be made clean? What else does the Prophet Isaiah mean when he says, 'Thou hast cast my sins behind Thy back'? Is not that where He chooses to not see them anymore?"

"They are good words, Sir. I could not bear Him to think of me and my sins both at once."

The old woman lay quiet after this, relieved in mind, though not in body. I hastened home to send some coals and other things, and then call upon Dr. Duncan, lest he should not know that his patient was worse.

From Dr. Duncan's I went to see old Samuel Weir, who likewise was ailing. I found him alone, in bed under the old embroidery. He greeted me with a withered smile, sweet and true, though no flash of white teeth broke forth to light up the welcome of the aged head.

"Are you not lonely, Mr. Weir?"

"No, Sir. I don't know as ever I was less lonely. I've got my stick, you see, Sir," he said, pointing to a thorn-stick which lay beside him.

"I do not quite understand you," I returned, knowing that the old man's sayings always meant something.

"You see, Sir, when I want anything, I've only to knock on the floor, and up comes my son out of the shop. And then again, when I knock at the door of the house up there, my Father opens it and looks out. So I have both my son on earth and my Father in heaven, and what can an old man want more?

"It's very strange," the old man resumed, after pause, "but as I lie here I begin to feel a child again. They say old age is a second childhood. Before I grew so old, I used to think that meant only that a man was helpless and silly again, as he used to be when he was a child. I never thought it meant that a man felt like a child again, as lighthearted and untroubled as I do now."

"Well, I suspect that is not what people do mean when they say so. But I am very glad—you don't know how pleased it makes me to hear that you feel so. I will hope to fare in the same way when my time comes."

"Indeed, I hope you will, Sir. Just before you came in now, I had quite forgotten that I was a toothless old man, and thought I was lying here waiting for my mother to come in and say goodnight to me before I went to sleep. Wasn't that curious, when I never saw my mother, as I told you before, Sir? But I have no end of fancies. There's one I see often—a man down on his knees at that cupboard nigh the floor there, searching and searching for somewhat; and I wish he would just turn round his face once for a moment that I might see him. I have a notion it's my own father."

"How do you account for that fancy, now, Mr. Weir?"

"I've often thought about it, Sir, but I never could account for it. I'm none willing to think it's a ghost. I've turned out that cupboard over and over, and there's nothing there I don't know."

"You're not afraid of it, are you?"

"No, Sir. Why should I be? I never did it no harm. And God can surely take care of me from all sorts."

I came simply to the conclusion that when he was a child, he had peeped in at the door of the same room where he now lay, and had actually seen a man in the position he described, half in the cupboard, searching for something. His mind had kept the impression after the conscious memory had lost its hold of the circumstance. It was a glimpse out of one of the many stories which haunted the old place.

A week had elapsed from the night I had sat up with Gerard Weir, and it did not seem likely his mother would ever rise from her bed again. On a Friday I went to see her just as the darkness was beginning to gather. The fire of life was burning itself out fast. It glowed on her cheeks, it burned in her hands, it blazed in her eyes—but the fever had left her mind. That was cool, oh, so cool now! Those fierce tropical storms of passion had passed away, and nothing of life was lost. Revenge had passed away, but revenge is of death and deadly. Forgiveness had taken its place, and forgiveness is the giving, and so the receiving of life. Gerard, his little head starred with sticking plaster, sat on her bed, happy over a spotted wooden horse with cylindrical body and jointless legs. But he dropped it when he saw me and flung himself upon my neck. Catharine's face gleamed with pleasure.

"Dear boy!" I said, "I am very glad to see you so much better." For this was the first time he had shown such a revival of energy. He had been quite sweet when he saw me but, until this evening, listless.

"Yes," he said, "I am quite well now." And he put his hand up to his head.

"Does it ache?"

"Not much now. The doctor says I had a bad fall."

"So you had, my child. But you will soon be well again."

The mother's face was turned aside, yet I could see one tear forcing its way from under her closed eyelid.

"Oh, I don't mind it," he answered. "Mammy is so kind to me! She lets me sit on her bed as long as I like."

"That is nice. But just run to Auntie in the next room. I think your mammy would like to talk to me for a little while."

The child ran off with overflowing obedience.

"I can even think of *him* now," said the mother, "without going into a passion. I hope God will forgive him. *I* do. I think He will forgive me."

"Did you ever hear," I asked, "of Jesus refusing anybody that wanted kindness from Him? He wouldn't always do exactly what they asked Him, because that would sometimes be of no use and would sometimes even be wrong—but He never pushed them away from Him, never repulsed their approach to Him. For the sake of His disciples, He made the Syro-Phoenician woman suffer a little while, but only to give her praise afterward and a wonderful granting of her prayer."

She said nothing for a little while, then murmured, "Shall I have to be ashamed to all eternity? I do not want to be ashamed. Shall I never be like other people—in heaven I mean?"

"If He is satisfied with you, you need not think anything more about yourself. If He lets you kiss His feet, you won't care about other people's opinions of you, even in heaven. But things will go very differently there from here, for everybody there will be more or less ashamed of himself, and will think worse of himself than of anyone else. If trouble about your past life were to show itself on your face there, they would all run to comfort you, telling you that you must think about yourself as He thinks about you. What He thinks is the rule, because it is the infallible right way. Leave all that to Him who has taken away our sins, and do not trouble yourself anymore about it. Such thoughts will not come to you at all when you have seen the face of Jesus Christ."

"Will He let us tell Him anything we please?"

"He lets you do that now; surely He will not be less our God and our Friend there."

"Oh, I don't mind how soon He takes me now! Only there's that poor child that I've behaved so badly to! I wish I could take him with me. I have no time to make it up to him here."

"You must wait till he comes there. He won't think hardly of you. There's no fear of that."

"What will become of him though? I can't bear the idea of burdening my father with him."

"Your father will be glad to have him, I know. He will feel it a privilege to do something for your sake, and the boy will do him good. If he does not want him, I will take him myself."

"Oh! Thank you—thank you, Sir." A burst of tears followed.

"He has often done me good," I said.

"Who, Sir—my father?"

"No. Your son."

"I don't quite understand what you mean, Sir."

"I mean just what I say. His words and behavior have both roused and comforted my heart again and again."

"To think of your saying that! The poor little innocent! Then it isn't all punishment?"

"If it were *all* punishment, we should perish utterly. He is your punishment—but look in what a lovely loving form your punishment has come, and say whether God has been good to you or not."

"If I had only received my punishment humbly, things would have been very different now. But I do take it—at least, I want to take it—just as He would have me take it. I will bear anything He likes. I suppose I must die?"

"I think He means you to die now. You are ready, I think. You have wanted to die for a long time, but you were not ready before."

"And now I want to live for my boy. But His will be done."

"Amen. There is no better prayer in the universe."

She lay silent. Mary tapped at the chamber door. "If you please, Sir, here's a little girl come to say that Mrs. Tomkins is dying and wants to see you."

"Then I must say good-night to you, Catharine. I will see you tomorrow morning. Think about old Mrs. Tomkins—she's a good old soul. When you find your heart drawn to her in the trouble of death, then lift it up to God for her, that He will please to comfort and support her and make her happier than health, stronger than strength, taking off the old worn garment of her body, and putting upon her the garment of salvation which will be a grand new body, like that the Saviour had when He rose again."

"I will try. I will think about her."

For I thought this would help to prepare her for her own death. In thinking lovingly about others, we think healthily about ourselves. And the things she thought of for the comfort of Mrs. Tomkins would return to comfort her in her own end.

TWENTY-EIGHT

CALM AND STORM

Again and again I was sent for to say farewell to Mrs. Tomkins, and again and again I returned home leaving her asleep, and for the time better. But on a Saturday evening young Tom came to me with the news that Catharine seemed much worse. I sent Tom on before and followed alone.

It was a brilliant starry night—no moon, no clouds, no wind, nothing but stars seeming to lean down toward the earth. It was, indeed, a glorious night—that is, I knew it was though I did not feel it. For the death, which I went to be near, came with a strange sense of separation between me and the nature around me. Here was death and there shone the stars.

I had very little knowledge of death. I had never yet seen a fellow creature—even my father—die. And the thought was oppressive to me. "To think," I said to myself, as I walked over the bridge to the village street, "to think that the one moment the person is here and the next, who shall say where? We know nothing of the region beyond the grave. Not even our risen Lord thought fit to bring back from Hades any news for the human family standing and straining their eyes after their brothers and sisters who have vanished in the dark. Surely it is well, all well, although we know nothing save that our Lord has been there, knows all about it, and does not choose to tell us." And so the oppression passed from me, and I was free.

But little as I knew of death, I was certain, the moment I saw Catharine, that the veil that hid the "silent land" from her had begun to lift. For a moment I almost envied her, that she was so

201

soon to see and know that after which our blindness and ignorance are always wondering and hungering. She could hardly speak. She looked more patient than calm. There was no light in the room but that of the fire. Thomas sat by the hearth with the child on his knee. Gerard's natural mood was so quiet and earnest that the solemnity about him did not oppress him. He looked as if he were present at some religious observance of which he felt more than he understood, and he was no more disquieted at the presence of death than the stars were.

And this was the end of the lovely girl—to leave the fair world still young because a selfish man had seen that she was fair! No time can change the relation of cause and effect. The poison that operates ever so slowly is yet poison and yet slays. And that man was now murdering her, with weapon long-reaching from the past. But no, thank God! This was not the end of her. Though there is woe for that man by whom the offense comes, yet there is provision for the offense. There is One who brings light out of darkness, joy out of sorrow, humility out of wrong. Back to the Father's house we go with the sorrows and sins which we gathered and heaped upon our weary shoulders, and an Elder Brother—different from that angry one who would not receive the prodigal—takes the burden from our shoulders, and leads us into the presence of the Good.

She put out her hand feebly and let it lie in mine. When I sat down by her bedside, she closed her eyes and said nothing. Her father was troubled, though his was a nature that ever sought concealment for its emotion. Gerard clambered up on my knee and laid his little hand upon his mother's. She opened her eyes, looked at the child, shut them again, and tears came out from between the closed lids.

"Has Gerard ever been baptized?" I asked her.

Her lips indicated a no.

"Then I will be his godfather, and that will be a pledge to you that I will never lose sight of him."

She pressed my hand, and the tears came faster.

Believing with all my heart that the dying should remember their dying Lord, and that the "Do this in remembrance of Me" can never be better obeyed, we kneeled. Then Thomas and I and Tom and Mary partook with the dying woman of the signs of that death wherein our Lord gave Himself entirely to us. Upon what that bread and that wine mean—the sacrifice of our Lord—the whole world of humanity hangs, for it is the redemption of men.

After she had received the holy sacrament, she lay still as before. I heard her murmur once, "Lord, I do not deserve it, but I do love Thee," and about two hours after, she quietly breathed her last. We all kneeled, and I thanked aloud the Father of us that He had taken her to Himself. Gerard had fallen fast asleep on his aunt's lap, and was now in his bed. Surely he slept a deeper sleep than his mother's, for had she not awakened even as she fell asleep?

When I came out once more, I knew better what the stars meant. They looked to me now as if they knew all about death, and therefore could not be sad to the eyes of men.

When I returned home my sister told me that Old Rogers had called and seemed concerned not to find me at home. He would have gone to find me, my sister said, had I been anywhere but by a deathbed. He would not leave any message, however, saying he would call in the morning.

I thought it better to go to his house. The stars were still shining as brightly as before, but a strong foreboding of trouble filled my mind, and once more the stars were far away. I could give no reason for my sudden fearfulness save this—that as I went to Catharine's house I had passed Jane Rogers on her way to her father's and, having just greeted her, had gone on. But, as it came back to me, she had looked at me strangely, and now her father had been to seek me. It must have something to do with Miss Oldcastle.

But it was past eleven when I came to the dark, still cottage, and I could not bring myself to rouse the weary man from his bed. So I turned and lingered by the old mill, and pondered on the profusion of strength that rushed past the wheel away to the great sea, doing nothing. "Nature," I thought, "does not demand that power should always be force. Power itself must repose. He that believes shall not make haste, says the Bible. But power needs strength to be still. Is my faith not strong enough to be still?" I looked up to the heavens once more, and the quietness of the stars seemed to reproach me. "We are safe up here," they seemed to say. "We shine, fearless and confident. We cannot fall out of His safety. Lift up your eyes on high and behold! Who hath created these things, that bringeth out our host by number? He calleth us all by name."

The night was very still and there was, I thought, no one awake within miles of me. The stars seemed to shine into me the divine reproach of those glorious words. "O my God!" I cried, and fell to my knees by the mill door.

I tried to say more to Him—but what that was ought not, cannot, be repeated to another.

When I opened my eyes, I saw the door of the mill was open too, and there in the door, his white head glimmering, stood Old Rogers, with a look on his face as if he had just come down from the mount. I started to my feet with that strange feeling of something like shame that seizes one at the very thought of other eyes than those of the Father. The old man came forward and bowed his head, but would have passed me without speech. I could not bear to part with him thus.

"Won't you speak to me, Old Rogers?" I said.

He turned at once with evident pleasure. "I beg your pardon, Sir. I was ashamed of having intruded on you, and I thought you would rather be left alone. I thought—I thought," hesitated the old man, "that you might like to go into the old mill, for the night's cold out o'doors."

"Thank you, Rogers. I won't now. I thought you had been in bed. How do you come to be out so late?"

"You see, Sir, when I'm in any trouble, it's no use to go to bed. I can't sleep. I only keep the old 'oman wakin'. And the key o' the mill allus hangin' at the back o' my door, and knowin' it to be a good place to—to—shut the door in, I came out as soon as she was asleep. I little thought to see you, Sir."

"I came to find you, not thinking how the time went. Catharine Weir is gone home."

"Poor woman. And perhaps something will come out now that will help us."

"I do not quite understand you," I said, with hesitation.

But Rogers made no reply.

"I am sorry to hear you are in trouble tonight. Can I help you?" I resumed.

"If you can help yourself, Sir, you can help me. But I have no right to say so. Only, if a pair of old eyes be not blind, a man may pray to God about anything he sees. I was prayin' hard about you in there, Sir, while you was on your knees o' the other side o' the door."

I could partly guess what the old man meant, and I could not ask him for further explanation.

"What did you want to see me about?" I inquired.

He hesitated for a moment.

"I dare say it was very foolish of me, Sir. But I just wanted to tell you that our Jane was down here from the Hall this afternoon—"

"I passed her on the bridge. Is she quite well?"

"Yes, yes, Sir. You know that's not the point."

The old man's tone seemed to reprove me for vain words, and I held my peace.

"The captain's there again."

An icy spear seemed to pass through my heart. I could make no reply, but turned away from the old man without a word. He made no attempt to detain me.

The first I remember after that, I was fighting with the wind of a gathering storm, out upon the common where I had dealt so severely with her who had this very night gone to a waveless sea. Is it the sea of death? No. The sea of life—a life too keen, too refined for our senses to know it and therefore we call it death, because we cannot lay hold upon it.

Next I found myself standing at the iron gate of Oldcastle Hall. I knew that I was there only when first I stood in the shelter of one of those great pillars and the monster on its top. I pushed the gate open and entered. The wind was roaring in the trees as I think I have never heard it roar since—the hail clashed upon the bare branches and twigs and mingled an unearthly hiss with the roar. The house stood like a tomb—dark, silent, without one dim light to show that sleep and not death ruled within. I passed round to the other side, but dared not stop to look up at the back of the house. I went on to the staircase in the rock and, by its rude and dangerous steps, descended to the little grove below. Here the wind roared overhead, yet could not reach me. But my heart was a well in which a storm boiled and raged, and all that was over my head was peace itself compared to what I felt. I sat down at the foot of a tree where I had first seen Miss Oldcastle reading, and then I looked up to the house. Yes, there was a light there! It must be in her window. She then could not rest anymore than I. Sleep was driven from her eyes because she must wed the man she would not, while sleep was driven from mine because I could not marry the woman I would. But was that all of it? Gladly would I have given her up forever to redeem her from such a bondage. "But it would be to marry another someday," suggested the tormentor within. And then the storm, which had a little abated, broke out afresh in my soul. But before I rose from her seat I was ready even for that—if only I might deliver her. Glancing once more at the dull light in her window, I rose and almost felt my way to the stair, and climbed again into the storm.

But I was quieter now, and able to go home. It must have been nearly morning when I reached my house.

When I fell asleep I dreamed I was again in the old quarry staring into the deep well. Mrs. Oldcastle was murdering her daughter in the house above, while I was spellbound where I should see her body float into the well from the subterranean passage. But as a white hand and arm appeared in the water below me, sorrow and pity more than horror broke the bonds of sleep, and I awoke to less trouble than that of my dreams, only because that which I feared had not yet come.

TWENTY-NINE

A SERMON TO MYSELF

Such a Sabbath morn! The day seemed all wan and weeping and gray with care. The wind dashed itself against the casement, laden with soft heavy sleet. The first thing I knew when I awoke was the raving of that wind. I could lie in bed not a moment longer. But how was I to do the work of my office? When a man's duty looks like an enemy, dragging him into the dark mountains, he has no less to go with it than when, like a friend with loving face, it offers to lead him along green pastures by the river's side. I had little power over my feelings. I could not prevent my mind from mirroring the nature around me, but I could address myself to the work I had to do. "My God!" was all the prayer I could pray before breakfast. But He knew what lay behind the utterance.

But how was I to preach? The subject on which I was pondering when young Weir came to me had retreated into the far past, on the far side of that black night. To speak upon that would have been vain, for I had nothing to say on the matter now. I could not even recall what I had thought and felt. I felt ashamed of yielding to personal trouble when the truths of God were all about me, although I could not feel them. Might not some hungry soul go away without being satisfied because I was faint and downhearted?

Then I remembered a sermon I had once preached upon the words of St. Paul: "Thou therefore which teachest another, teachest thou not thyself?" And I said to myself, "Might I not try the other way now, and preach to myself? In teaching myself, might I not teach others?" All this passed through my mind as I

207

sat in my study after breakfast, within an hour of churchtime.

I took my Bible, read and thought, and found myself in my vestry not quite unwilling to read the prayers and speak to my people. There were very few present. The day was violently stormy and, to my relief, the Hall pew was empty. Instead of finding myself a mere minister to the prayers of others, I found as I read that my heart went out in crying to God for the divine presence of His Spirit. And if I thought more of myself in my prayers than was well, yet as soon as I was converted, would I not strengthen my brethren? And the sermon I preached was that which the stars had preached to me and thereby driven me to my knees. I took for my text, "The glory of the Lord shall be revealed."

I preached to myself that the power of God is put side by side with the weakness of men—not that He may glory over His feeble children, but that He may say, "You will never be strong but with *My* strength, and that you can get only by trusting in Me. Look how strong I am. You wither like the grass. Do not fear; let the grass wither. Lay hold of My Word, and that will be life in you that the withering wind cannot reach. I am coming with My strong hand to do My work—to feed My flock like a shepherd, to gather the lambs with My arm and carry them in My bosom, and to gently lead those who are with young. I come to you with help. Look at the stars I have made—I know every one of them. Not one goes wrong, because I keep them right. I give *power* to the *faint*, and plenty of strength to them that have no might."

"Thus," I went on to say, "God brings His strength to destroy our weakness by making us strong. This is a God indeed! Shall we not trust Him?" And then I tried to show that it is in the commonest troubles of life, as well as in spiritual fears and perplexities, that we are to trust in God. For God made the outside as well as the inside, and when outside things such as pain or difficulties in money, are referred to God and His will, they too become spiritual affairs; for nothing in the world can appear commonplace or unclean to the man who sees God in everything.

All the time I was speaking, the rain, mingled with sleet, was dashing against the windows. The wind was howling over the graves all about, but the dead were not troubled by the storm. Over my head a sparrow flitted from beam to beam, taking refuge in the church till the storm should cease. "This," I said aloud, "is what the Church is for: as the sparrow finds there is a house from the storm, so the human heart escapes thither to hear the still small voice of God, when its faith is too weak to find Him in the storm." A dim watery gleam fell on the chancel floor, and the comfort of the sun awoke in my heart. I received that pale sunray of hope as comfort for the race, and for me as one of the family—even as the rainbow that was set in the cloud—a promise of light for them that sit in darkness.

I descended from the pulpit comforted by the sermon I had preached to myself. But I felt justified in telling my people that in consequence of the continued storm (for there had been no more sunshine than just that watery gleam), there would be no service in the afternoon.

The people were very slow in dispersing. There was so much putting on of clogs, gathering up of skirts over the head, and expanding of umbrellas (although worse than useless in the violent wind), that the porches were crowded. I lingered with these.

"I am sorry you will have such a wet walk home," I said to the wife of the shoemaker, a sweet little wizened creature with more wrinkles than hair.

"It's very good of you to let us off this afternoon, Sir. Not as I minds the wet—it finds out the holes in people's shoes, and gets my husband more work." Nor was there anything necessarily selfish in her response, for if there are holes in people's shoes, the sooner they are found out the better.

Mr. Stoddart, whose love for the old organ had been stronger than his dislike to the storm, approached me.

"I never saw you down in the church before, Mr. Stoddart," I said, "though I have heard you often enough. You use your own private door always."

"I thought to go that way now, but there came such a fierce burst of wind and rain in my face that my courage failed me, and I turned back, like the sparrow, for refuge."

"A thought strikes me," I said. "Come home with me and have some lunch, and then we will go together to see some of my poor people. I have often wished to ask you."

His face fell. "It is such a day!" he answered, but not positively refusing.

"So it was when you set out this morning," I returned, "but you would not deprive us of the aid of your music for the sake of a charge of wind and a rattle of raindrops."

"But I shan't be of any use. You are going, and that is enough."

"I beg your pardon. Your very presence will be of use. Nothing yet given him or done for him by his fellow ever did any man so much good as the recognition of the brotherhood by the common signs of friendship and sympathy. The best good of given money depends on the degree to which it is the sign of that friendship and sympathy. Our Lord did not make little of visiting: 'I was sick, and ye visited Me.' 'Inasmuch as ye did it not to one of the least of these, ye did it not to Me.' "

"But I cannot pretend to feel any interest. Why then should I go?"

"To please me, your friend. That is a good human reason. You need not say a word—you must not pretend anything. Go as my companion, not as their visitor. Will you come?"

"I suppose I must."

"Thank you. You will help me, for I seldom have a companion."

So, when the storm-fit had abated for the moment, we hurried to the vicarage, had a good though hasty lunch, and set out for the village. The rain was worse than ever. There was no sleet, and the wind was not cold, but the windows of heaven were opened.

"Don't you find some pleasure in fighting the wind?" I said.

"I have no doubt I should," answered Mr. Stoddart, "if I thought I were going to do any good. But, to tell the truth, I would rather be by my own fire, with my folio Dante on the reading desk."

"Well, I would rather help the poorest woman in creation than contemplate the sufferings of the greatest and wickedest."

"There are two things you forget," returned Mr. Stoddart. "First, that the works of Dante are not nearly occupied with the sufferings of the wicked. And next, that what I have complained of in this expedition—a wild-goose chase, were it not your doing—is that I am not going to help anybody."

"You would have the best of the argument entirely," I replied, "if your expectation were correct."

We had come within a few yards of the Tomkins' cottage, which lay low down toward the river, and I saw that the water was at the threshold. I turned to Mr. Stoddart who, to do him justice, had not yet grumbled in the least.

"Perhaps you had better go home, after all," I said, "for you must wade into Tomkins' if you go at all. Poor old man! What can he be doing, with his wife dying and the river in his house?"

210

"You have constituted yourself my superior officer, Mr. Walton. I never turned my back on my leader yet, though I confess I wish I could see the enemy a little clearer."

"There is the enemy," I said, pointing to the water and walking into it.

Mr. Stoddart followed me without a moment's hesitation.

When I opened the door, I saw a small stream of water running straight to the fire on the hearth, which it had already drowned. The old man was sitting by his wife's bedside. Life seemed rapidly going from the old woman. She lay breathing very hard.

"Oh, Sir," said the old man, as he rose, almost crying, "you've come at last!"

"Did you send for me?" I asked.

"No, Sir. I had nobody to send. Leastways I asked the Lord if He wouldn't fetch you. I been prayin' hard for you for the last hour. I couldn't leave her to come for you. And I do believe the wind 'ud ha' blown me off my two old legs."

"Well, I am come, you see. I would have come sooner, but I had no idea you would be flooded."

"It's not that I mind, Sir, though it *is* cold sin' the fire went out. But she *is* goin' now, Sir. She ha'n't spoken a word this two hours and more, and her breathin's worse and worse. She don't know me now, Sir."

A moan of protestation came from the dying woman.

"She does know you, and loves you too, Tomkins," I said. "And you'll both know each other better by and by."

The old woman made a feeble motion with her hand. I took it in mine. It was cold and deathlike. The rain was falling in large slow drops from the roof onto the bedclothes. But she would be beyond the reach of all storms before long, and it did not matter much.

"If you can find a basin or plate, Mr. Stoddart, put it to catch the drop here," I said, for I wanted to give him the first chance of being useful.

"There's one in the press there," said the old man, rising feebly.

"Keep your seat," said Mr. Stoddart. "I'll get it." And he got a basin from the cupboard and put it on the bed to catch the drop.

The old woman held my hand in hers, but by its motion I knew she wanted something, and I made her husband take hold of her other hand. This seemed to content her. So I went and whispered to Mr. Stoddart, who stood looking on, "You heard me say I would visit some of my sick people this afternoon. You must go instead of me and tell them that I cannot come, because old Mrs. Tomkins is dying—but I will see them soon."

He seemed rather relieved at the commission. I gave him the necessary directions to find the cottages, and he left me. He was one of those men who make excellent front-line men, but are quite unfit for officers. He did what he was told without flinching, but he had to be told.

(This was the beginning of a relation between Mr. Stoddart and the poor of the parish, a very slight one, indeed, for it consisted only in his knowing two or three of them, so as to ask after their health when he met them, and give them an occasional half crown. But it led to better things. I once came upon him in the avenue, standing in dismay over the fragments of a jug of soup which he had dropped. "What am I to do?" he said. "Poor Jones expects his soup today."

"Why, go back and get some more."

"But what will cook say?" He was more afraid of the cook than of a squadron of cavalry.

"Never mind the cook. Tell her you must have some more as soon as it can be got ready." He stood uncertain for a moment, and then his face brightened.

"I will tell her I want my soup. And I'll get out through the greenhouse and carry it to Jones."

"Very well," I said, "that will do capitally." And I went on, without determining whether the gift of his own soup arose more from love of Jones or fear of the cook.)

I resumed my seat by the bedside, where the old woman was again moaning. As soon as I took her hand she ceased, and so I sat till it began to grow dark.

"Are you there, Sir?" she would murmur.

"Yes, I am here. I have your hand."

"I can't feel you, Sir."

"But you can hear me, and you can hear God's voice in your heart. I am here, though you can't feel me; and God is here, though you can't see Him."

"Are you there, Tomkins?"

"Yes, my woman, I'm here," he answered, "but I wish I was there instead, wheresomever it be you're goin', old girl."

And all that I could hear of her answer was, "bym-by—bym-by."

Why should I linger over the deathbed of an illiterate woman, old and plain? Here was a woman with a heart like my own, who needed the same salvation I needed, to whom the love of God was the one blessed thing, who was passing through the same dark passage that the Lord had passed through before her, and that I had to pass through after her. And now her old age and plainness were about to vanish, and all that had made her youth attractive to Tomkins was about to return to her, only rendered tenfold more beautiful.

At length, after a long silence, the peculiar sounds of obstructed breathing indicated the end at hand. The jaw fell, and the eyes were fixed. The old man closed the mouth and the eyes of his old companion, weeping like a child, and I prayed aloud, giving thanks to God for taking her to Himself. It went to my heart to leave the old man alone with the dead, but it was better to let him be alone for a while.

I went to Old Rogers and asked him what was to be done.

"I'll go and bring him home, Sir, directly. He can't be left there."

"But how can you bring him in such a night?"

"Would your mare go with a cart, do you think?"

"Quite quietly. She brought a load of gravel from the common a few days ago. But where's a cart? I haven't got one."

"There's one at Weir's to be repaired, Sir. It wouldn't be stealing to borrow it."

How he managed with Tomkins I do not know. He only said afterward that he could hardly get the old man away from the body. When I went in the next day, I found Tomkins sitting disconsolate but comfortable in the easy chair by the fire. Mrs. Rogers was bustling about cheerily. The storm had died in the night, and the sun was shining. It was the first of the spring weather. The whole country was gleaming with water, which soon would sink away and leave the grass the thicker for its rising.

THIRTY

A COUNCIL OF FRIENDS

I was in danger of a return of my last attack. I had been sitting for hours in wet clothes, with my boots full of water, and now I had to suffer for it. But, as I was not to blame and had had no choice whether I should be wet or dry, I felt no depression at the prospect of illness. Indeed, I was too depressed from other causes to care much. I was unable to leave my bed, and knew that Captain Everard was at the Hall, and knew nothing besides. No voice reached me from that quarter any more than if Oldcastle Hall had been beyond the grave.

One pleasant thing happened. My sister came into my room and said that Miss Crowther had called and wanted to see me.

"Which Miss Crowther is it?" I asked.

"The little lady that looks like a bird, and chirps when she talks."

"You told her I had a bad cold, did you not?"

"Oh, yes. But she says if it is only a cold, it will do you no harm to see her."

"But you told her I was in bed, didn't you?"

"Of course. But it makes no difference. She says she's used to seeing sick folk in bed, and if you don't mind seeing her, she doesn't mind seeing you."

"Well, I suppose I must see her," I said.

So my sister made me a little tidier, and introduced Miss Crowther.

"O Dear Mr. Walton, I am so sorry! But you're not very ill, are you?"

"I hope not, Miss Jemima. Indeed, I think I will get off easier than I expected."

"I am glad of that. Now listen to me. I won't keep you, and it is a matter of some importance. I hear that one of your people is dead, and has left a little boy behind her. Now I have been wanting for a long time to adopt a child—"

"But," I interrupted her, "what would Miss Hester say?"

"My sister is not so very dreadful as perhaps you think her, Mr. Walton. Besides, when I do want my own way—which is not often, for there are not so many things worth insisting upon—I always have it. I stand upon my right of primogeniture. Well, I think I know something this child's father. I am sorry to say I don't know much good of him, and that's the worst of the boy. Still—"

"The boy is an uncommonly sweet and lovable child, whoever was his father," I interposed.

"Then I am the more determined to adopt him. What friends has he?"

"He has a grandfather, and an uncle and aunt, and will have a godfather—me—in a few days, I hope."

"There will be no opposition on the part of the relatives, I presume?"

"I am not so sure of that. I fear I shall object for one, Miss Jemima."

"I didn't expect that of you, Mr. Walton, I must say." And there was a tremor in the old lady's voice more of disappointment and hurt than of anger.

"I will think it over, though, and talk about it to his grandfather, and we shall find out what's best. You must not think I should not like you to have him."

"Thank you, Mr. Walton. Then I won't stay longer now. But I warn you I will call again very soon, if you don't come to see me. Good morning."

And the dear old lady left me rather hurriedly, turning at the door, however, to add, "Mind, I've set my heart upon having the boy, Mr. Walton. I've seen him often."

What would have made her take such a fancy to the boy? Of course, I talked the matter over with Thomas Weir but, as I had suspected, I found that he was now unwilling to part with the boy.

At the very time Miss Jemima was with me (as I found out some years later), Old Rogers turned into Thomas Weir's workshop and said, "Don't you think, Mr. Weir, there's summat the matter wi' Parson?"

"Overworked," returned Weir. "He's lost two, ye see, and had to see them both safe over within the same day. He's got a bad cold besides. Have ye heard of him today?"

"Yes, he's badly, and in bed. But that's not what I mean. There's summat on his mind," said Old Rogers.

"Well, I don't think it's for you or me to meddle with Parson's mind," returned Weir.

"I'm not so sure o' that," persisted Rogers. "But if I had thought, Mr. Weir, as how you would be ready to take me up short for mentionin' of the thing, I wouldn't ha' opened my mouth to you about Parson—leastways about his in'ards. I means this— as how Parson's in love. There, that's paid out."

"Suppose he was, I don't see yet what business that is of yours or mine either."

"Well, I do. I'd go to Davie Jones for that man."

"But what can we do?" returned Weir. Perhaps he was less inclined to listen, seeing that he was busy with a coffin for his daughter.

"I tell you what, Mr. Weir, this here's a serious business, and it seems to me it's not shipshape o' you to go on with that plane o' yours when we're talkin' about Parson."

"Well, Old Rogers, I meant no offense. Here goes. Now, what have you to say? Though if it's offense to Parson you're speakin' of, I know, if I were Parson, who I'd think was takin' the greatest liberty, me wi' my plane, or you wi' your fancies."

"Belay there and hearken." So Old Rogers went into as many particulars as he thought fit to prove his suspicion.

"Supposing all you say, Old Rogers," remarked Thomas, "I don't yet see what we've got to do with it. Parson ought to know best what he's about."

"But my daughter tells me," said Rogers, "that Miss Oldcastle has no mind to marry Captain Everard, and she thinks if parson would only speak out he might have a chance."

Weir made no reply and was silent so long, with his head bent, that Rogers grew impatient. "Well, Man, ha' you nothing to say now—not for your best friend—on earth, I mean—and that's Parson? It may seem a small matter to you, but it's no small matter to Parson."

"Small to me!" said Weir, and, taking up his tool—a constant recourse with him when agitated—he began to plane furiously.

Old Rogers now saw that there was more in it than he had thought, and he held his peace and waited. After a minute or two of fierce activity, Thomas lifted up a face more white than the deal-board he was planing, and said, "You should have come to the point a little sooner, Old Rogers."

He then laid down his plane and went out of the workshop, leaving Rogers standing there in bewilderment. But he was not gone many minutes. He returned with a letter in his hand. "There," he said, giving it to Rogers.

"I can't read hand o' write," returned Rogers. "I ha' enough ado with straight-foret print. But I'll take it to Parson."

"On no account," returned Thomas, emphatically. "That's not what I gave it you for. Neither you nor Parson has any right to read that letter. Can Jane read writing?"

"I don't know as she can. What makes lasses take to writin' is when their young man's over the seas, not in the mill over the brook."

"I'll be back in a minute," said Thomas, and taking the letter from Rogers' hand, he left the shop again.

He returned once more with the letter sealed up in an envelope and addressed to Miss Oldcastle.

"Now you tell your Jane to give that to Miss Oldcastle from me—mind, from me—and she must give it into her own hands, and let no one else see it. And I must have it again. Mind you tell Jane all that, Old Rogers. Can you trust her not to go talking about it?"

"I think I can. I ought to, anyhow. But she can't know anythink in the letter now, Mr. Weir."

"I know that, but Marshmallows is a talkin' place, and poor Kate ain't right out o' hearin' yet. You'll come and see her buried tomorrow, won't ye, Old Rogers?"

"I will, Thomas. You've had a troubled life but, thank God, the sun came out a bit before she died."

"That's true, Old Rogers. It's all right, I do think, though I grumbled long and sore. But Jane mustn't speak of that letter."

"No, that she shan't."

"I'll tell you some day what's in it, but I can't bear to talk about it yet." And so they parted.

I was too unwell either to bury my dead or to comfort my living the next Sunday. I got help from Addicehead, however, and the dead were laid aside in the ancient wardrobe of the tomb. They were both buried by my vestry door, Catharine in the grave of her mother (where I had found young Tom lying), and old Mrs. Tomkins on the other side of the path. On Sunday Rogers gave his daughter the letter, and she carried it to the Hall.

That night when her bell rang, Jane went up and found Miss Oldcastle so pale and haggard that she was frightened. She had thrown herself back on the couch, with her hands lying by her sides, as if she cared for nothing in this world or out of it. But when Jane entered, she started and sat up, and tried to look like herself.

"Here is a letter," said Jane, "that Mr. Weir the carpenter sent to you, Miss."

"What is it about, Jane?" she asked, listlessly.

Then a sudden flash broke from her eyes, and she held out her hand eagerly to take it. She opened it and read it with changing color, but when she had finished it her cheeks were crimson, and her eyes glowing like fire.

"The wretch!" she said, and threw the letter into the middle of the floor. Jane stooped to pick it up, but had hardly raised herself when the door opened, and in came Mrs. Oldcastle. The moment she saw her mother, Ethelwyn rose, and, advancing to meet her, said, "Mother, I will *not* marry that man. You may do what you please with me, but I *will not*."

"Heighho!" exclaimed Mrs. Oldcastle, with spread nostrils, and turning suddenly upon Jane, snatched the letter out of her hand.

She opened and read it, her face getting more still and stony as she read. Miss Oldcastle stood and looked at her mother with cheeks now pale, but with eyes still flashing. Her mother finished the letter and walked swiftly to the fire, tearing the letter as she went. She thrust it between the bars, pushing it in fiercely with the poker and muttering, "A vile forgery of those wretches! As if he would ever have looked upon one of *their* women! A low conspiracy to get money from a gentleman!"

And for the first time since she went to the Hall, Jane said, there was color in that dead white face. She turned once more upon Jane and screamed, "You leave the house—*this instant!*"

And she came from the fire toward Jane, whose absolute fear drove her from the room before she knew what she was about. The locking of the door behind her let her know that she had abandoned her young mistress, but it was too late. She lingered by the door and listened, but beyond the occasional hoarse tone of suppressed rage, she heard nothing. Then the lock suddenly turned, and she was surprised by Mrs. Oldcastle, for if she was not listening, she at least was where she had no right to be.

Opposite Miss Oldcastle's bedroom was another room, seldom used, the door of which was now standing open. Mrs. Oldcastle gave Jane a violent push into this room and shut the door and locked it. Jane examined the door to see if she could escape, but she found the lock at least as strong as the door. Being a sensible girl and self-possessed, as her parents' child ought to be, she made no noise, but waited patiently through the night. At length, hearing a step in the passage, she tapped gently at the door, and called, "Who's there?"

The cook's voice answered her.

"Let me out," said Jane. "The door's locked."

The cook promised to get her out, but found no key. Meantime, all she could do was hand Jane a loaf of bread on a stick from the next window. Finally the door was unlocked, and she was left at liberty. Unable to find her young mistress, she packed her box and escaped to her father. As soon as she had told him her story, he came straight to me.

But Judy found me first.

THIRTY-ONE

THE NEXT THING

Judy hurriedly opened my study door and entered. She looked about the room with a quick glance to see that we were alone, then caught my hand in both of hers, and burst out crying.

"Why, Judy," I said, "what is the matter?"

But the sobs would not allow her to answer. I was frightened and so stood silent, my chest feeling like an empty tomb waiting for death to fill it. With a strong effort, she checked the succession of her sobs and spoke, "They are killing Auntie! She looks like a ghost already."

"Tell me, Judy, what *can* I do for her?"

"You must find out, Mr. Walton. If you loved her as much as I do, you would find out what to do."

"But she will not let me do anything for her."

"Yes, she will. She says you promised to help her someday."

"Did she send you, then?"

"Oh, you exact people! You must have everything square and in print before you move. If it had been me now, wouldn't I have been off like a shot! Do get your hat, Mr. Walton."

"Then I will go at once."

In a moment we were in the open air. It was a still night, and a pale half-moon hung in the sky. I offered Judy my arm, but she took my hand, and we walked on through the village and out upon the road.

"Now, Judy," I said at last, "tell me what they are doing to your aunt."

"I don't know what they are doing. But I am sure she will die

She is as white as a sheet and will not leave her room. Grannie must have frightened her dreadfully. Everybody is frightened at her but me, and I begin to be frightened too. And what will become of Auntie then?"

"But what can her mother do to her?"

"I don't know. I think it is her determination to have her own way that makes Auntie afraid she will get it somehow—and she says now she will rather die than marry Captain Everard. No one is allowed to wait on her but Sarah, and what has become of Jane I don't know. I haven't seen her all day, and the servants are whispering together more than usual. Auntie won't eat what Sarah brings her, I am sure, else I should almost fancy she was starving herself to death to keep clear of that Captain Everard."

"Is he still at the Hall?"

"Yes. But I don't think it is altogether his fault. Grannie won't let him go. I don't believe he knows how determined Auntie is not to marry him. To be sure, though Grannie never lets her have more than five shillings at a time, she will be worth something when she is married."

"Nothing can make her worth more than she is, Judy," I said, perhaps with some discontent in my tone.

"That's as you and I think, Mr. Walton, not as Grannie and the captain think at all. I dare say he would not care much more than Grannie whether she was willing or not, so long as she married him."

"But, Judy, we must have some plan laid before we reach the Hall, else my coming will be of no use."

"Of course. I know how much I can do, and you must arrange the rest with her. Auntie and the captain will be at dinner. I will take you to the little room upstairs, the octagon just under Auntie's room. I will leave you there, and tell Auntie that you want to see her."

"But, Judy—"

"Don't you want to see her, Mr. Walton?"

"Yes, I do, more than you can think."

"Then I will tell her so."

"But will she come to me?"

"I don't know. We have to find that out."

"Very well. I leave myself in your hands."

I was now perfectly collected. Judy and I scarcely spoke from the moment we entered the gate till I found myself at a side door.

Judy went in and opened it and led me along a passage and up a stair into the little drawing room. There was no light. She led me to a seat at the farther end and, opening a door beside me, left me in the dark.

There I sat so long that I fell into a fit of musing. Castle after castle I built up; castle after castle fell to pieces in my hands. Suddenly from out of the dark a hand settled on my arm. I looked up and could just see the whiteness of Ethelwyn's face. She said in a broken half-whisper, "Will you save me, Mr. Walton?"

I reached for her hand and held it. All my trembling was gone in a moment, and the suppressed feelings of many months rushed to my lips. What I said I do not know, but I know that I told her I loved her. And she did not draw her hand from mine, even as I said, "If all I am, all I have will save you—"

"But I am saved already," she interposed, "if you love me, for I love you."

And for some moments there were no words to speak. Holding her hand, I was conscious only of God and her. At last I said, "There is no time now but for action. You should go with me at once. Will you come home to my sister? Or I will take you wherever you please."

"I will go with you anywhere you think best. Only take me away."

"Put on your bonnet, then, and a warm cloak, and we will settle it as we go."

She had scarcely left the room when Mrs. Oldcastle came to the door. "Sarah, bring candles," she said, "and tell Captain Everard to come to the octagon room." Then she continued to herself, "Where can that little Judy be? The child gets more and more troublesome, I do think. I must take her in hand."

How was I to let her know that I was there? To announce yourself to a lady by a voice out of the darkness, or to wait for her to discover you where she thought she was quite alone—neither is a pleasant way of presenting yourself. But I was helped out once more by that blessed little Judy.

"Here I am, Grannie," she said. "But I won't be taken in hand by you or anyone else. I tell you that, so mind. And Mr. Walton is here too, and Aunt Ethelwyn is going with him."

"What do you mean, you silly child?"

"I mean what I say," and "Miss Judy speaks the truth," fell together from her lips to mine.

"Mr. Walton," began Mrs. Oldcastle, indignantly, "it is scarcely like a gentleman to come where you are not wanted—"

Here Judy interrupted her. "I beg your pardon, Grannie, Mr. Walton was wanted—very much wanted. I fetched him."

But Mrs. Oldcastle went on, unheeding, "—and to be sitting in my room in the dark too!"

"That couldn't be helped, Grannie. Here comes Sarah with candles."

"Sarah," said Mrs. Oldcastle, "ask Captain Everard to be kind enough to step this way."

"Yes, Ma'am," answered Sarah, with an untranslatable look at me as she set down the candles.

We could now see each other. Knowing words to be but idle breath, I did not complicate matters by speech, but stood silent, regarding Mrs. Oldcastle. She did not flinch, but returned my look with one both haughty and contemptuous. In a few moments Captain Everard entered, bowed slightly, and looked to Mrs. Oldcastle as if for an explanation, whereupon she spoke, but to me. "Mr. Walton," she said, "will you explain to Captain Everard to what we owe the *unexpected* pleasure of a visit from you?"

"Captain Everard has no claim to any explanation from me. To you, Mrs. Oldcastle, I would have answered, had you asked me, that I was waiting for Miss Oldcastle."

"Pray inform Miss Oldcastle, Judy, that Mr. Walton insists upon seeing her at once."

"That is quite unnecessary. Miss Oldcastle will be here presently," I said.

Mrs. Oldcastle, livid with wrath, walked toward the door beside me. I stepped between her and it, and said, "Pardon me, Mrs. Oldcastle. That is the way to Miss Oldcastle's room. I am here to protect her."

Without saying a word, she turned and looked at Captain Everard. He advanced with a long stride of determination. But then the door behind me opened, and Miss Oldcastle appeared in her bonnet and shawl, carrying a small bag in her hand. She put her hand on my arm and stood fronting the enemy with me. Judy was on my right, her eyes flashing and her cheeks red, prepared to do battle.

"Ethelwyn, go to your room instantly, I *command* you," said her mother, and she approached to remove her hand from my arm. I put my other arm between her and her daughter.

"No, Mrs. Oldcastle," I said, "you have lost all a mother's rights by ceasing to behave like a mother. Miss Oldcastle will never more do anything in obedience to your commands, whatever she may do in compliance with your wishes."

"Allow me to remark," said Captain Everard, with attempted nonchalance, "that that is strange doctrine for your cloth."

"So much the worse for my cloth, then," I answered, "and the better for yours, if it leads you to act more honorably."

He smiled haughtily, and gave a look of dramatic appeal to Mrs. Oldcastle.

"At least," said that lady, "do not disgrace yourself, Ethelwyn, by leaving this house in this unaccountable manner at night and on foot. If you *will* leave the protection of your mother's roof, wait at least till tomorrow."

"I would rather spend the night in the open air than pass another night under your roof, Mother. You have been a strange mother to me—and to Dorothy too!"

"At least do not put your character in question by going in this unmaidenly fashion. People will talk to your prejudice—and Mr. Walton's too."

Ethelwyn smiled. She was now as collected as I was, seeming to have cast off all her weakness. She knew her mother too well to be caught by the change in her tone. She answered nothing, but only looked at me. So I said, "They will hardly have time to do so, I trust, before it will be out of their power. It rests with Miss Oldcastle herself to say when that shall be."

As if she had never suspected that such was the result of her scheming, Mrs. Oldcastle's demeanor changed utterly. She made a spring at her daughter and seized her by her arm.

"Then I forbid it," she screamed, "and I *will* be obeyed. I stand on my rights. Go to your room, you minx."

"There is no law, human or divine, to prevent her from marrying whom she will," I said. "How old are you, Ethelwyn?"

"Twenty-seven," answered Miss Oldcastle.

"Is it possible you can be so foolish, Mrs. Oldcastle, as to think you have any hold on your daughter's freedom? Let her go."

But she kept her grasp.

"You hurt me, Mother," said Miss Oldcastle.

"Hurt you! You smooth-faced hypocrite, I will hurt you, then!"

But I took Mrs. Oldcastle's arm in my hand, and she let go her hold.

"How dare you touch a woman!" she said.

"Because she has so far ceased to be a woman as to torture her own daughter."

Here Captain Everard stepped forward, saying, "The riot act ought to be read, I think. It is time for the military to interfere."

"Well put, Captain Everard," I said. "Our side will disperse if you will only leave room for us to go."

"Possibly *I* may have something to say in the matter."

"Say on."

"This lady has jilted me."

"Have you, Ethelwyn?"

"I have not."

"Then, Captain Everard, you lie."

"You dare to tell me so?" And he strode a pace nearer.

"It needs no daring. I know you too well, and so does another who trusted you and found you as false as hell."

"You presume on your cloth, but—" he said, lifting his hand.

"You may strike me, presuming on my cloth," I answered, "and I will not return your blow. Insult me as you will, and I will bear it. Call me coward, and I will say nothing. But lay one hand on me to prevent me from doing my duty, and I will knock you down—or find you more of a man than I take you for."

Conscience—or something not so good—made a coward of him, and he turned on his heel. "I really am not sufficiently interested in the affair to oppose you. You may take the girl. Both your cloth and the presence of ladies protect your insolence. I do not like brawling where one cannot fight. You shall hear from me before long, Mr. Walton."

"No, Captain Everard, I shall not hear from you. I know that of you which, even on the code of the duelist, would justify any gentleman in refusing to meet you. Stand out of my way!"

I advanced with Miss Oldcastle on my arm, and he drew back. As we reached the door, Judy bounded after us, threw her arms round her aunt's neck, then round mine, kissing us both, and returned to her place on the sofa. Mrs. Oldcastle gave a scream and sunk fainting on a chair—a last effort to detain her daughter. Miss Oldcastle would have returned, but I would not permit her.

"No," I said, "she will be better without you. Judy, ring the bell for Sarah."

"How dare you give orders in my house?" exclaimed Mrs. Oldcastle, sitting bolt upright in the chair and shaking her fist at us.

Then assuming the heroic, she added, "From this moment she is no daughter of mine. Nor can you touch one farthing of her money, Sir. You have married a beggar after all, and that you'll both know before long."

"Thy money perish with thee!" I said, and repented the moment I had said it. It sounded like an imprecation, and I had no correspondent feeling—after all, she was the mother of my Ethelwyn. But the allusion to money made me so indignant that the words burst from me before I could consider their import.

The cool wind greeted us like the breath of God as we left the house and closed the door behind us. The moon was shining alone in the midst of a lake of blue. We had not gone far from the house when Miss Oldcastle began to tremble violently. When we reached the vicarage, I gave her in charge to my sister while I went for Dr. Duncan.

THIRTY-TWO

OLD ROGERS' THANKSGIVING

I found Dr. Duncan seated at his dinner, which he left immediately when he heard that Miss Oldcastle needed his help. I told him as we went what had befallen at the Hall. He listened with the interest of a boy reading a romance, asking twenty questions about the particulars. Then he shook me warmly by the hand, saying, "You have fairly won her, Walton, and I am glad of it. She is well worth all you must have suffered. Perhaps this will remove the curse from that wretched family. You have saved her from a fate worse than her sister's."

"I fear she will be ill, though," I said, "after all that she has gone through." But even I did not suspect how ill she would be.

An excited Old Rogers arrived and was shown into the study, where I allowed him to tell out his daughter's story without interruption. He ended by saying, "Now, Sir, you really must do summat. This won't do in a Christian country. We ain't aboard ship here with a nor'easter a-walkin' the quarterdeck."

"There's no occasion, my dear old fellow, to do anything."

He was taken aback. "Well, I don't understand you, Mr. Walton. You're the last man I'd have expected to hear argufy for faith without works. It's right to trust in God, but if you don't stand to your halliards, your craft'll miss stays, and your faith'll be blown out of the boltropes in the turn of a marlinspike."

I suspect there was some confusion in the figure, but the old man's meaning was plain enough. Nor would I keep him in a moment more of suspense. "Miss Oldcastle is in the house, Old Rogers," I said.

"What house, Sir?" returned the old man, his gray eyes opening wider as he spoke.

"This house, to be sure."

I shall never forget the look he cast upward to the Father. And never shall I find one who will listen to my story with more interest than Old Rogers did, as I recounted the adventures of the evening. There were few to whom I could have told them; to Old Rogers I felt that it was right and natural and dignified to tell the story even of my love's victory.

He rose, took my hand, and said, "Mr. Walton, you *will* preach now. I thank God for the good we shall all get from the trouble you have gone through."

"I ought to be the better for it," I answered.

"You *will* be the better for it," he returned. "I've allus been the better for any trouble as ever I had to go through. I couldn't quite say the same for every bit of good luck I had—leastaways I consider trouble the best luck a man can have. And I wish you a good-night, Sir. Thank God! Again."

My design had been to go at once to London and make preparation for as early a wedding as Miss Oldcastle would consent to, but now life and not marriage was the question. Dr. Duncan looked very grave, and all his encouragement did not amount to much. There was such a lack of vitality about her! Her life was nearly quenched from lack of hope, and her whole complaint appeared in excessive weakness. Finding that she fainted after every little excitement, I left her for four weeks entirely to my sister and Dr. Duncan. It was long before I could venture to stay in her room more than a minute or two, but by the summer she was able to be wheeled into the garden in a chair.

I had some painful apprehensions as to the treatment Judy herself might meet with from her grandmother, and had been doubtful whether I ought not to have carried her off as well as her aunt. But Judy came often to the vicarage, and on her first visit to Ethelwyn (which was the next day) she set my mind at rest.

"But does your grannie know where you are?" I had asked her.

"So well, Mr. Walton," she replied, "that there was no occasion to tell her. Why shouldn't I rebel as well as Aunt Wynnie, I wonder?" she added, looking archness itself.

"How does she bear it?"

"Bear what, Mr. Walton?"

"The loss of your aunt."

"You don't think Grannie cares about that, do you? She's vexed enough at the loss of Captain Everard. Do you know, I think he had too much wine yesterday, or he wouldn't have made quite such a fool of himself."

"I fear he hadn't had quite enough to give him courage, Judy. I dare say he was brave enough once, but a bad conscience soon destroys a man's courage."

"Why do you call it a bad conscience, Mr. Walton? I should have thought that a bad conscience was one that would let a girl go on anyhow and say nothing about it to make her uncomfortable."

"You are quite right, Judy. That is certainly the worst kind of conscience. But tell me, how does Mrs. Oldcastle bear it?"

"Grannie never says a word about you, or Auntie either."

"But you said she was vexed: how do you know that?"

"Because ever since the captain went away this morning, she won't speak a word even to Sarah."

"Are you not afraid of her locking you up someday or other?"

"Not a bit of it. Grannie won't touch me. And you shouldn't tempt me to run away from her like Auntie. I won't. Grannie is a naughty old lady, and I don't believe anybody loves her but me—certainly not Sarah. Therefore, I can't leave her, and I won't leave her, Mr. Walton, whatever you may say about her."

"Indeed, I don't want you to leave her, Judy."

(And Judy did not leave her as long as she lived, and the old lady's love to that child was one redeeming point in her fierce character. And a quarrel took place between that old woman and Sarah, which I regarded as a hopeful sign. And once she folded her granddaughter in her arms and wept long and bitterly. Perhaps the thought of her dying child came back upon her, along with the reflection that the only friend she had was the child of that marriage which she had persecuted to dissolution. Only a few years passed, however, before her soul was required of her. And to this day, Judy has never heard how her old grannie treated her mother.)

229

THIRTY-THREE
TOM'S STORY

It was summer when Ethelwyn and I were married. She was now quite well, and no shadow hung upon her half-moon forehead. We went for a fortnight into Wales, and then returned to the vicarage and the duties of the parish, in which she was quite ready to assist me. She saw that the best thing she could do for our parishioners was to help me—to serve me and not them.

I began to arrange my work again, and it came to my mind that I had been doing very little for Tom Weir. I could not blame myself much for this, and I was sure neither he nor his father blamed me at all. I called him to my house the next morning and proceeded to acquaint myself with what he had been doing. I found that he had made considerable progress both in Latin and mathematics, and I resolved that I would now push him a little. I found this only brought out his mettle, and his progress was extraordinary.

Although I carefully abstained from making the suggestion to him, I was more than pleased when I discovered that he would gladly give himself to the service of the Church. At the same time, I felt compelled to be cautious, in fear that the prospect of the social elevation involved might be a temptation to him, as it has been to many a man of humble birth. However, as I continued to observe him closely, my conviction was deepened that he was rarely fitted for ministering to his fellows. And I found that Thomas, so far from being unfavorably inclined to the proposal, was prepared to spend the few savings of his careful life upon Tom's education. To this, however, I could not listen, because there was

230

his daughter Mary, and his grandchild too, for whom he ought to make what little provision he could.

I therefore took the matter in my own hands, and managed (at less expense than most suppose) to maintain my young friend at Oxford till such time as he gained a fellowship. I felt justified in doing so, as someday Mrs. Walton would inherit the Oldcastle property. Certain other moneys of hers were now in the trust of her mother and two gentlemen in London, though she could not touch it as long as her mother lived and chose to refuse her the use of it. But I did not lose a penny, for of the very first money Tom received after his fellowship, he brought the half to me, and eventually repaid me every shilling. As soon as he was in deacon's orders he came to assist me as curate, and I found him a great help and comfort.

But, in looking back and trying to account for the snare into which I fell, I see plainly enough that I thought too much of what I had done for Tom, and too little of the honor God had done me in allowing me to help Tom. I took the throne over him, not consciously, but still with a contemptible condescension of heart that the nature in me called only fatherly friendship.

One evening a gentle tap came at my door, and Tom entered. He looked pale and anxious and uncertain in his motions.

"What is the matter, Tom?" I asked.

"I wanted to say something to you, Sir," answered Tom.

"Say on," I returned cheerily.

"It is not easy to say, Sir," rejoined Tom, with a faint smile. "Miss Walton, Sir—"

"Well, what of her? There's nothing happened to her? She was here a few minutes ago—"

Here a suspicion of the truth flashed on me and struck me dumb. I am now covered with shame to think how it swept away for the moment all my fine theories about the equality of men in Christ. How could Tom Weir, whose father was a joiner, who had been a lad in a London shop himself, dare to propose marrying my sister? Instead of thinking of what he really was, my regard rested upon this and that stage through which he had passed to reach his present condition. In fact, I regarded him rather as of my making than of God's.

I have known good people who were noble and generous toward their so-called inferiors, and full of the rights of the race, until it touched their own family, and just no longer. Yea, I, when Tom

Weir wanted to marry my sister, judged according to appearances in which I did not even believe, and judged not righteous judgment.

What answer I returned to Tom I hardly know. I remember that the poor fellow's face fell, and that he murmured something which I did not heed. And then I found myself walking in the garden under the great cedar, having stepped out of the window almost unconsciously and left Tom standing there alone. It was very good of him ever to forgive me.

Wandering about in the garden, my wife saw me from her window and met me as I turned a corner in the shrubbery.

"What is the matter with you?" she asked.

"Oh, not much," I answered, "only that Weir has been making me feel rather uncomfortable."

"What has he been doing?" she inquired, in some alarm. "It is not possible he has done anything wrong."

My wife trusted him as much as I did.

"No-o-o," I answered, "not anything exactly wrong."

"It must be very nearly wrong to make you look so miserable."

I began to feel ashamed and more uncomfortable. "He has fallen in love with Martha," I said, "and I fear he may have made her fall in love with him too."

My wife laughed merrily. "What a wicked curate!"

"Well, but you know it is not exactly agreeable."

"Why?"

"You know well enough."

"I am not going to take it for granted. Is he not a good man, and well educated?"

"Yes."

"Is he not clever, and a gentleman?"

"One of the cleverest fellows I ever met, and I have no fault to find with his manners."

"Nor with his habits or his ways of thinking?" my wife went on.

"No. But, Ethelwyn, you know what I mean quite well. His family, you know—"

"Well, is his father not a respectable man?"

"Oh yes, certainly. Thoroughly respectable."

"He wouldn't borrow money of his tailor instead of paying for his clothes, would he?"

"Certainly not."

"And if he were to die today, he would carry no debts to heaven

232

with him? Does he bear false witness against his neighbor?"

"No."

"Well, I think Tom very fortunate in having such a father. I wish my mother had been as good."

"That is all true, and yet—"

"And yet, suppose a young man you liked had a fashionable father who had ruined half a score of tradespeople—would you object to him because of his family?"

"Perhaps not."

"Then, with you, position outweighs honesty, in fathers, at least."

To this I was not ready with an answer, and my wife went on. "Do you know why I would not accept your offer of taking my name when I should succeed to the property?"

"You said you liked mine better," I answered.

"So I did. But I did not tell you that I was ashamed that my good husband should take a name which for centuries had been borne by hard-hearted, worldly-minded people, who were neither gentle nor honest, nor high-minded."

"Still, Ethelwyn, you know there is something in it, though it is not easy to say what. And you avoid that. I suppose Martha has been talking you over to her side."

"For the first time, I am almost ashamed of you," my wife said with a shade of solemnity. "And I will punish you by telling you the truth. Do you think I had nothing of that sort to get over when I began to find that I was thinking a little more about you than was convenient under the circumstances? Your manners, though irreproachable, just had not the tone that I had been accustomed to. There was a diffidence about you also that did not at first advance you in my regard."

"Yes, yes," I answered, a little piqued, "I have no doubt you thought me a boor. But it is quite bad enough to have brought you down to my level, without sinking you still lower now."

"Now there you are wrong, and that is what I want to show you. I found that my love to you would not be satisfied with simply making an exception in your favor. I must see what force there really was in the notions I had been bred in."

"Ah!" I said, "I see. You looked for a principle in what you had thought was an exception."

"Yes," returned my wife, "and I soon found one. The next step was to throw away all false judgment in regard to such things.

Would you hesitate a moment between Tom Weir and the dissolute son of an earl?"

"You know I would not."

"Well, just carry out the considerations that suggests."

"But his sister?"

"You were preaching last Sunday about the way God thinks of things, and you said that was the only true way of thinking about them. Would the Mary who poured the ointment on the head of Jesus have refused to marry a good man because he was the brother of that Mary who poured it on His feet? Have you thought what God would think of Tom for a husband to Martha?"

I did not answer, and when I lifted my eyes from the ground, thinking Ethelwyn stood beside me, she was gone. I was ashamed to follow and find her, so I got my hat instead and strolled out.

What was it that drew me toward Thomas Weir's shop? It must have been incipient repentance—a feeling that I had wronged the man. But just as I turned the corner, and the smell of the wood reached me, the picture so often associated in my mind with such a scene of human labor rose before me. I saw the Lord of Life bending over His bench, fashioning some lowly utensil for a housewife of Nazareth. And He would receive payment for it too, for He, at least, could see no disgrace in the order of things that His Father had appointed. It is the vulgar mind that looks down on the earning and worships the inheriting of money.

And the thought sprung up at once in my mind, "If I ever see our Lord face to face, how shall I feel if He says to me, 'Didst thou do well to murmur that thy sister espoused a certain man, for that in his youth he had earned his bread as I earned Mine? Where was then thy right to say unto Me, Lord, Lord?' "

I hurried into the workshop. "Has Tom told you about it?" I said.

"Yes, Sir. And I told him to mind what he was about, for he was not a gentleman, and you was, Sir."

"I hope I am. And Tom is as much a gentleman as I have any claim to be."

Thomas Weir held out his hand. "Now, Sir, I do believe you mean in my shop what you say in your pulpit, and there is *one* Christian in the world at least. But what will your good lady say? She's higher born than you—no offense, Sir."

"Ah! Thomas, you shame me. I am not so good as you think me. It was my wife that brought me to reason about it."

"God bless her."

"Amen. I'm going to find Tom."

At the same moment Tom entered the shop, with a very melancholy face. He started when he saw me and looked confused.

"Tom, my boy," I said, "I behaved very badly to you. I am sorry for it. Come back with me and have a walk with my sister. I don't think she'll be sorry to see you." His face brightened up at once, and we left the shop together.

Tom was the first to speak. "I know, Sir, how many difficulties my presumption must put you in."

"Not another word about it, Tom. You are blameless. I wish I were. Take my sister, in God's name, Tom, and be good to her."

Tom went to find Martha, and I to find Ethelwyn.

"It is all right," I said, "even to the shame I feel at having needed your reproof."

"Don't think of that. God gives us all time to come to our right minds, you know," answered my wife.

"But how did you get on so far ahead of me?"

Ethelwyn laughed. "Why," she said, "I only told you back again what you have been telling me for the last seven or eight years."

So to me the message had come first, but my wife had answered first with the deed.

Next to her and my children, Tom has been my greatest comfort for many years. He is still my curate, and I do not think we shall part till death separates us for a time. He has distinguished himself in the literary world, and when I read his books, I am yet prouder of my brother-in-law. My sister is worth twice what she was before.

Thomas Weir is now too old to work any longer. His father is dead, and Thomas occupies his chair in the large room of the old house. The workshop I have turned into a schoolroom. A great part of Tom's time is devoted to the children, for he and I agree that the pastoral care ought to be equally divided between the sheep and the lambs.

Jane Rogers was married to young Brownrigg about a year after we were married. Old Brownrigg is all but confined to the chimney corner now, and Richard manages the farm, though not quite to his father's satisfaction, of course. The old mill has been superseded by one of new and rare device (built by Richard), but the cottage where Old Rogers and his woman lived has slowly moldered back to the dust, for the old people have been dead for years.

Often in the summer, as I go to or come from the vestry, I sit down for a moment on the turf that covers my old friend Rogers, and think that this body of mine is everyday moldering away, till it shall fall a heap of dust into its appointed place. But what is that to me? It is to me the drawing nigh of the fresh morning of life when I shall be young and strong again, glad in the presence of the wise and beloved dead, and unspeakably glad in the presence of God.

I am seated now in that little octagonal room overlooking the Hall quarry, with its green lining of trees and its deep central well. It is my study now. My wife is not yet too old to prefer her old little room, although the stair is high and steep. Nor do I object, for I see her the oftener.

And Ethelwyn bends her smooth forehead over me—for she has a smooth forehead still. One of the good things that come of being married is that there is one face which you can still see the same through all the shadows which years have gathered and heaped upon it. No, I have a better way of putting it: there is one face whose final beauty you can see the more clearly as the bloom of youth departs, and the loveliness of wisdom and the beauty of holiness take its place.

I myself am getting old—faster and faster. When my voice quavers, I feel that it is mine and not mine, that it just belongs to me like my watch which does not run well now, though it did thirty years ago. And my knees shake—even walking across the floor of my study—like that old mare of my father's, which came at last to have the same weakness in her knees that I have in mine. But these things are not me, I say. I *have* them, and please God, shall soon have better. For, of all children, how can the children of God be old?

A Quiet Neighborhood

Family Trees

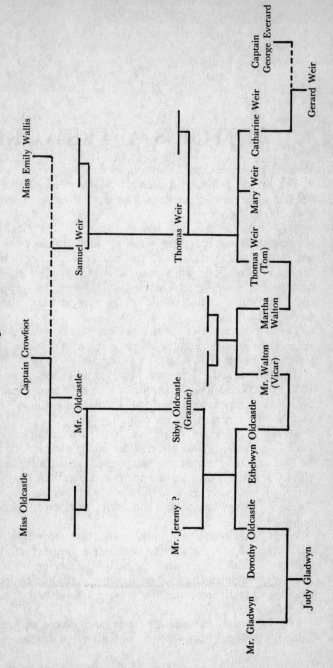

EDITOR'S AFTERWORD

Writing styles change. Good stories don't.

The first statement explains why George MacDonald's novels are not widely read these days. The second statement explains why they should be.

A Quiet Neighborhood was not written as a "historical novel"—it was a *contemporary* magazine serial as published in 1866. MacDonald's works were written from life, and reflect his deep insight into the natures of God, fallen man, and redeemed man. The places and people were largely taken from places and people around him—he began writing of the things near at hand, the things he knew best.

The "Marshmallows" of this book is MacDonald's name for the village of Arundel, situated directly south of London and only a few miles north of the English Channel.

Arundel was the scene of MacDonald's first pastorate, from 1850 to 1853. He was the pastor of a small Congregational assembly, whose chapel stood (and still stands) only a hundred yards or so from the larger Anglican church.

MacDonald's years there were not without pleasure and turmoil; in Arundel he was married, he first contracted the tuberculosis that would so torture and shape the rest of his life, and his first child was born. Those years ended on a less than happy note: the elders of his congregation, unhappy with certain aspects of his theology, halved his salary and ultimately forced him from the pulpit.

When MacDonald took up his pen a few years later to write *A Quiet Neighborhood*, he carried forward a number of Arundelian memories: Old Rogers and the mill, the bridge over the River Arun, the Anglican church with its stone walls and the poor-graves near the church door, and the mysterious old hall at the edge of the village.

Old Rogers is indeed the name and image of one of MacDonald's Arundel flock—a man who attended services regularly in his round frock, red cotton handkerchief, and tall beaver hat. The mill once stood near the bridge, but both the mill and the bridge are gone. A chemist's shop (drug store, to us Americans) stands where the mill stood, and a newer (though still elegant) stone bridge has replaced the old one where MacDonald did, in truth, first meet his Old Rogers.

Oldcastle Hall is patterned after the main part of the huge castle which overshadows all Arundel: a lover of castles and staircases (as MacDonald was) could not but take away strong memories of that imposing, sprawling structure. (I suspect that the very name "Oldcastle Hall" is a private joke, for one might refer to the living quarters at Arundel castle as "the old castle hall.")

And the Anglican church itself nestles in the walls that surround the castle. The side door is still there, which Walton used as a private exit—and the path from that door yet wanders among quiet graves whose quiet is that of patient and enduring hope in Christ.

A Quiet Neighborhood, hailed as one of MacDonald's greatest successes, was reprinted in numerous editions throughout his lifetime. But after MacDonald died in Surrey in 1905, *A Quiet Neighborhood* and its sequels began a slow fade from the public eye. Old copies of the books traded hands quietly over the ensuing years, but no attempt was made to reprint them.

This version of *A Quiet Neighborhood* began in 1982—more than 100 years after the first publication. Although I had long been aware of the existence of MacDonald's twenty-nine novels for adults, I had never seen a copy for sale. Then, in a used bookstore in the wilds of Vermont, I encountered a first American edition of *Annals of a Quiet Neighborhood*—and paid without tremor or regret the full marked price: 35 cents. Seldom has my money been better invested.

My wife, Elizabeth, and I began reading, and were immediately charmed. Buried among the debris of an outmoded and difficult literary style was an absolutely readable and relevant mystery/romance/adventure novel. True to the literary conventions of his age (which held that any novel worth reading would occupy no less than three thick volumes) MacDonald wrote at great length about small events, and used the events as springboards for doctrinal digressions and religious rhapsodizing. These descriptions, dialectics, and dissertations, while fascinating in themselves, do nothing to advance the story and are not crucial to the main spiritual impact of the book.

So we edited the book, striving to achieve a balance between brevity and breadth that would be economical to print, interesting to the reader of the 1980s, and faithful to the heart of MacDonald's vision. We do not pretend that this version is *better* than the original—merely shorter and easier to read. The excesses of the Victorian style have been trimmed away—but none, I hope, of MacDonald's jewels have perished along with the trivia.

MacDonald's books *should* be read in the original versions, wherever patience and availability permit. One of the finest American collections of his works is open to the public: The Wade Collection, Wheaton College, Wheaton, Illinois.

Dan Hamilton
Indianapolis, Indiana
September 1984